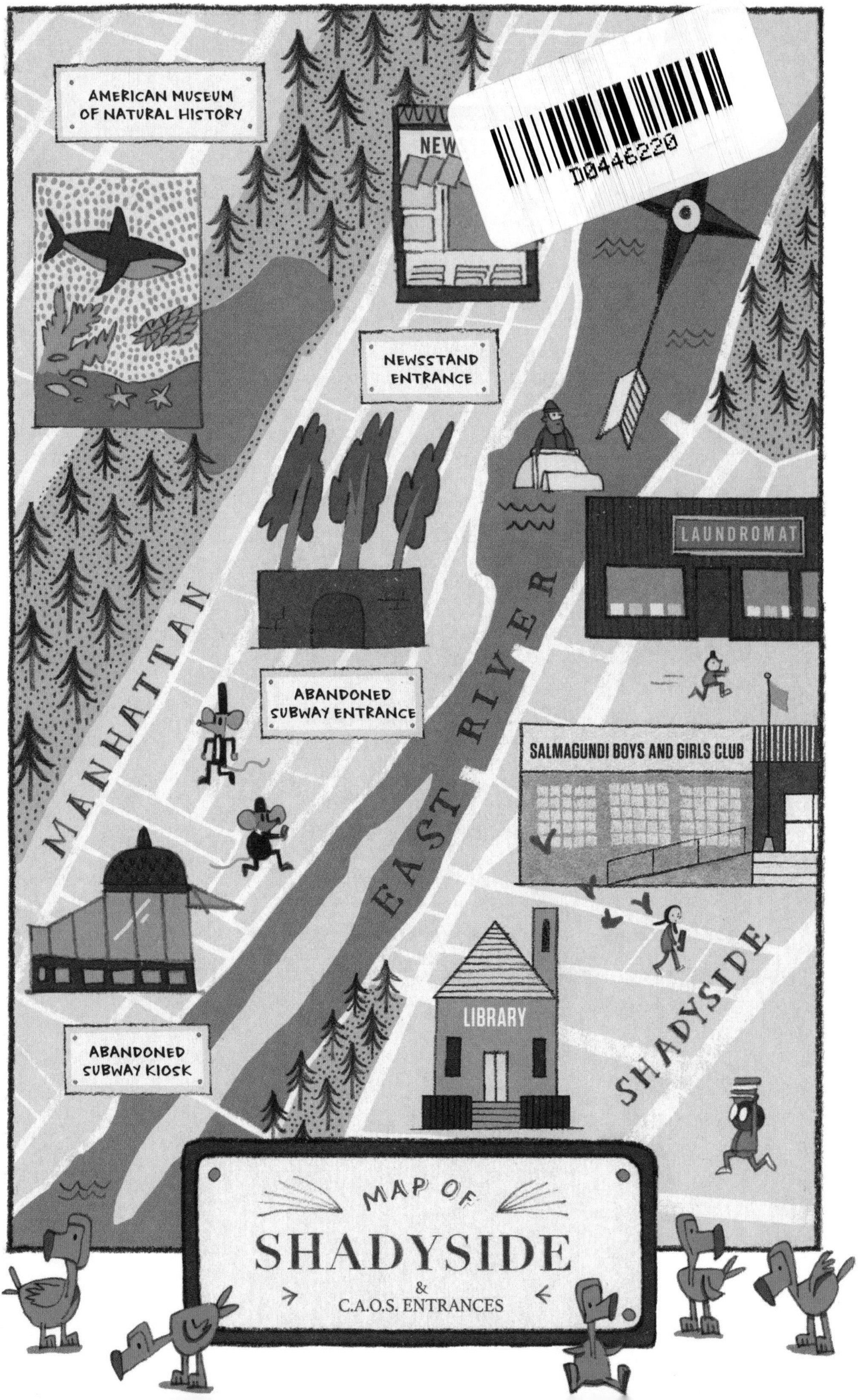

AMERICAN MUSEUM OF NATURAL HISTORY
NEWSSTAND ENTRANCE
LAUNDROMAT
MANHATTAN
EAST RIVER
ABANDONED SUBWAY ENTRANCE
SALMAGUNDI BOYS AND GIRLS CLUB
LIBRARY
SHADYSIDE
ABANDONED SUBWAY KIOSK
MAP OF
SHADYSIDE
&
C.A.O.S. ENTRANCES

For our planet and all the creatures and living things that let us share space.

Ivanna (for her eagle-eye and grace under pressure), Niamh (joke polisher extraordinaire, keeper of order first class), Fion (for the coloring assist—we'd still be in the weeds without you), and Sam (for letting us have all this fun).

To my fellow storytellers and friends for their camaraderie and indispensable advice: Mika Song, Angela Dominguez, Aram Kim, Pilar Valdes, and Tim Miller.

Thank you, Owen, for being the best husband, first reader, editor, and meal preparer in Queens. There would be no book 2 without you.

First edition published in 2022 by Flying Eye Books,
an imprint of Nobrow Ltd. 27 Westgate Street, London, E8 3RL.

Text and Illustrations © Isabel Roxas 2022.
Colours by Isabel Roxas and Fion Fitzgerald.

Isabel Roxas has asserted her right under the Copyright, Designs and Patents Act, 1988, to be identified as the Author and Illustrator of this Work.

1 3 5 7 9 10 8 6 4 2

Published in the US by Nobrow (US) INC.
Printed in Latvia on FSC® certified paper.

ISBN: 978-1-83874-055-9
flyingeyebooks.com

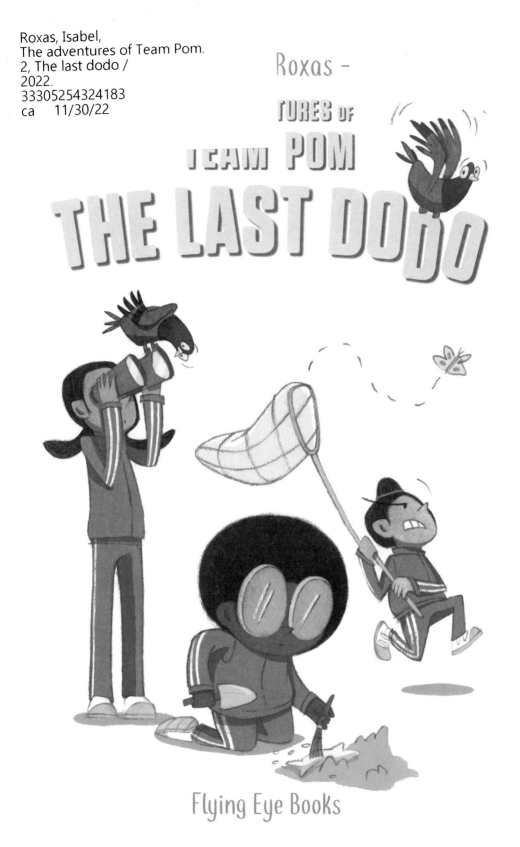

Roxas -

TURES OF

TEAM POM

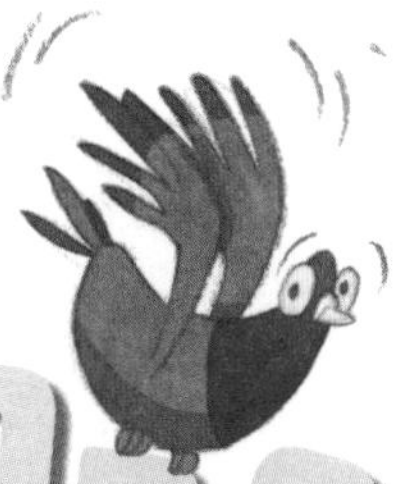

THE LAST DODO

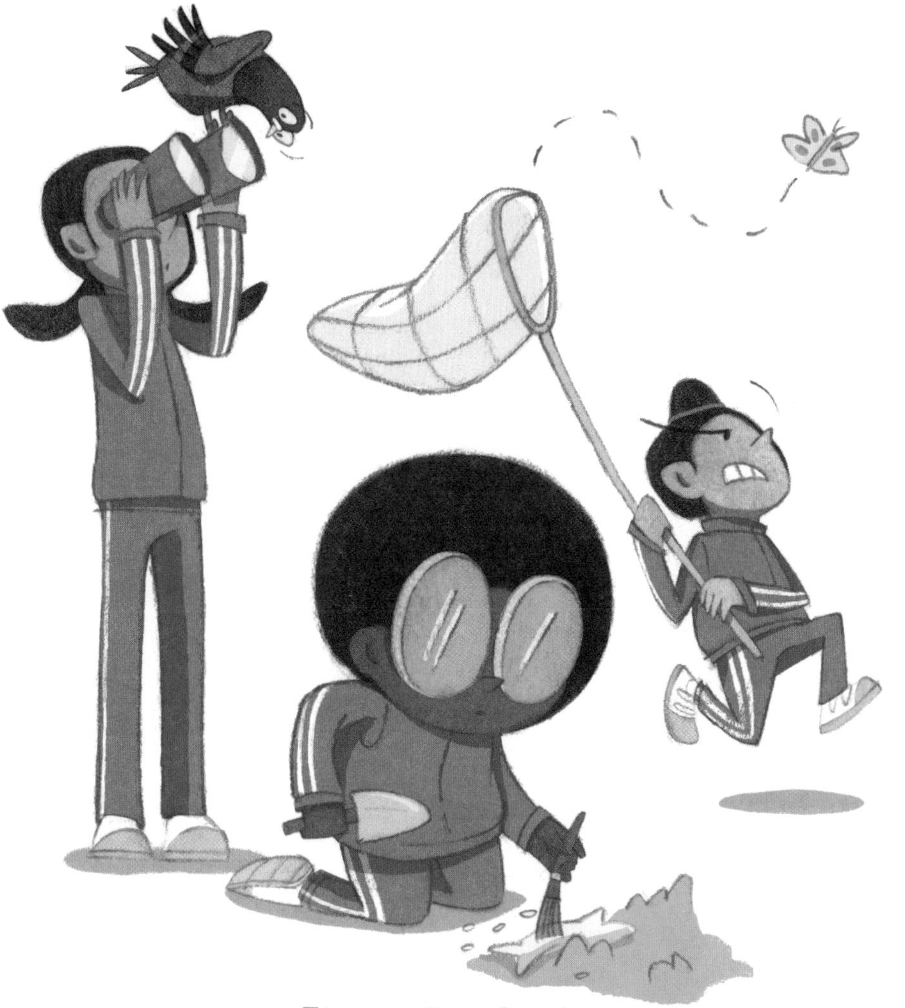

Flying Eye Books

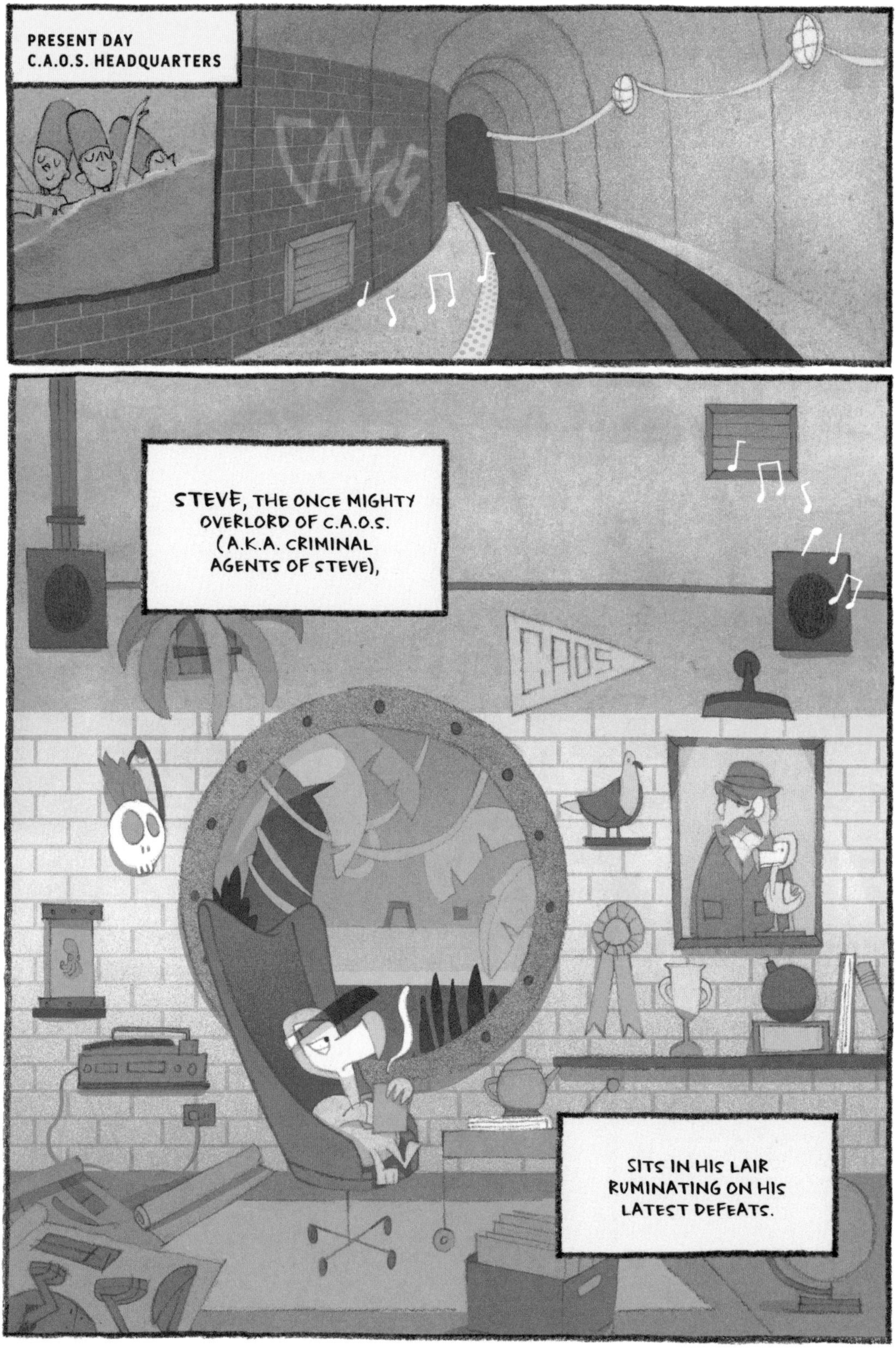
PRESENT DAY
C.A.O.S. HEADQUARTERS
STEVE, THE ONCE MIGHTY OVERLORD OF C.A.O.S. (A.K.A. CRIMINAL AGENTS OF STEVE),
SITS IN HIS LAIR RUMINATING ON HIS LATEST DEFEATS.

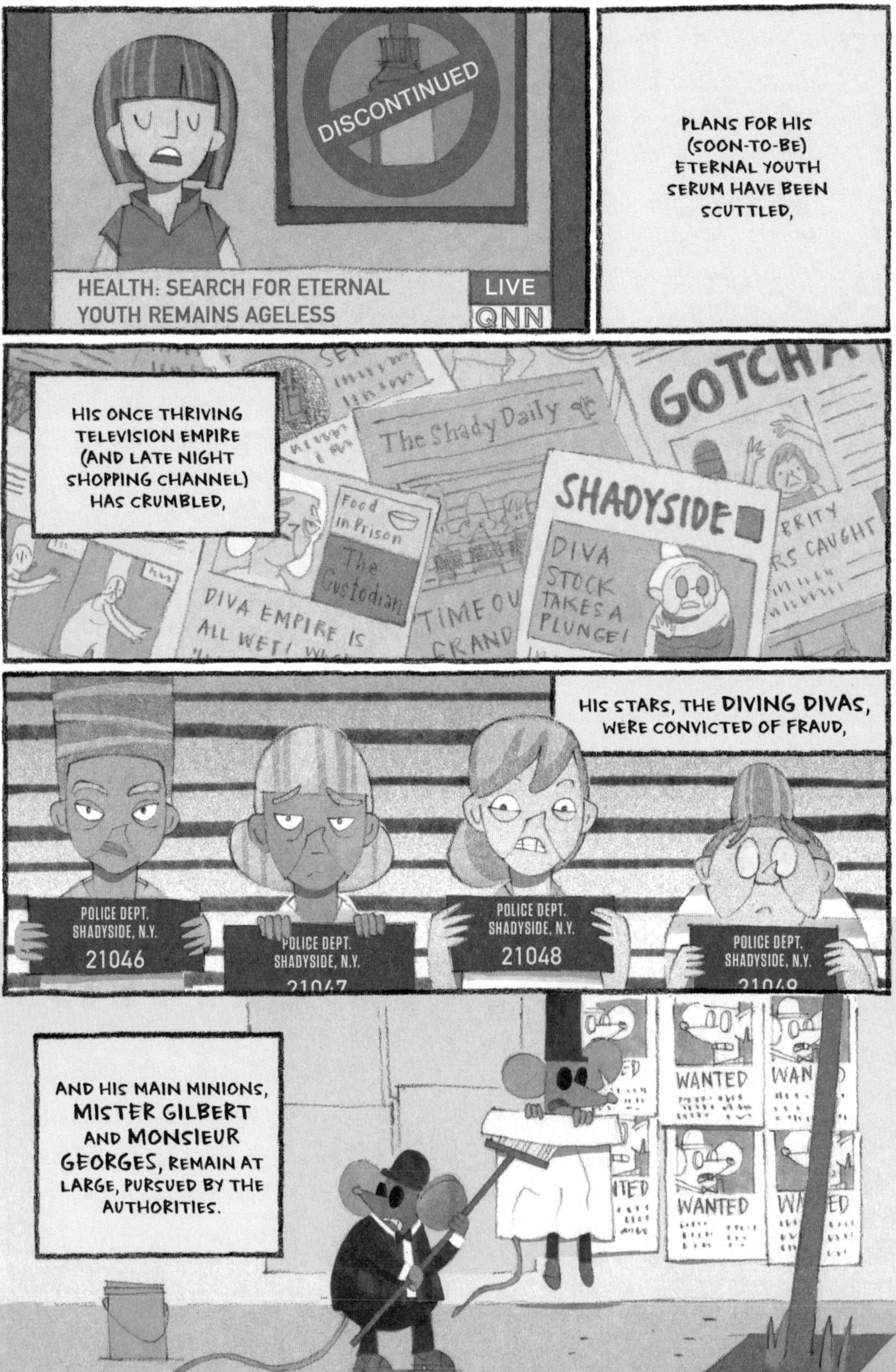
DISCONTINUED
HEALTH: SEARCH FOR ETERNAL YOUTH REMAINS AGELESS
LIVE
QNN
PLANS FOR HIS (SOON-TO-BE) ETERNAL YOUTH SERUM HAVE BEEN SCUTTLED,
HIS ONCE THRIVING TELEVISION EMPIRE (AND LATE NIGHT SHOPPING CHANNEL) HAS CRUMBLED,
GOTCHA
The Shady Daily
Food in Prison
The Custodian
SHADYSIDE
DIVA STOCK TAKES A PLUNGE!
HIS STARS, THE **DIVING DIVAS**, WERE CONVICTED OF FRAUD,
POLICE DEPT. SHADYSIDE, N.Y. 21046
POLICE DEPT. SHADYSIDE, N.Y.
POLICE DEPT. SHADYSIDE, N.Y. 21048
POLICE DEPT. SHADYSIDE, N.Y.
AND HIS MAIN MINIONS, **MISTER GILBERT** AND **MONSIEUR GEORGES**, REMAIN AT LARGE, PURSUED BY THE AUTHORITIES.
WANTED
WANTED

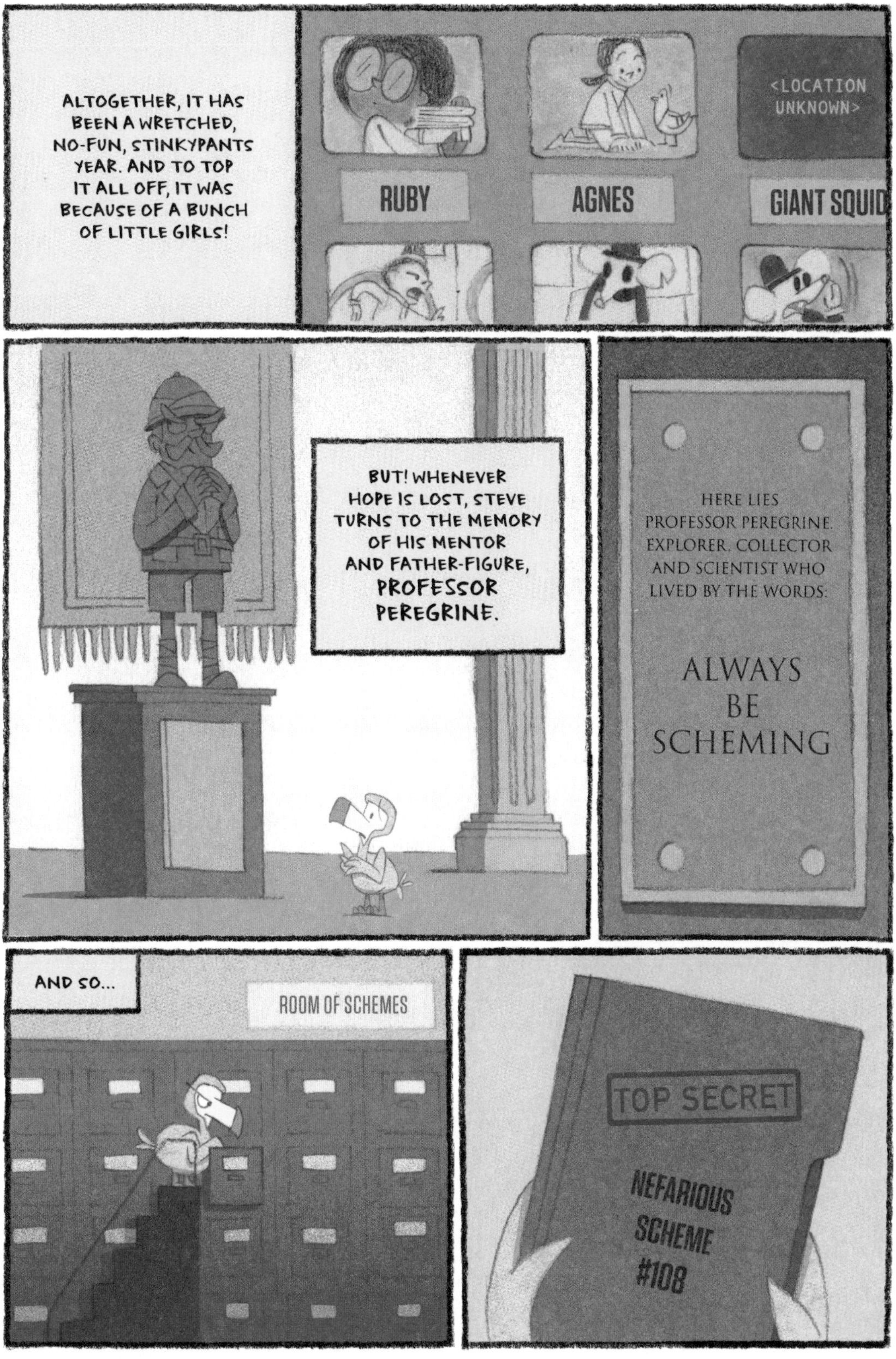
ALTOGETHER, IT HAS BEEN A WRETCHED, NO-FUN, STINKYPANTS YEAR. AND TO TOP IT ALL OFF, IT WAS BECAUSE OF A BUNCH OF LITTLE GIRLS!
<LOCATION UNKNOWN>
RUBY
AGNES
GIANT SQUID
BUT! WHENEVER HOPE IS LOST, STEVE TURNS TO THE MEMORY OF HIS MENTOR AND FATHER-FIGURE, PROFESSOR PEREGRINE.
HERE LIES PROFESSOR PEREGRINE. EXPLORER. COLLECTOR AND SCIENTIST WHO LIVED BY THE WORDS:
ALWAYS BE SCHEMING
AND SO...
ROOM OF SCHEMES
TOP SECRET
NEFARIOUS SCHEME #108

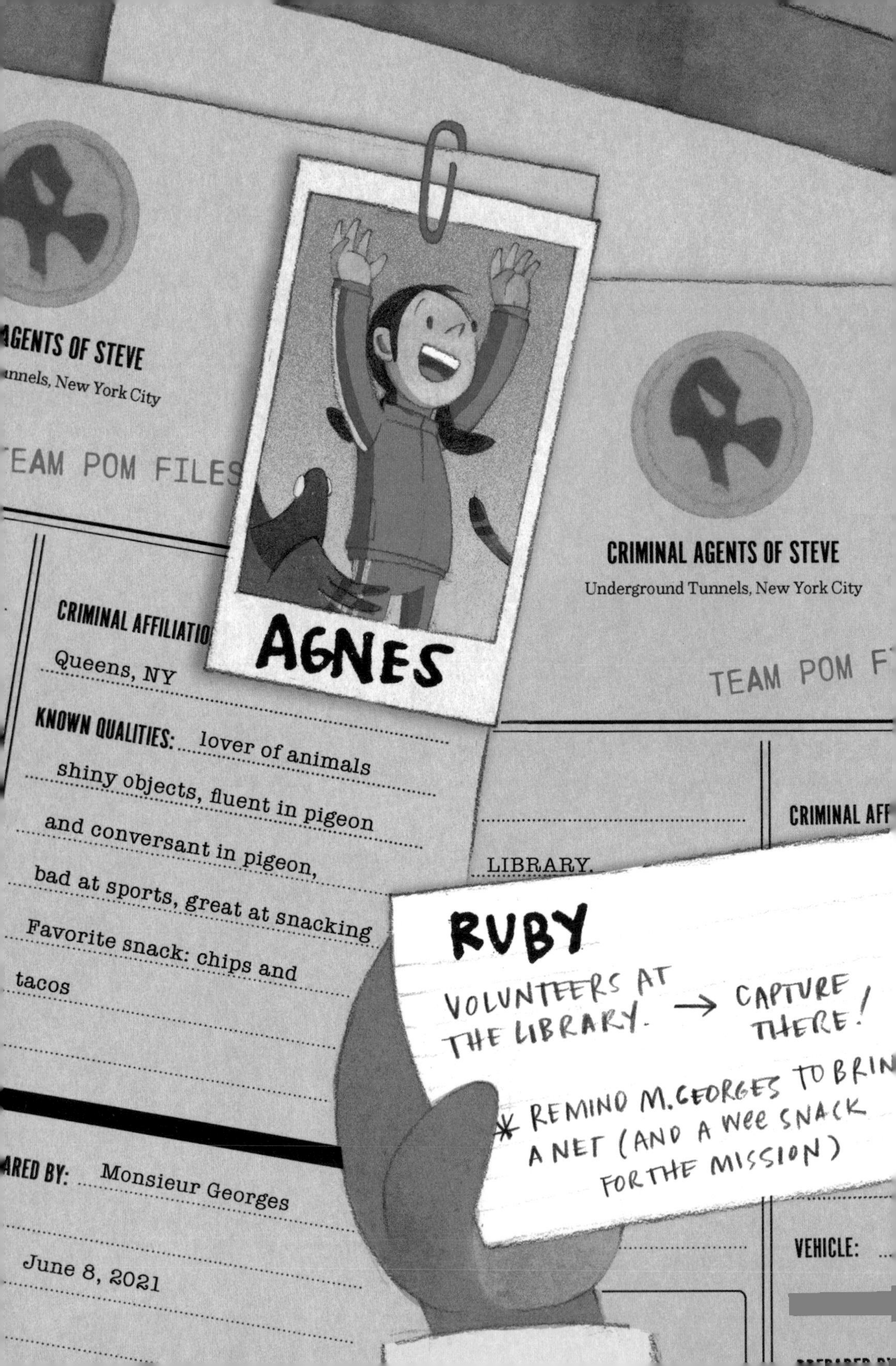
AGENTS OF STEVE
nnels, New York City
TEAM POM FILES
CRIMINAL AFFILIATIO
Queens, NY
KNOWN QUALITIES: lover of animals
shiny objects, fluent in pigeon
and conversant in pigeon,
bad at sports, great at snacking
Favorite snack: chips and
tacos
ARED BY: Monsieur Georges
June 8, 2021
AGNES
CRIMINAL AGENTS OF STEVE
Underground Tunnels, New York City
TEAM POM F
CRIMINAL AFF
LIBRARY.
VEHICLE:
RUBY
VOLUNTEERS AT THE LIBRARY. → CAPTURE THERE!
* REMIND M. GEORGES TO BRIN
A NET (AND A WEE SNACK
FOR THE MISSION)

RUBY

n stuff, Miscellan

am genius

ngi foraging

e mollusks

can speak a little squid

right-hand human

(see file #20045)

dio flyer

ster Gilbert

ROBERTA
- TEAM LEADER
- VERY NOSY
- TTLE BOSS
- VES CRANE CLAW
- FAVORITE
  SNACK
  ↓ BAOS!
- S OBSTACLE
  COURSES

ROBERT

feet 1 in (ish)

S OF STEVE

CRIMIN

Salm

KNOW

Litt

The

fa

ba

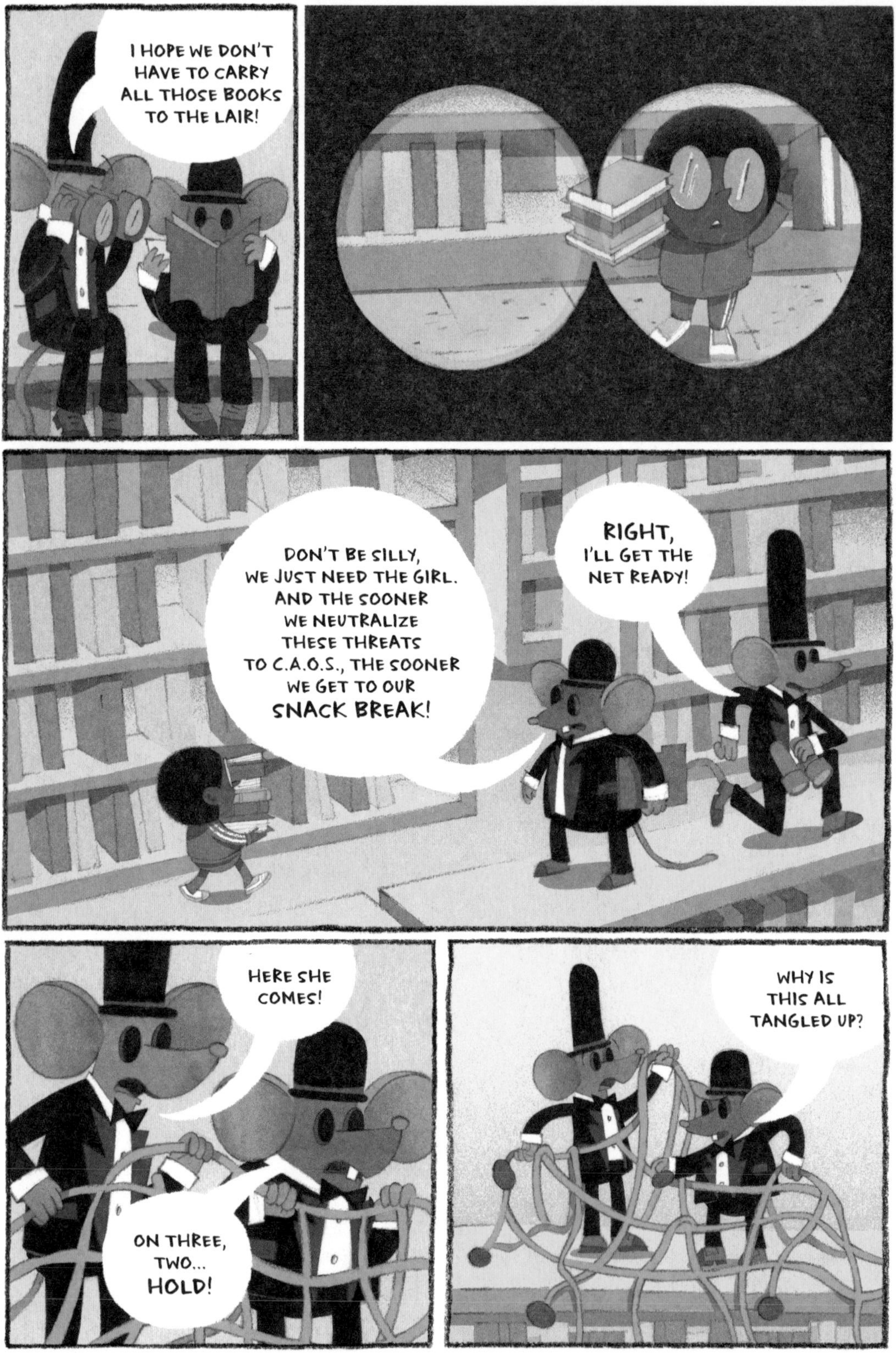
I HOPE WE DON'T HAVE TO CARRY ALL THOSE BOOKS TO THE LAIR!
DON'T BE SILLY, WE JUST NEED THE GIRL. AND THE SOONER WE NEUTRALIZE THESE THREATS TO C.A.O.S., THE SOONER WE GET TO OUR SNACK BREAK!
RIGHT, I'LL GET THE NET READY!
HERE SHE COMES!
ON THREE, TWO... HOLD!
WHY IS THIS ALL TANGLED UP?

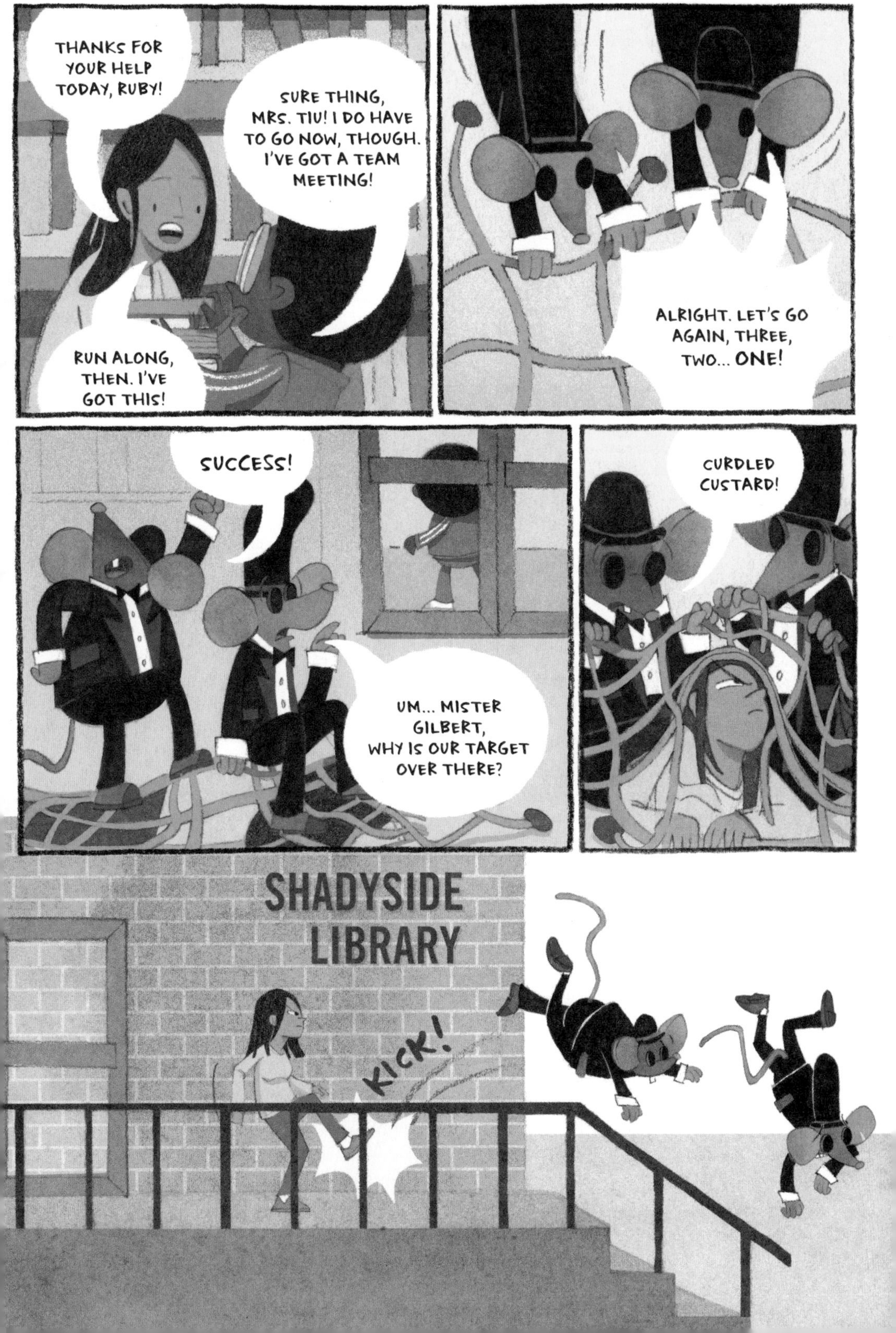
THANKS FOR YOUR HELP TODAY, RUBY!
SURE THING, MRS. TIU! I DO HAVE TO GO NOW, THOUGH. I'VE GOT A TEAM MEETING!
RUN ALONG, THEN. I'VE GOT THIS!
ALRIGHT. LET'S GO AGAIN, THREE, TWO... ONE!
SUCCESS!
UM... MISTER GILBERT, WHY IS OUR TARGET OVER THERE?
CURDLED CUSTARD!
SHADYSIDE LIBRARY
KICK!

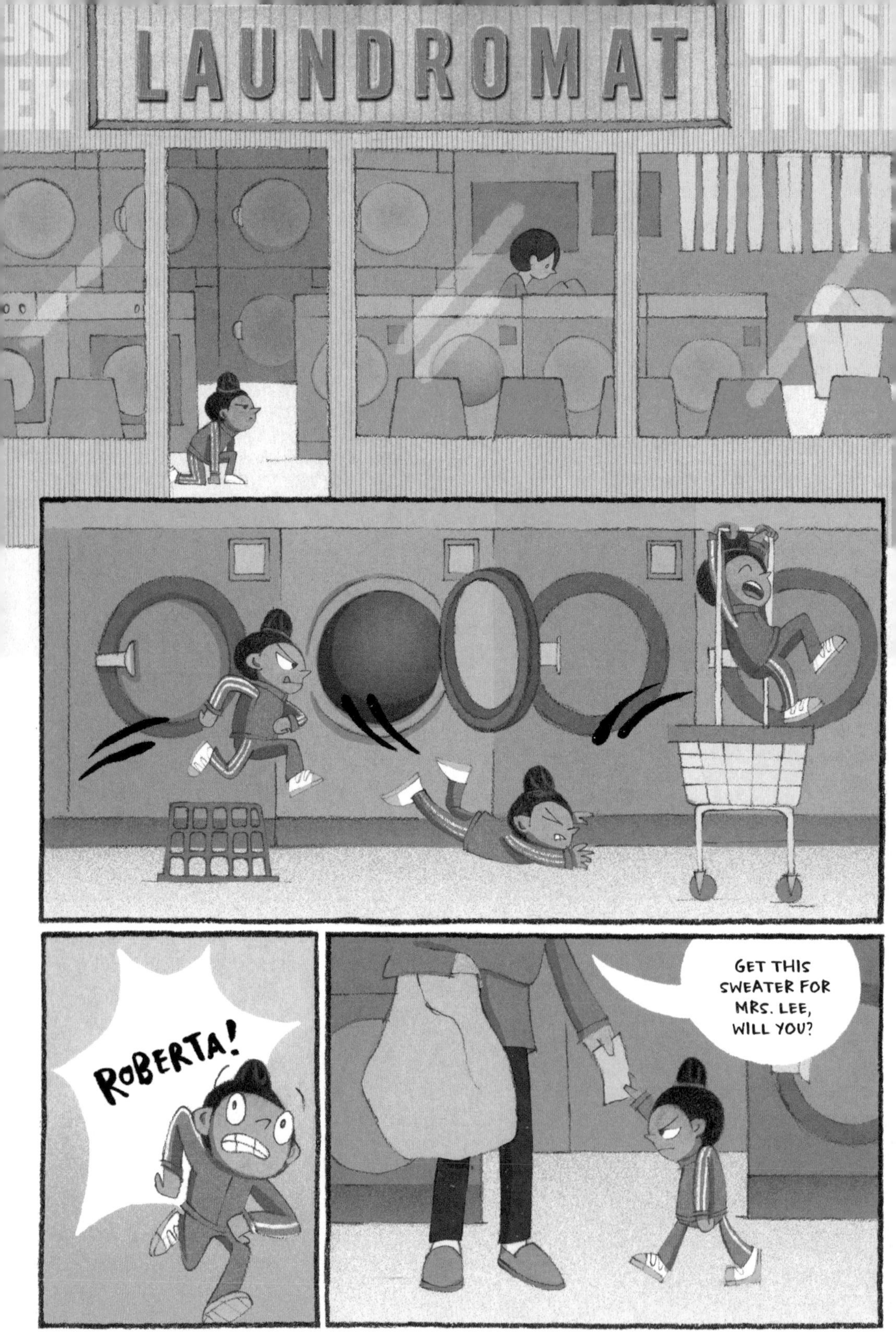
LAUNDROMAT
ROBERTA!
GET THIS SWEATER FOR MRS. LEE, WILL YOU?

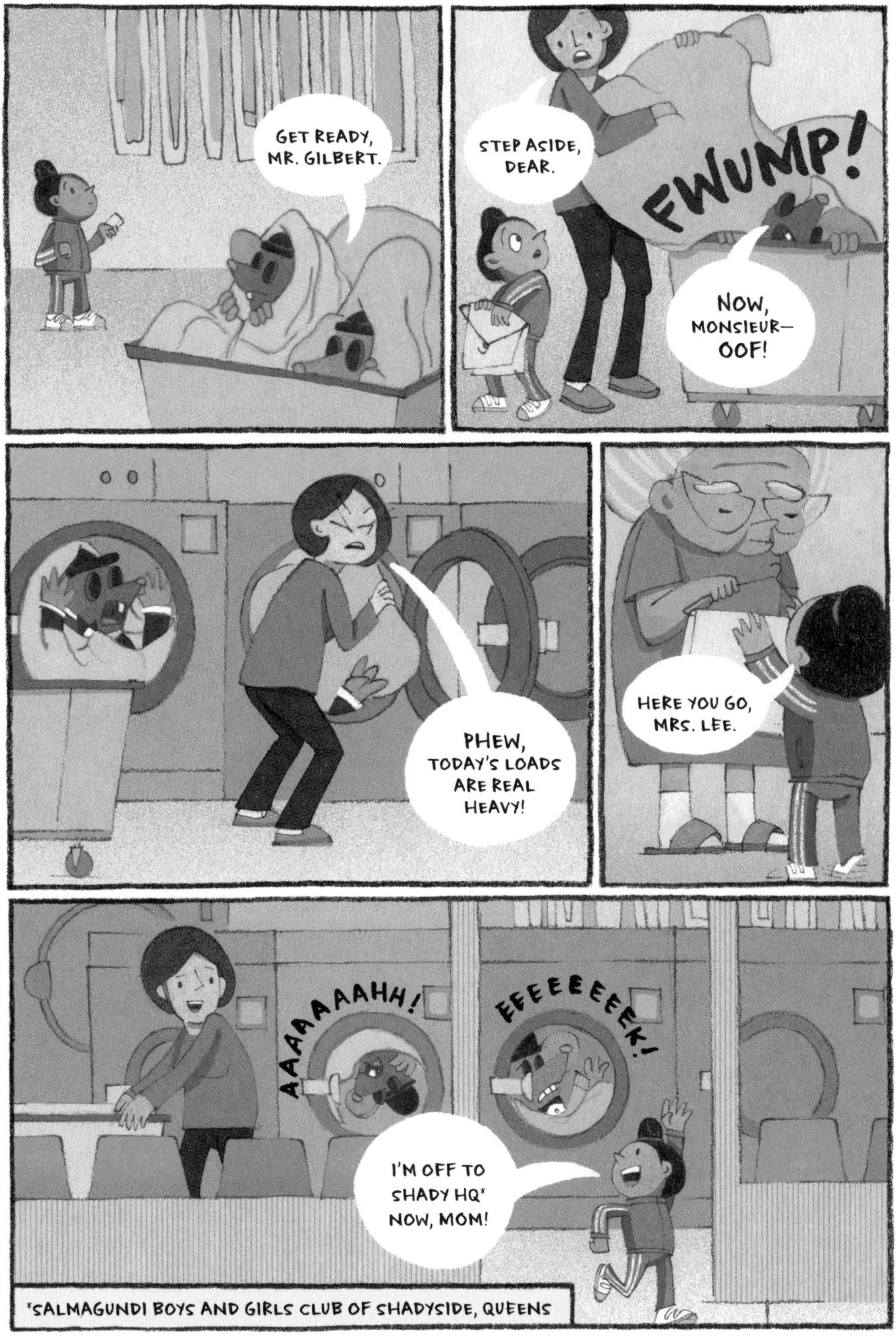
GET READY, MR. GILBERT.
STEP ASIDE, DEAR.
FWUMP!
NOW, MONSIEUR— OOF!
PHEW, TODAY'S LOADS ARE REAL HEAVY!
HERE YOU GO, MRS. LEE.
AAAAAAAHH!
EEEEEEEEK!
I'M OFF TO SHADY HQ* NOW, MOM!
*SALMAGUNDI BOYS AND GIRLS CLUB OF SHADYSIDE, QUEENS

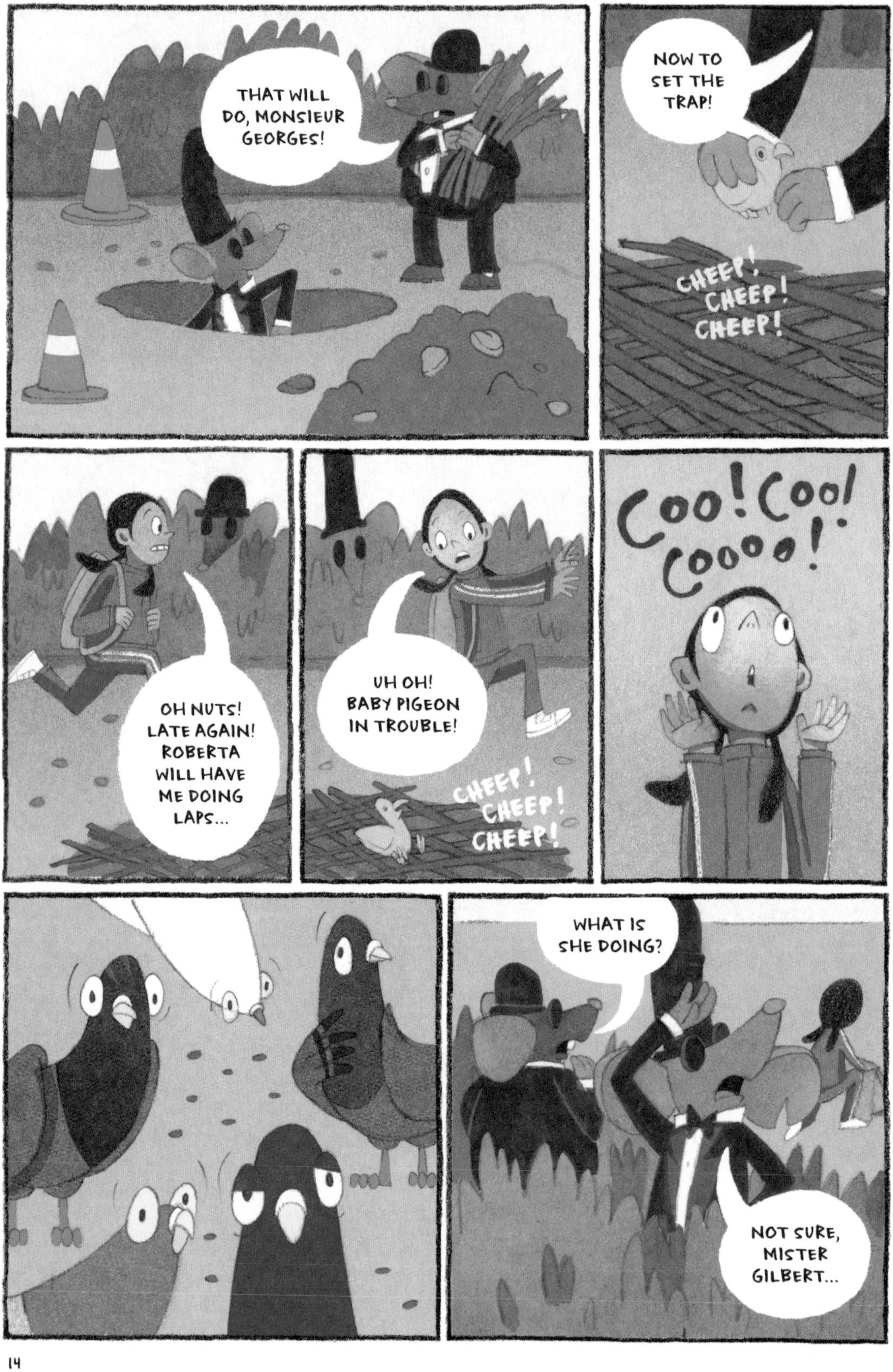
THAT WILL DO, MONSIEUR GEORGES!
NOW TO SET THE TRAP!
CHEEP! CHEEP! CHEEP!
OH NUTS! LATE AGAIN! ROBERTA WILL HAVE ME DOING LAPS...
UH OH! BABY PIGEON IN TROUBLE!
CHEEP! CHEEP! CHEEP!
COO! COO! COOOO!
WHAT IS SHE DOING?
NOT SURE, MISTER GILBERT...

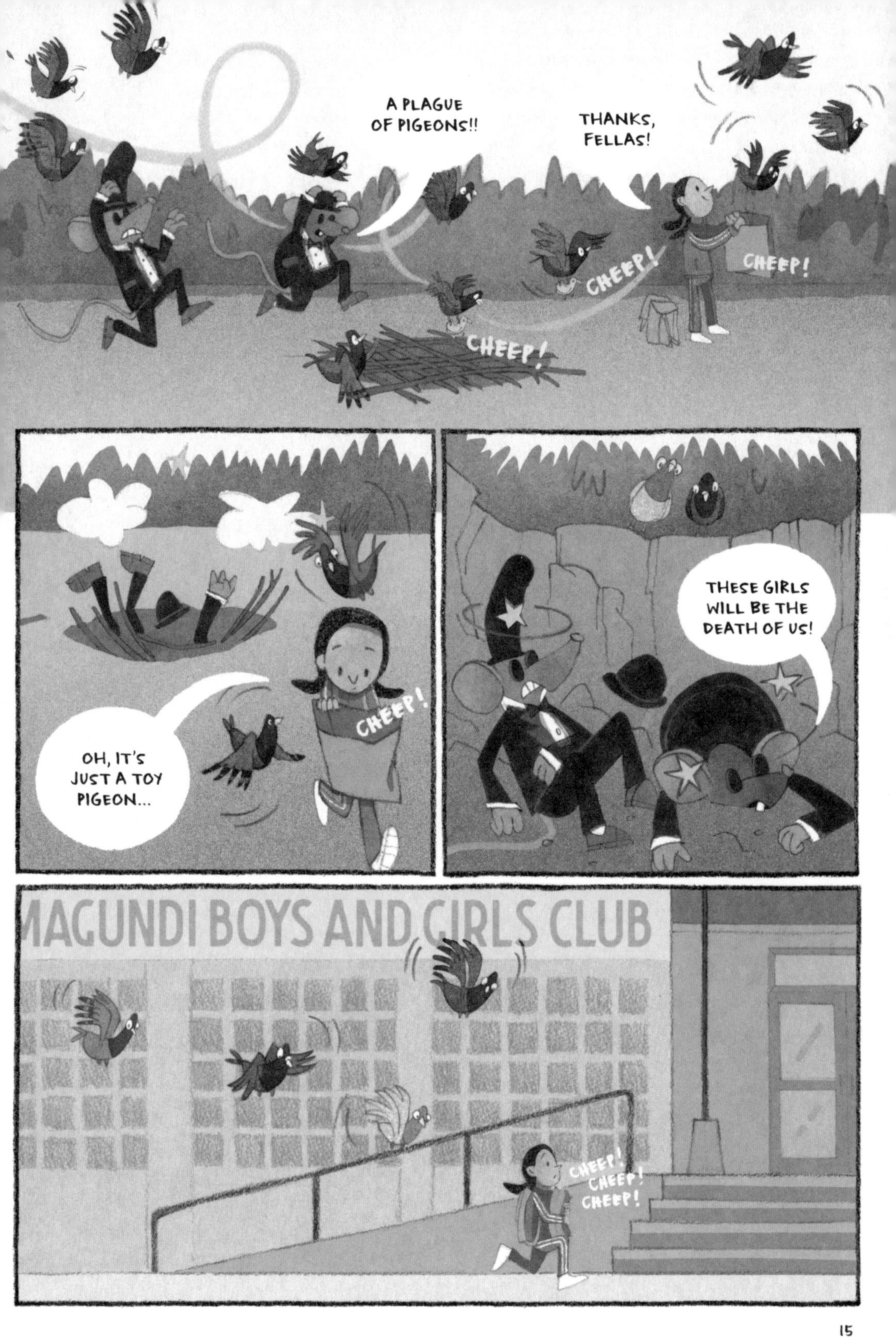
A PLAGUE OF PIGEONS!!
THANKS, FELLAS!
CHEEP!
CHEEP!
CHEEP!
OH, IT'S JUST A TOY PIGEON...
CHEEP!
THESE GIRLS WILL BE THE DEATH OF US!
MAGUNDI BOYS AND GIRLS CLUB
CHEEP!
CHEEP!
CHEEP!

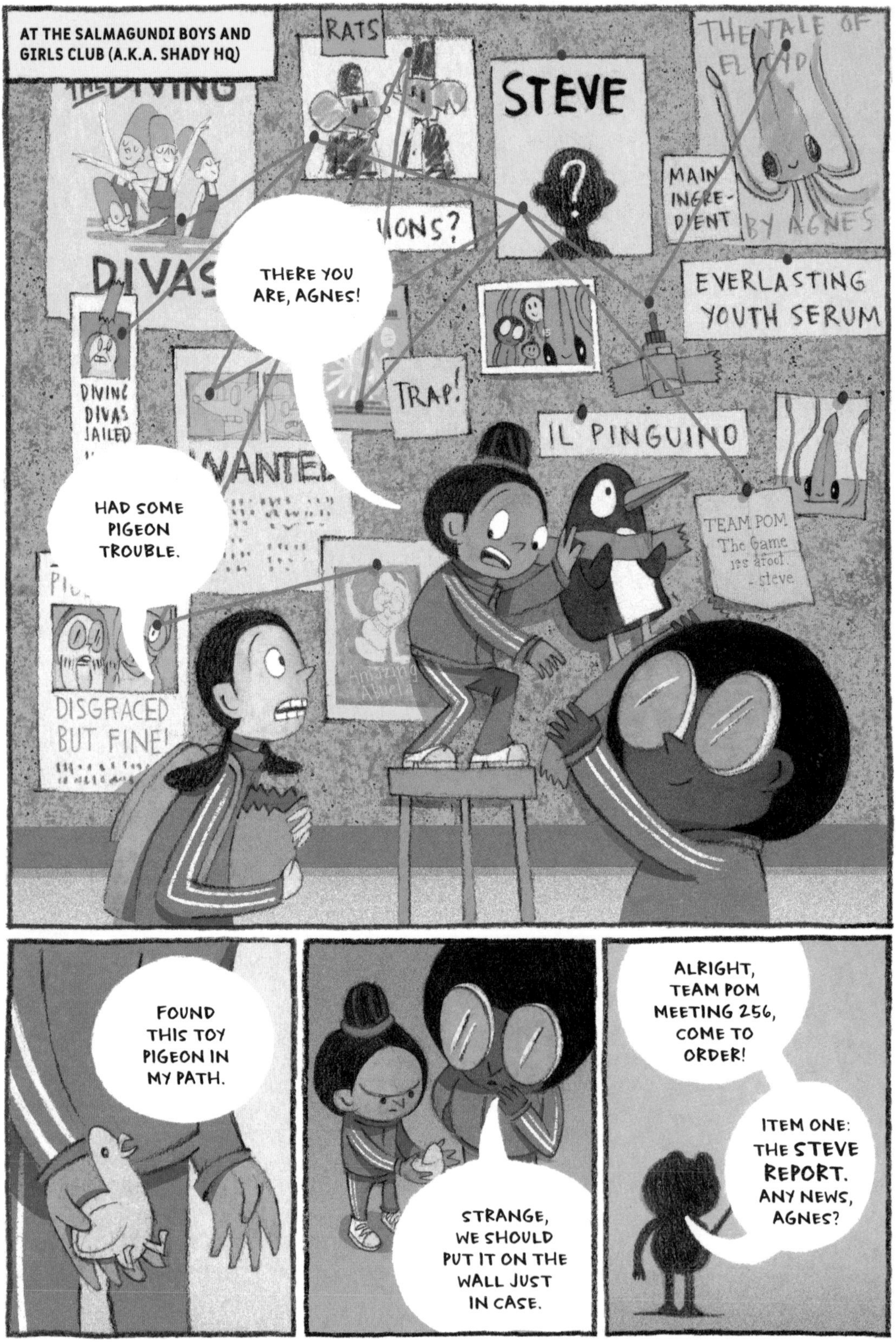
AT THE SALMAGUNDI BOYS AND GIRLS CLUB (A.K.A. SHADY HQ)
RATS
STEVE
THE DIVING DIVAS
MAIN INGRE-DIENT
BY AGNES
EVERLASTING YOUTH SERUM
DIVING DIVAS JAILED
WANTED
TRAP!
IL PINGUINO
TEAM POM The Game is afoot. - steve
DISGRACED BUT FINE!
THERE YOU ARE, AGNES!
HAD SOME PIGEON TROUBLE.
FOUND THIS TOY PIGEON IN MY PATH.
STRANGE, WE SHOULD PUT IT ON THE WALL JUST IN CASE.
ALRIGHT, TEAM POM MEETING 256, COME TO ORDER!
ITEM ONE: THE STEVE REPORT. ANY NEWS, AGNES?

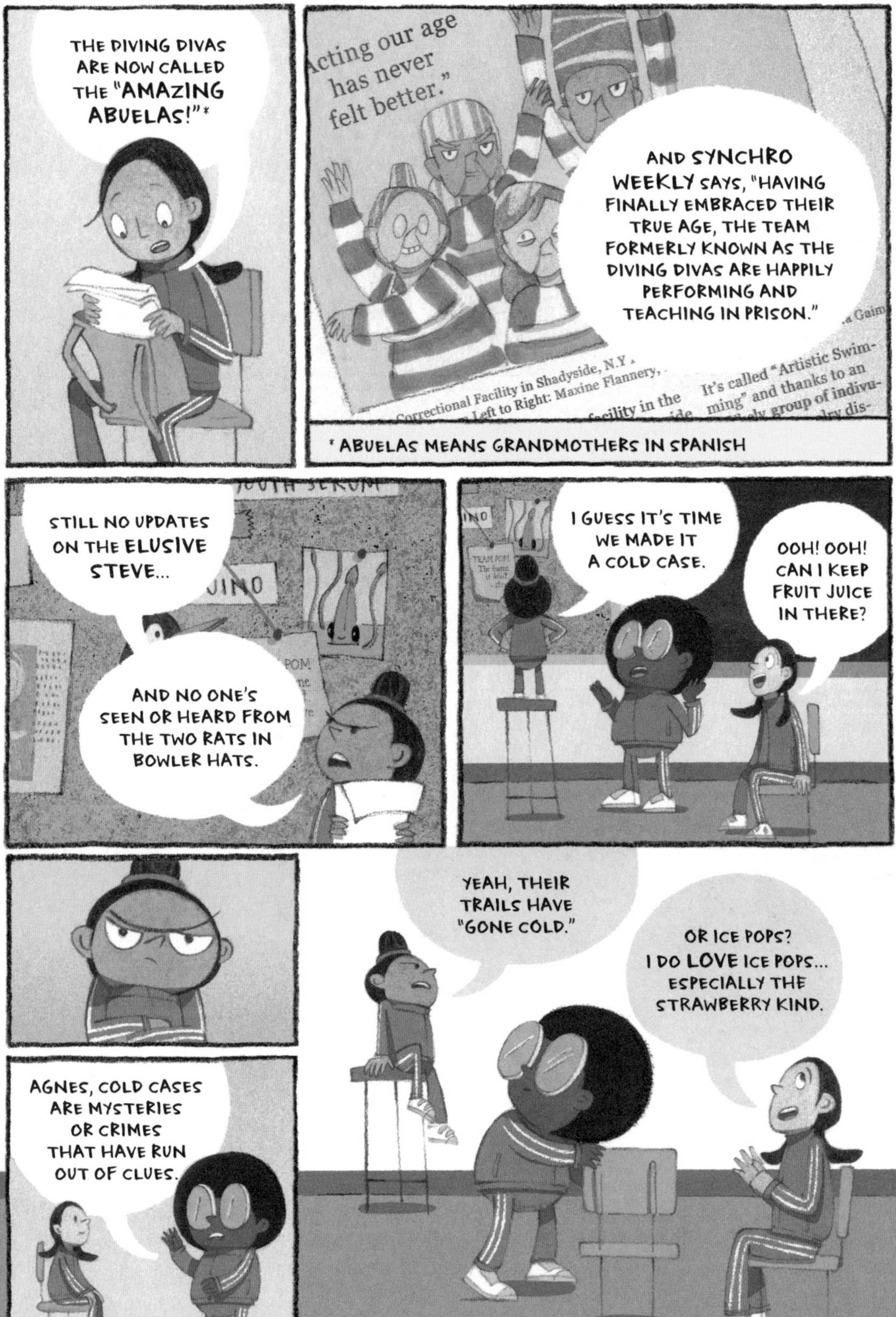
THE DIVING DIVAS ARE NOW CALLED THE "AMAZING ABUELAS!"*
cting our age has never felt better."
AND SYNCHRO WEEKLY SAYS, "HAVING FINALLY EMBRACED THEIR TRUE AGE, THE TEAM FORMERLY KNOWN AS THE DIVING DIVAS ARE HAPPILY PERFORMING AND TEACHING IN PRISON."
* ABUELAS MEANS GRANDMOTHERS IN SPANISH
STILL NO UPDATES ON THE ELUSIVE STEVE...
AND NO ONE'S SEEN OR HEARD FROM THE TWO RATS IN BOWLER HATS.
I GUESS IT'S TIME WE MADE IT A COLD CASE.
OOH! OOH! CAN I KEEP FRUIT JUICE IN THERE?
AGNES, COLD CASES ARE MYSTERIES OR CRIMES THAT HAVE RUN OUT OF CLUES.
YEAH, THEIR TRAILS HAVE "GONE COLD."
OR ICE POPS? I DO LOVE ICE POPS... ESPECIALLY THE STRAWBERRY KIND.

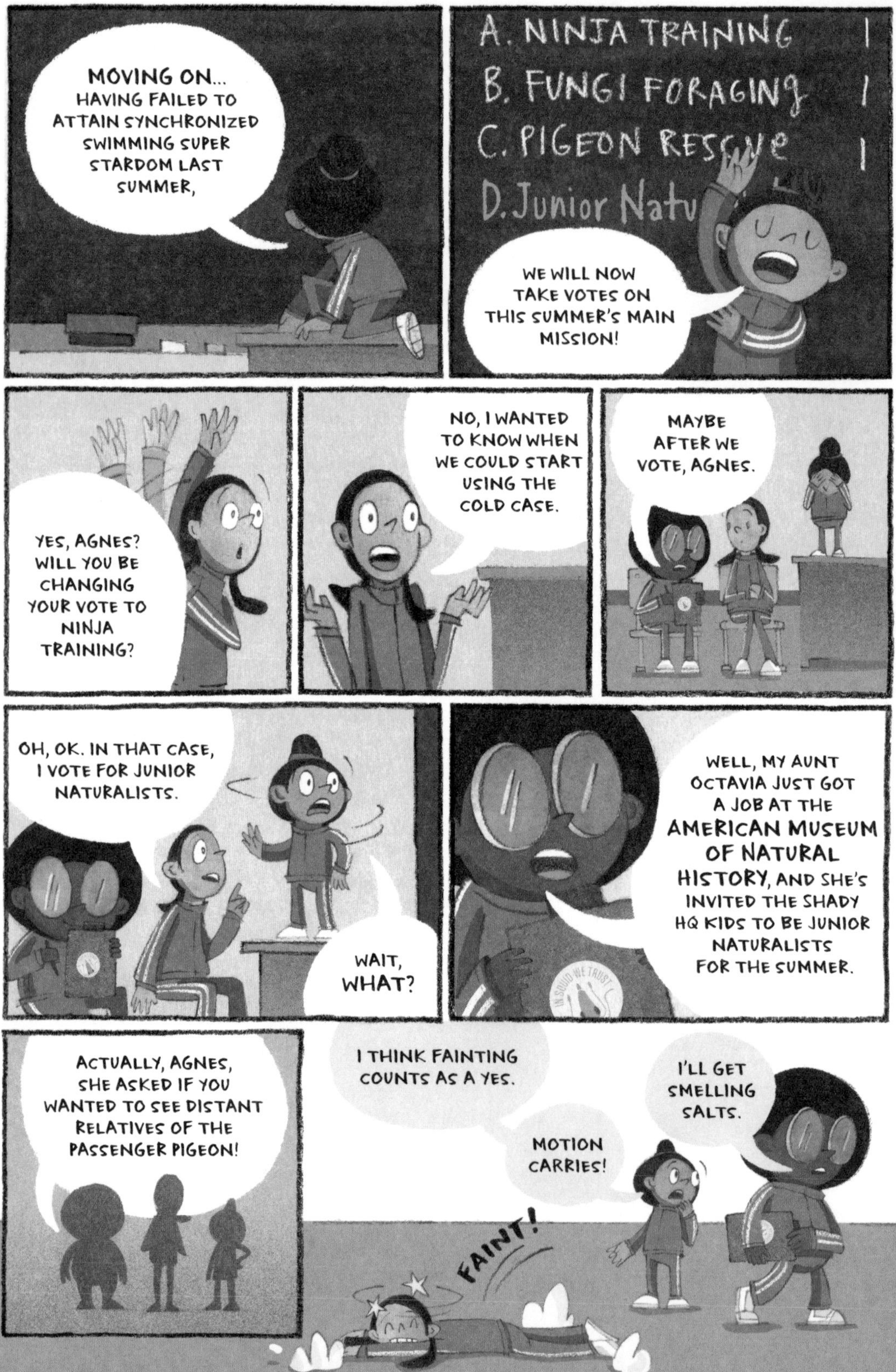
MOVING ON... HAVING FAILED TO ATTAIN SYNCHRONIZED SWIMMING SUPER STARDOM LAST SUMMER,
A. NINJA TRAINING I
B. FUNGI FORAGING I
C. PIGEON RESCUE I
D. Junior Natu
WE WILL NOW TAKE VOTES ON THIS SUMMER'S MAIN MISSION!
YES, AGNES? WILL YOU BE CHANGING YOUR VOTE TO NINJA TRAINING?
NO, I WANTED TO KNOW WHEN WE COULD START USING THE COLD CASE.
MAYBE AFTER WE VOTE, AGNES.
OH, OK. IN THAT CASE, I VOTE FOR JUNIOR NATURALISTS.
WAIT, WHAT?
WELL, MY AUNT OCTAVIA JUST GOT A JOB AT THE AMERICAN MUSEUM OF NATURAL HISTORY, AND SHE'S INVITED THE SHADY HQ KIDS TO BE JUNIOR NATURALISTS FOR THE SUMMER.
IN SQUID WE TRUST
ACTUALLY, AGNES, SHE ASKED IF YOU WANTED TO SEE DISTANT RELATIVES OF THE PASSENGER PIGEON!
I THINK FAINTING COUNTS AS A YES.
MOTION CARRIES!
I'LL GET SMELLING SALTS.
FAINT!

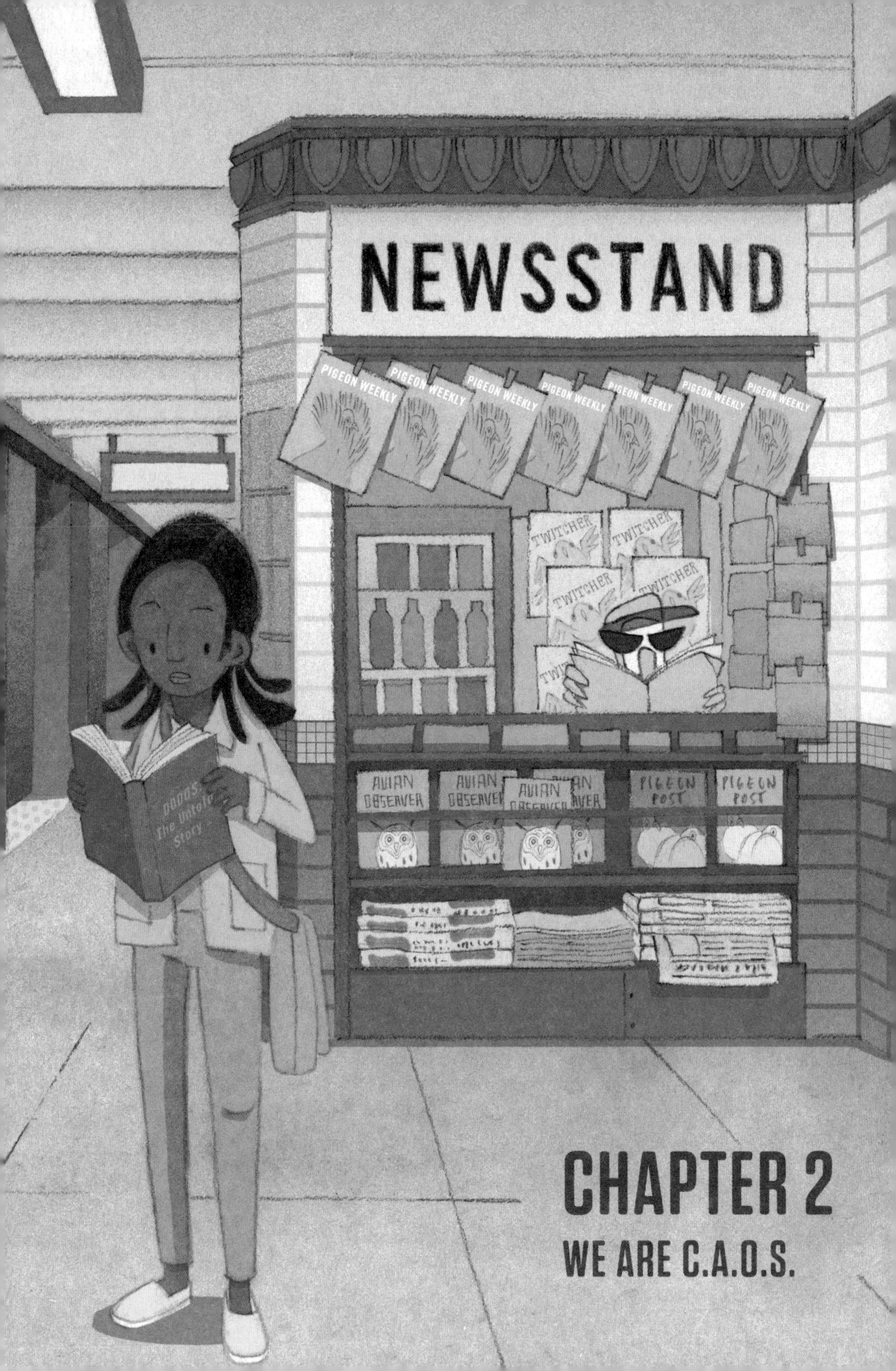
NEWSSTAND
PIGEON WEEKLY
TWITCHER
AVIAN OBSERVER
PIGEON POST

CHAPTER 2

WE ARE C.A.O.S.

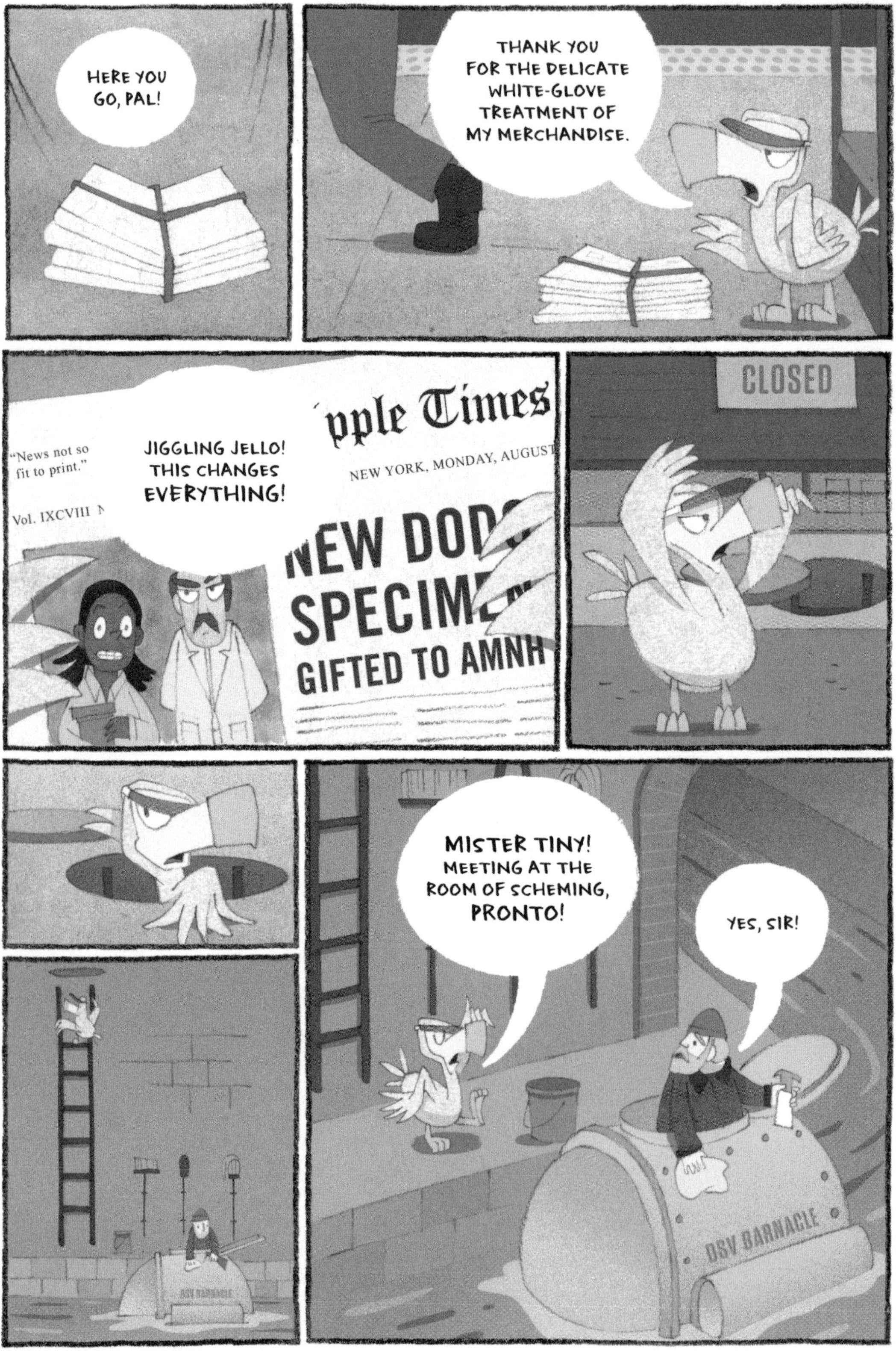
HERE YOU GO, PAL!
THANK YOU FOR THE DELICATE WHITE-GLOVE TREATMENT OF MY MERCHANDISE.
pple Times
"News not so fit to print."
NEW YORK, MONDAY, AUGUST
Vol. IXCVIII
JIGGLING JELLO! THIS CHANGES EVERYTHING!
NEW DOD
SPECIME
GIFTED TO AMNH
CLOSED
DSV BARNACLE
MISTER TINY! MEETING AT THE ROOM OF SCHEMING, PRONTO!
YES, SIR!
DSV BARNACLE

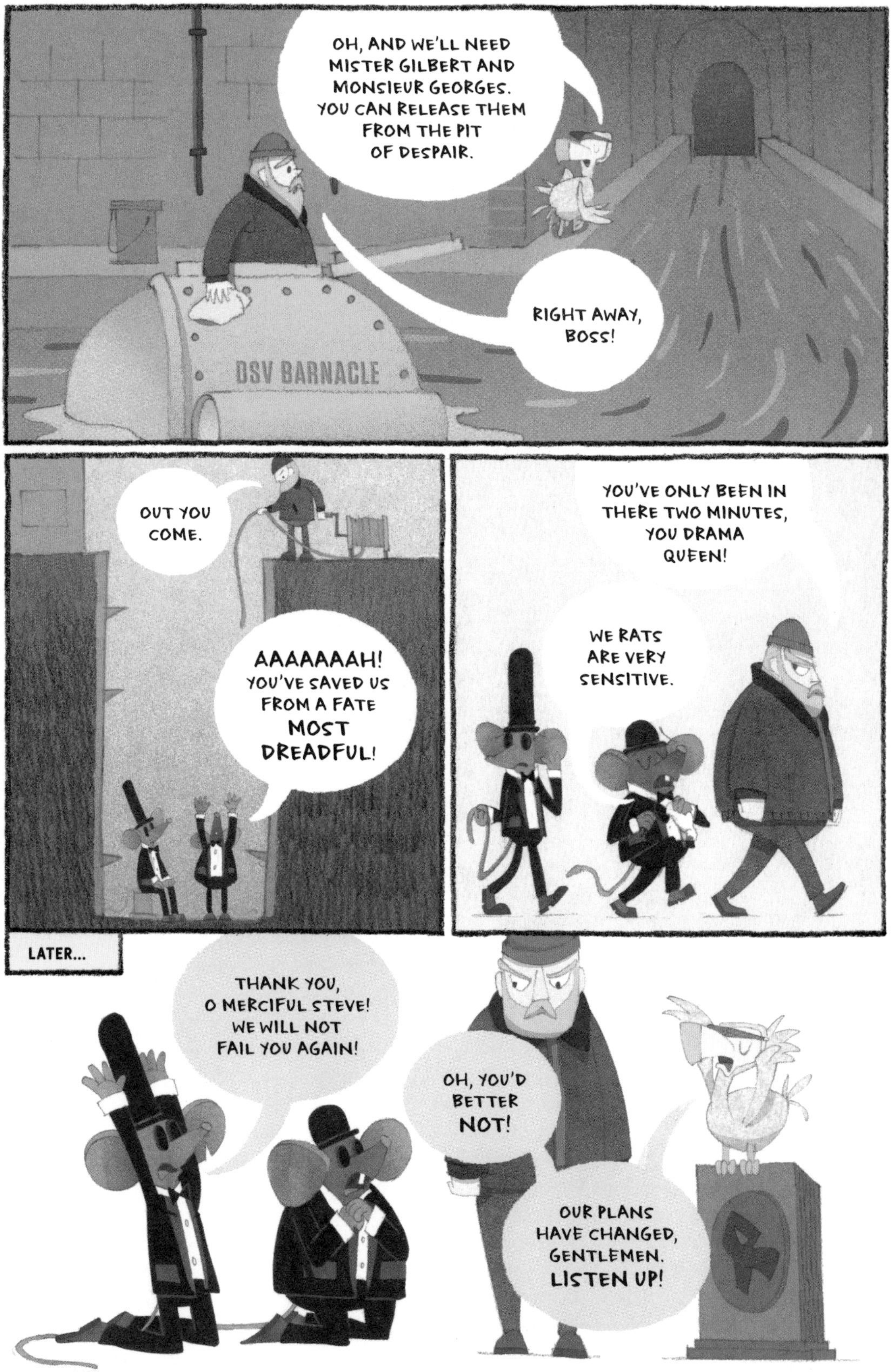
OH, AND WE'LL NEED MISTER GILBERT AND MONSIEUR GEORGES. YOU CAN RELEASE THEM FROM THE PIT OF DESPAIR.
RIGHT AWAY, BOSS!
DSV BARNACLE
OUT YOU COME.
AAAAAAAH! YOU'VE SAVED US FROM A FATE MOST DREADFUL!
YOU'VE ONLY BEEN IN THERE TWO MINUTES, YOU DRAMA QUEEN!
WE RATS ARE VERY SENSITIVE.
LATER...
THANK YOU, O MERCIFUL STEVE! WE WILL NOT FAIL YOU AGAIN!
OH, YOU'D BETTER NOT!
OUR PLANS HAVE CHANGED, GENTLEMEN. LISTEN UP!

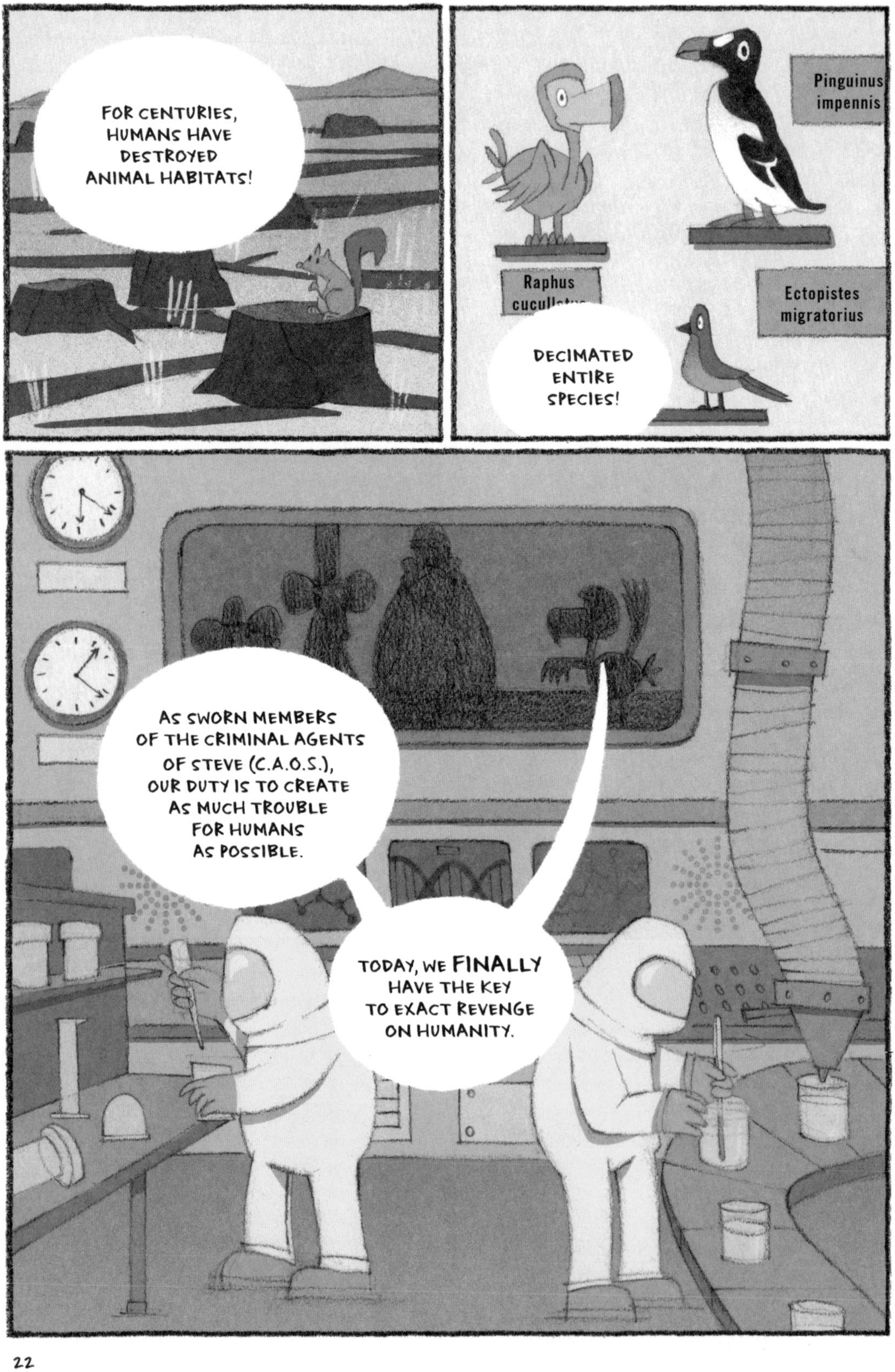
FOR CENTURIES, HUMANS HAVE DESTROYED ANIMAL HABITATS!
Pinguinus impennis
Raphus
Ectopistes migratorius
DECIMATED ENTIRE SPECIES!
AS SWORN MEMBERS OF THE CRIMINAL AGENTS OF STEVE (C.A.O.S.), OUR DUTY IS TO CREATE AS MUCH TROUBLE FOR HUMANS AS POSSIBLE.
TODAY, WE FINALLY HAVE THE KEY TO EXACT REVENGE ON HUMANITY.

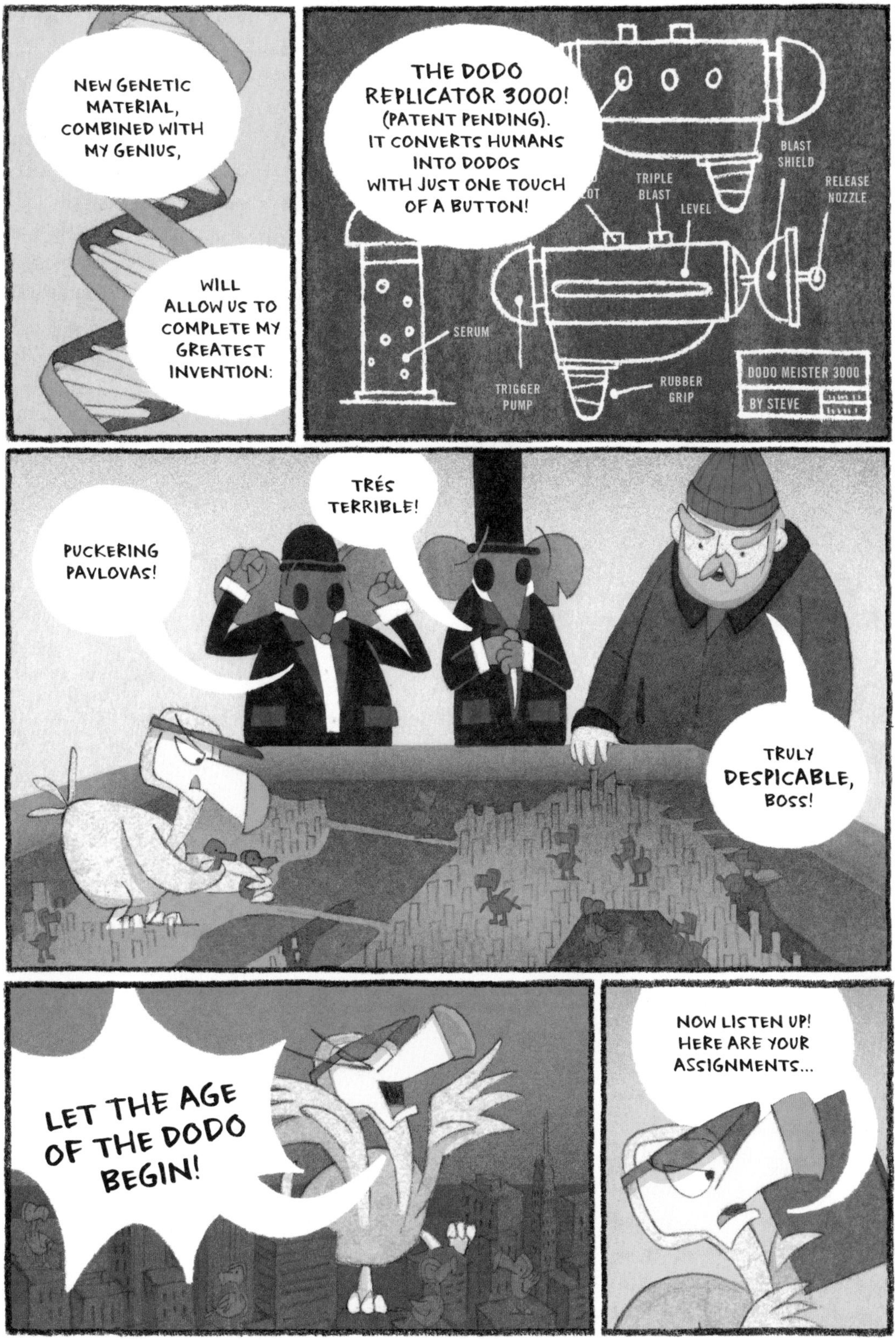
NEW GENETIC MATERIAL, COMBINED WITH MY GENIUS,
WILL ALLOW US TO COMPLETE MY GREATEST INVENTION:
THE DODO REPLICATOR 3000! (PATENT PENDING). IT CONVERTS HUMANS INTO DODOS WITH JUST ONE TOUCH OF A BUTTON!
BLAST SHIELD
RELEASE NOZZLE
TRIPLE BLAST
LEVEL
SERUM
TRIGGER PUMP
RUBBER GRIP
DODO MEISTER 3000
BY STEVE
PUCKERING PAVLOVAS!
TRÉS TERRIBLE!
TRULY DESPICABLE, BOSS!
LET THE AGE OF THE DODO BEGIN!
NOW LISTEN UP! HERE ARE YOUR ASSIGNMENTS...

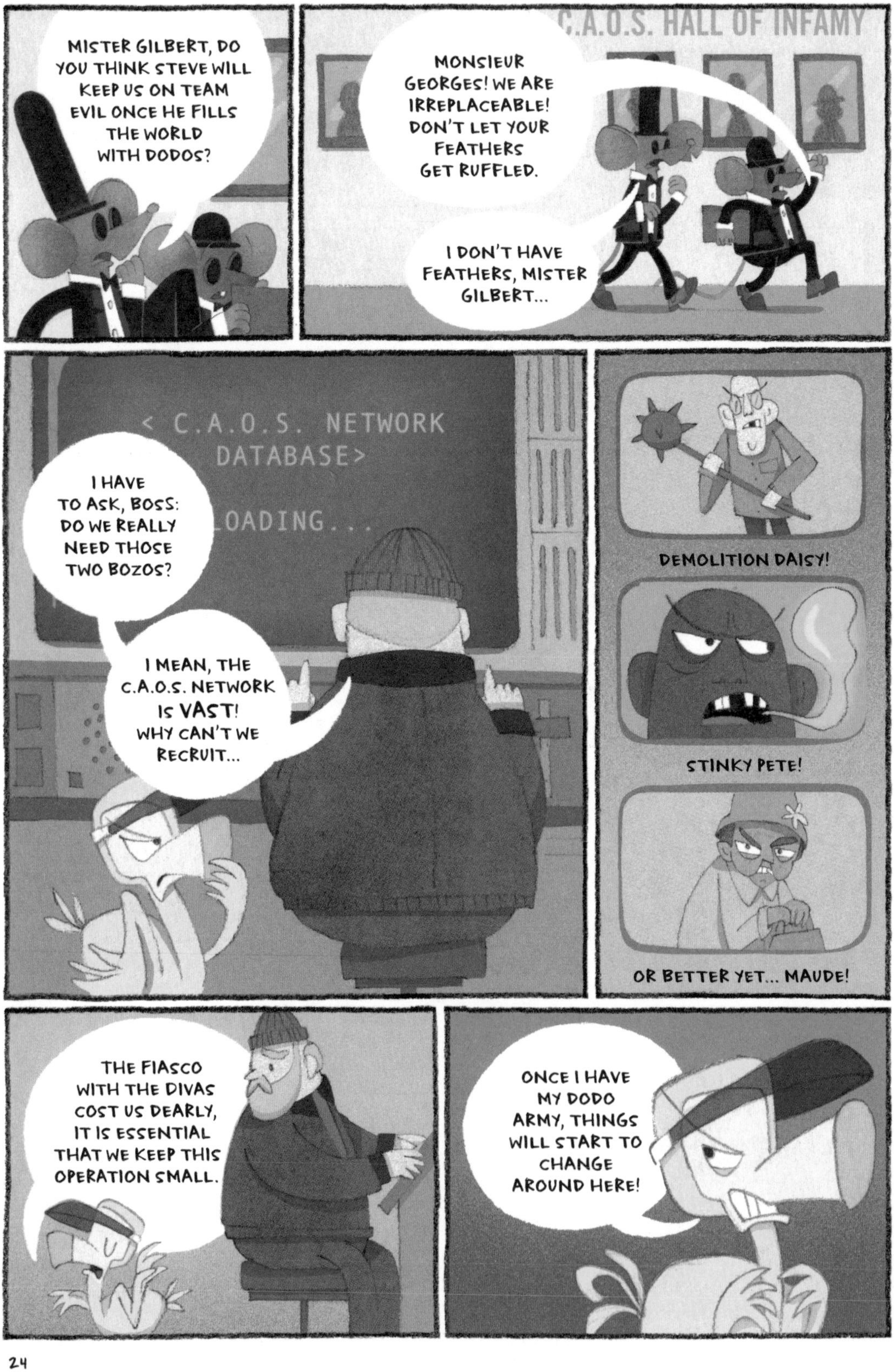
MISTER GILBERT, DO YOU THINK STEVE WILL KEEP US ON TEAM EVIL ONCE HE FILLS THE WORLD WITH DODOS?
C.A.O.S. HALL OF INFAMY
MONSIEUR GEORGES! WE ARE IRREPLACEABLE! DON'T LET YOUR FEATHERS GET RUFFLED.
I DON'T HAVE FEATHERS, MISTER GILBERT...
< C.A.O.S. NETWORK DATABASE>
LOADING...
I HAVE TO ASK, BOSS: DO WE REALLY NEED THOSE TWO BOZOS?
I MEAN, THE C.A.O.S. NETWORK IS VAST! WHY CAN'T WE RECRUIT...
DEMOLITION DAISY!
STINKY PETE!
OR BETTER YET... MAUDE!
THE FIASCO WITH THE DIVAS COST US DEARLY, IT IS ESSENTIAL THAT WE KEEP THIS OPERATION SMALL.
ONCE I HAVE MY DODO ARMY, THINGS WILL START TO CHANGE AROUND HERE!

CHAPTER 3
JUNIOR NATURALISTS

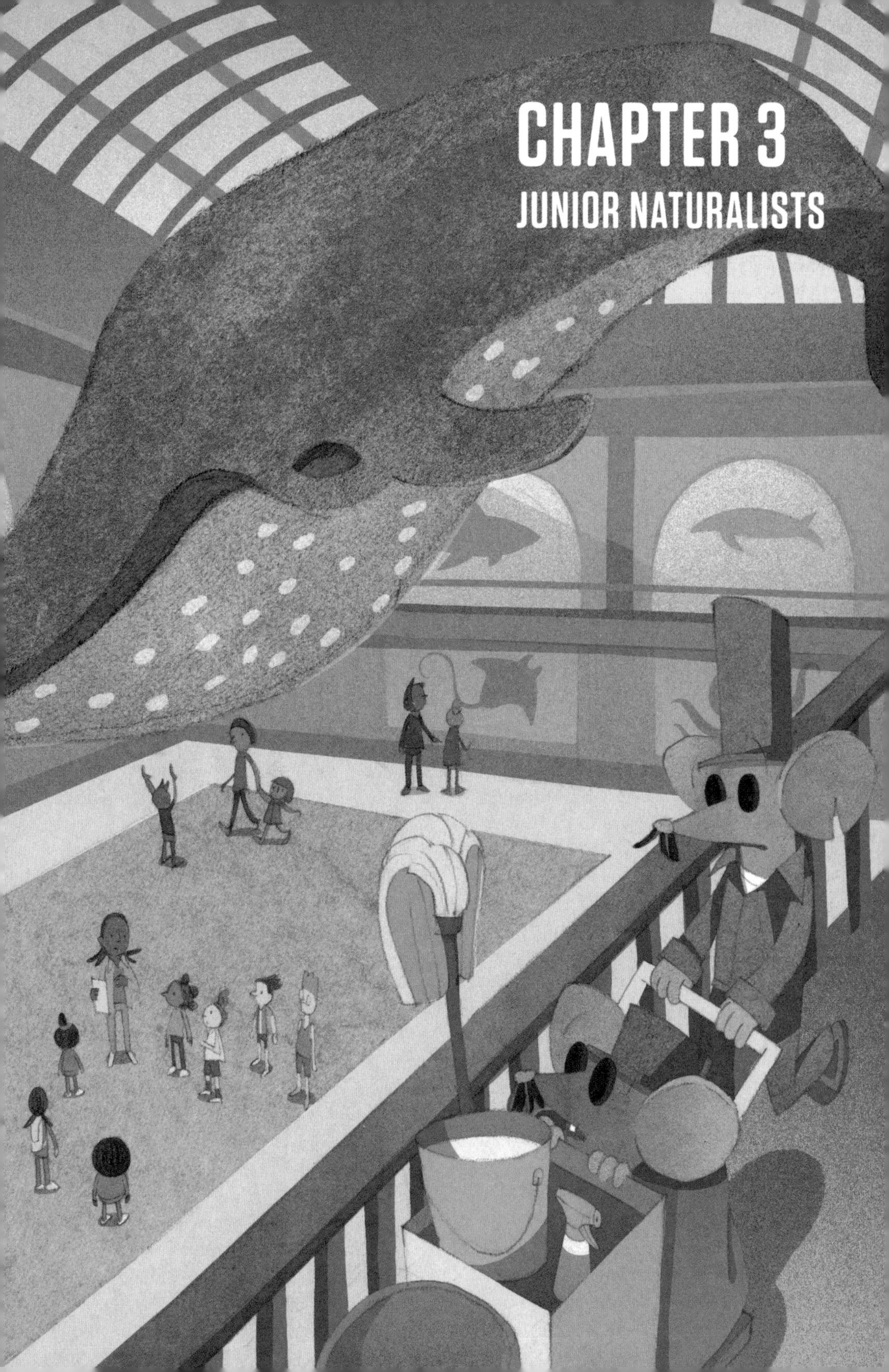

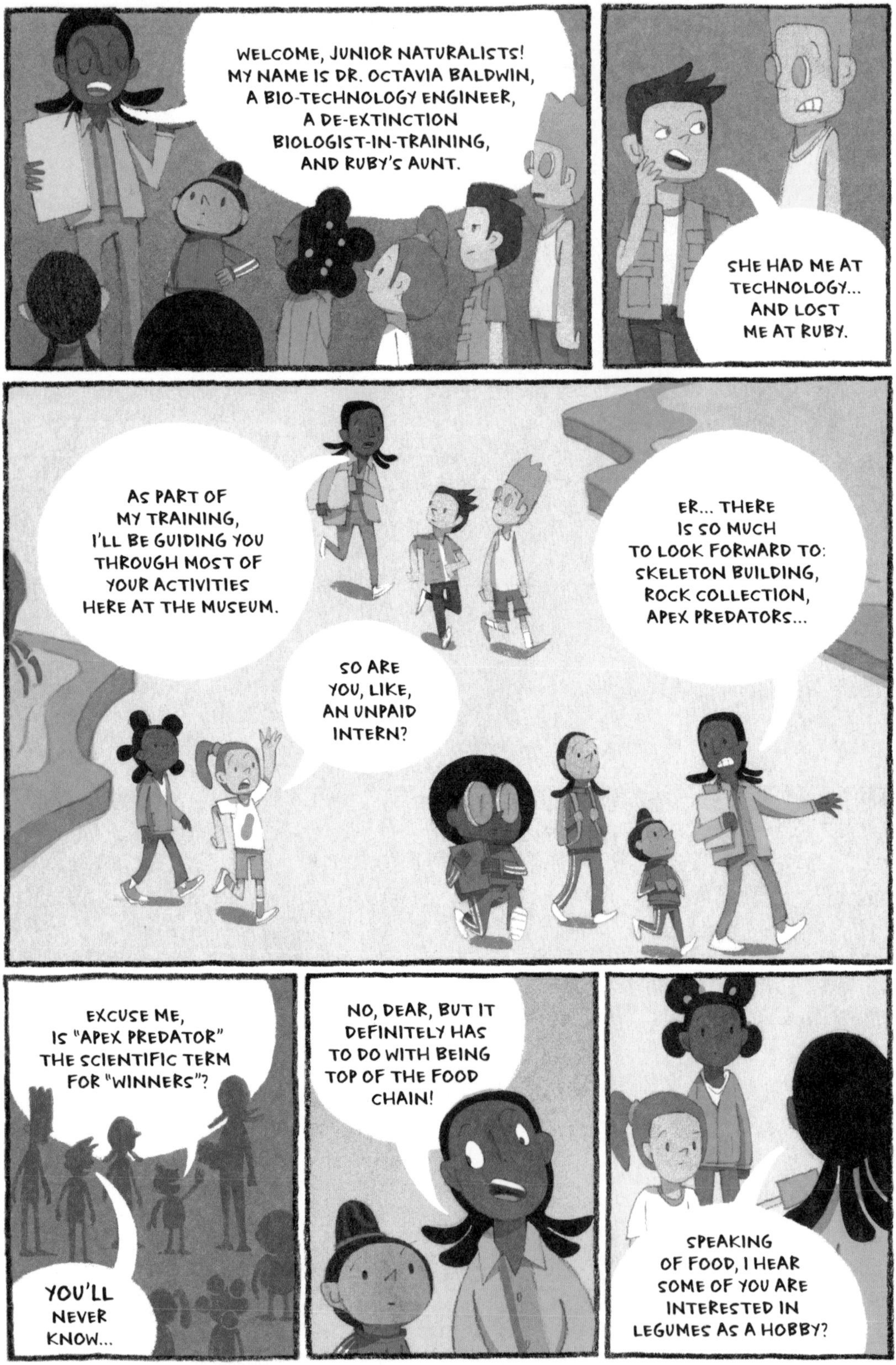
WELCOME, JUNIOR NATURALISTS! MY NAME IS DR. OCTAVIA BALDWIN, A BIO-TECHNOLOGY ENGINEER, A DE-EXTINCTION BIOLOGIST-IN-TRAINING, AND RUBY'S AUNT.
SHE HAD ME AT TECHNOLOGY... AND LOST ME AT RUBY.
AS PART OF MY TRAINING, I'LL BE GUIDING YOU THROUGH MOST OF YOUR ACTIVITIES HERE AT THE MUSEUM.
SO ARE YOU, LIKE, AN UNPAID INTERN?
ER... THERE IS SO MUCH TO LOOK FORWARD TO: SKELETON BUILDING, ROCK COLLECTION, APEX PREDATORS...
EXCUSE ME, IS "APEX PREDATOR" THE SCIENTIFIC TERM FOR "WINNERS"?
YOU'LL NEVER KNOW...
NO, DEAR, BUT IT DEFINITELY HAS TO DO WITH BEING TOP OF THE FOOD CHAIN!
SPEAKING OF FOOD, I HEAR SOME OF YOU ARE INTERESTED IN LEGUMES AS A HOBBY?

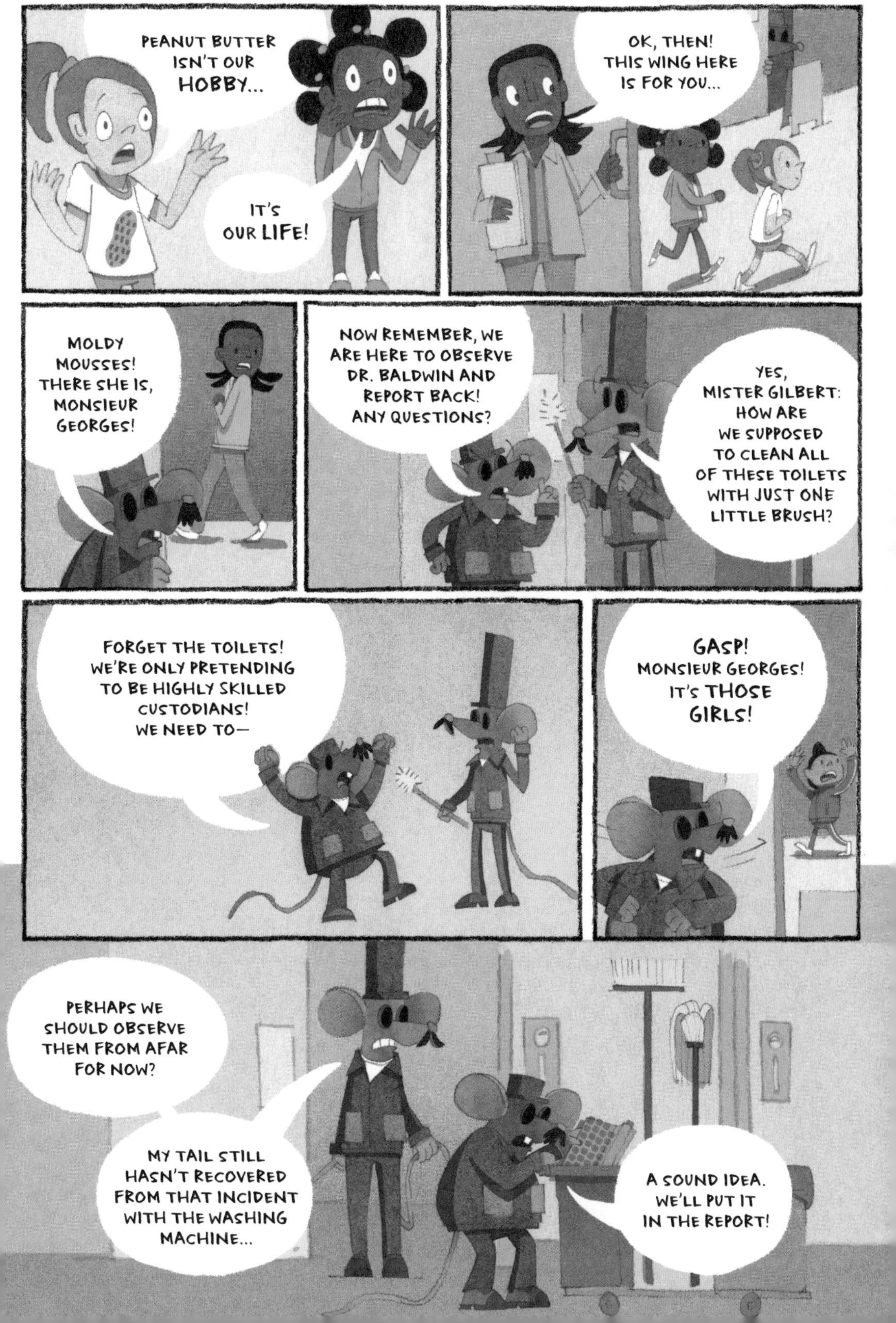
PEANUT BUTTER ISN'T OUR HOBBY...
IT'S OUR LIFE!
OK, THEN! THIS WING HERE IS FOR YOU...
MOLDY MOUSSES! THERE SHE IS, MONSIEUR GEORGES!
NOW REMEMBER, WE ARE HERE TO OBSERVE DR. BALDWIN AND REPORT BACK! ANY QUESTIONS?
YES, MISTER GILBERT: HOW ARE WE SUPPOSED TO CLEAN ALL OF THESE TOILETS WITH JUST ONE LITTLE BRUSH?
FORGET THE TOILETS! WE'RE ONLY PRETENDING TO BE HIGHLY SKILLED CUSTODIANS! WE NEED TO—
GASP! MONSIEUR GEORGES! IT'S THOSE GIRLS!
PERHAPS WE SHOULD OBSERVE THEM FROM AFAR FOR NOW?
MY TAIL STILL HASN'T RECOVERED FROM THAT INCIDENT WITH THE WASHING MACHINE...
A SOUND IDEA. WE'LL PUT IT IN THE REPORT!

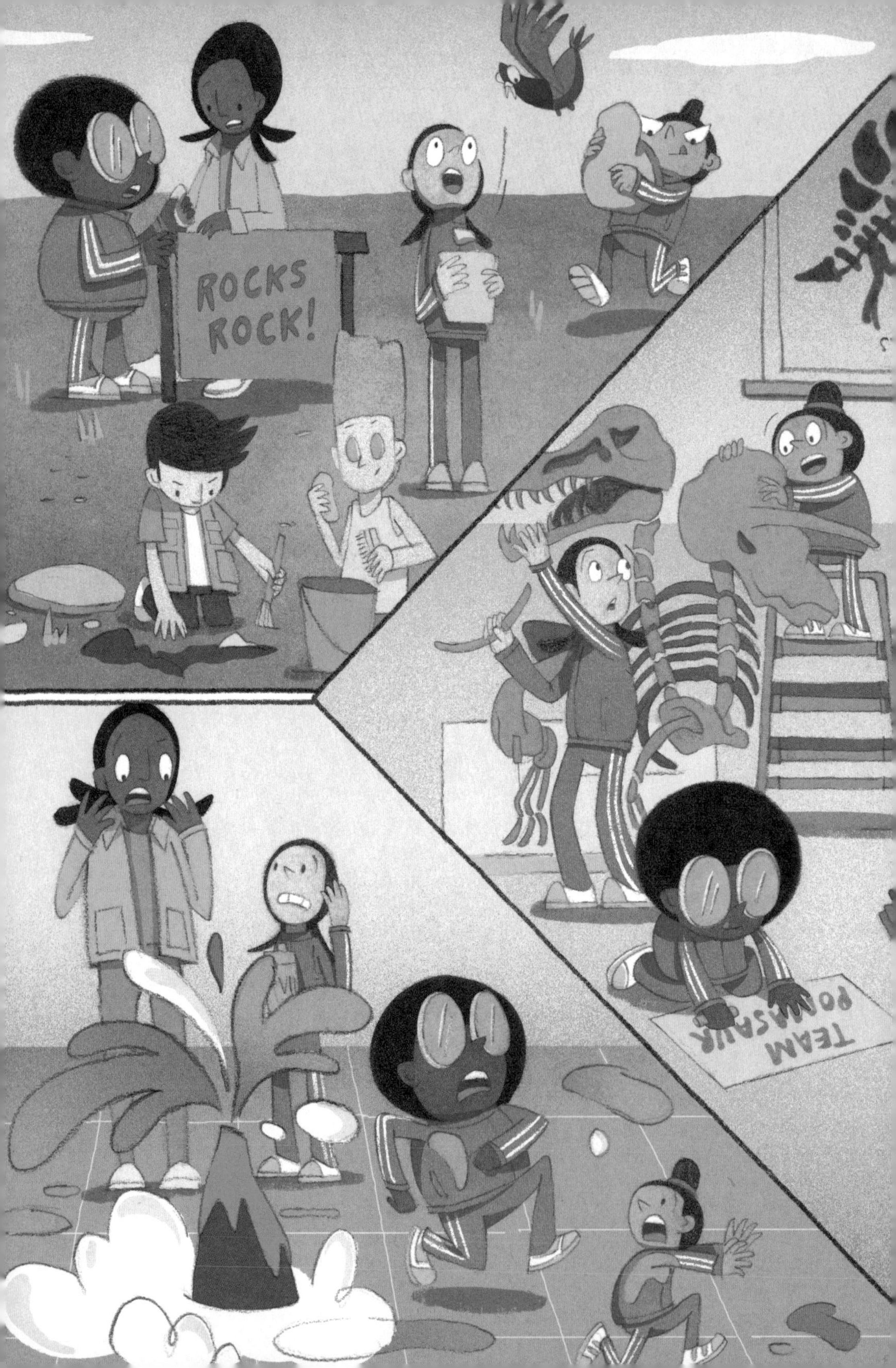
ROCKS ROCK!
TEAM

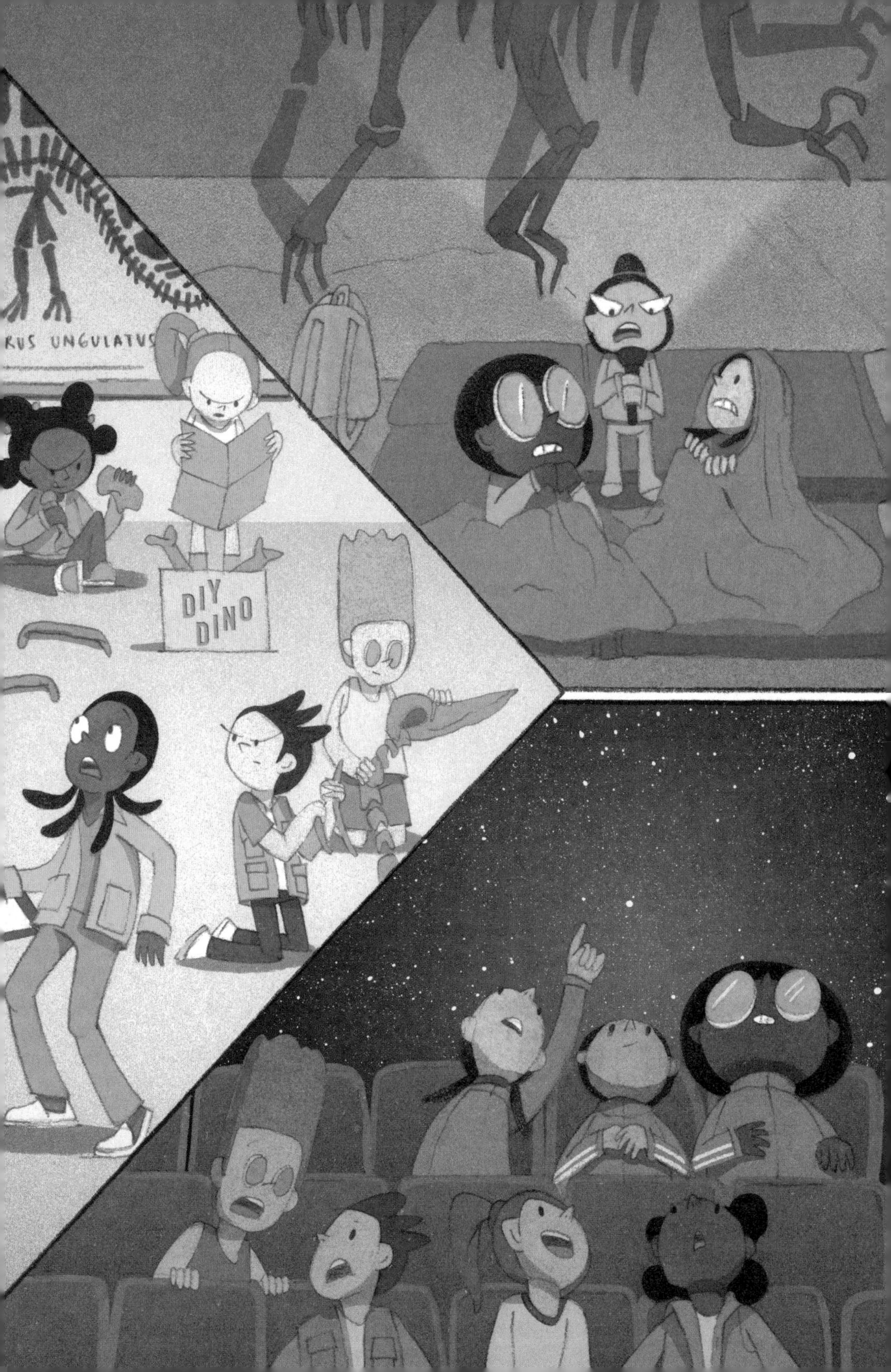
RUS UNGULATUS
DIY DINO

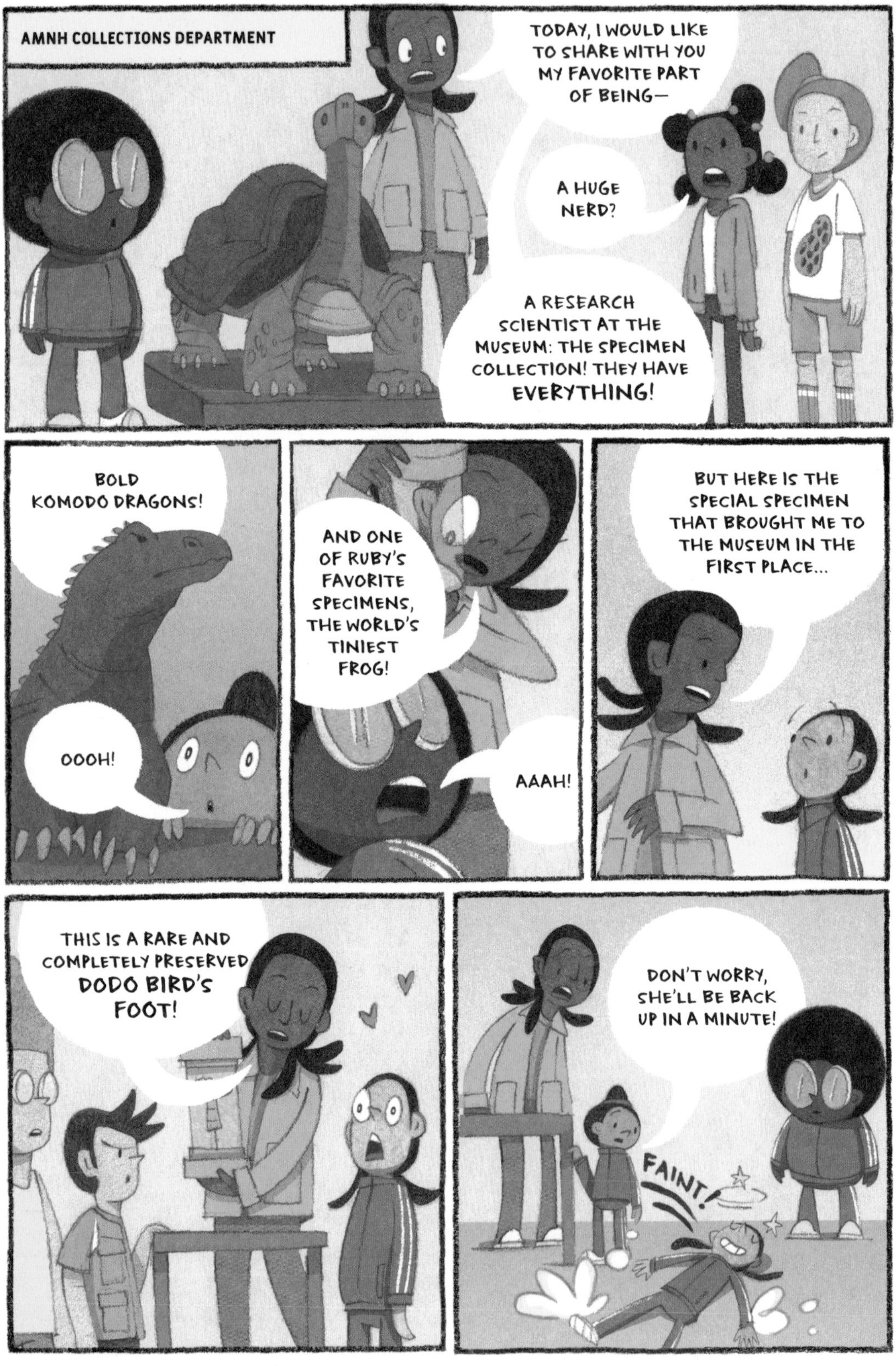
AMNH COLLECTIONS DEPARTMENT
TODAY, I WOULD LIKE TO SHARE WITH YOU MY FAVORITE PART OF BEING—
A HUGE NERD?
A RESEARCH SCIENTIST AT THE MUSEUM: THE SPECIMEN COLLECTION! THEY HAVE EVERYTHING!
BOLD KOMODO DRAGONS!
OOOH!
AND ONE OF RUBY'S FAVORITE SPECIMENS, THE WORLD'S TINIEST FROG!
AAAH!
BUT HERE IS THE SPECIAL SPECIMEN THAT BROUGHT ME TO THE MUSEUM IN THE FIRST PLACE...
THIS IS A RARE AND COMPLETELY PRESERVED DODO BIRD'S FOOT!
DON'T WORRY, SHE'LL BE BACK UP IN A MINUTE!
FAINT!

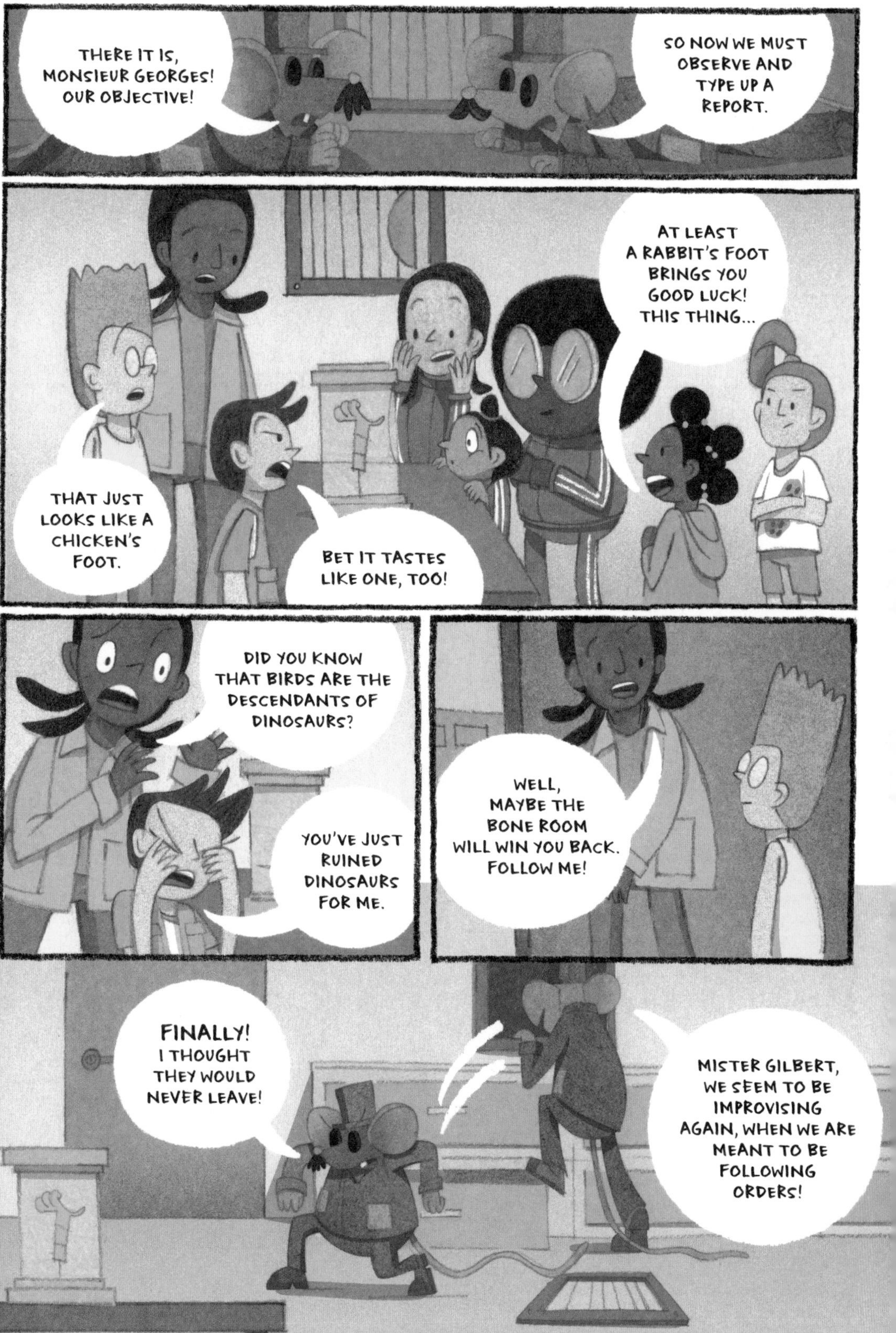
THERE IT IS, MONSIEUR GEORGES! OUR OBJECTIVE!
SO NOW WE MUST OBSERVE AND TYPE UP A REPORT.
AT LEAST A RABBIT'S FOOT BRINGS YOU GOOD LUCK! THIS THING...
THAT JUST LOOKS LIKE A CHICKEN'S FOOT.
BET IT TASTES LIKE ONE, TOO!
DID YOU KNOW THAT BIRDS ARE THE DESCENDANTS OF DINOSAURS?
YOU'VE JUST RUINED DINOSAURS FOR ME.
WELL, MAYBE THE BONE ROOM WILL WIN YOU BACK. FOLLOW ME!
FINALLY! I THOUGHT THEY WOULD NEVER LEAVE!
MISTER GILBERT, WE SEEM TO BE IMPROVISING AGAIN, WHEN WE ARE MEANT TO BE FOLLOWING ORDERS!

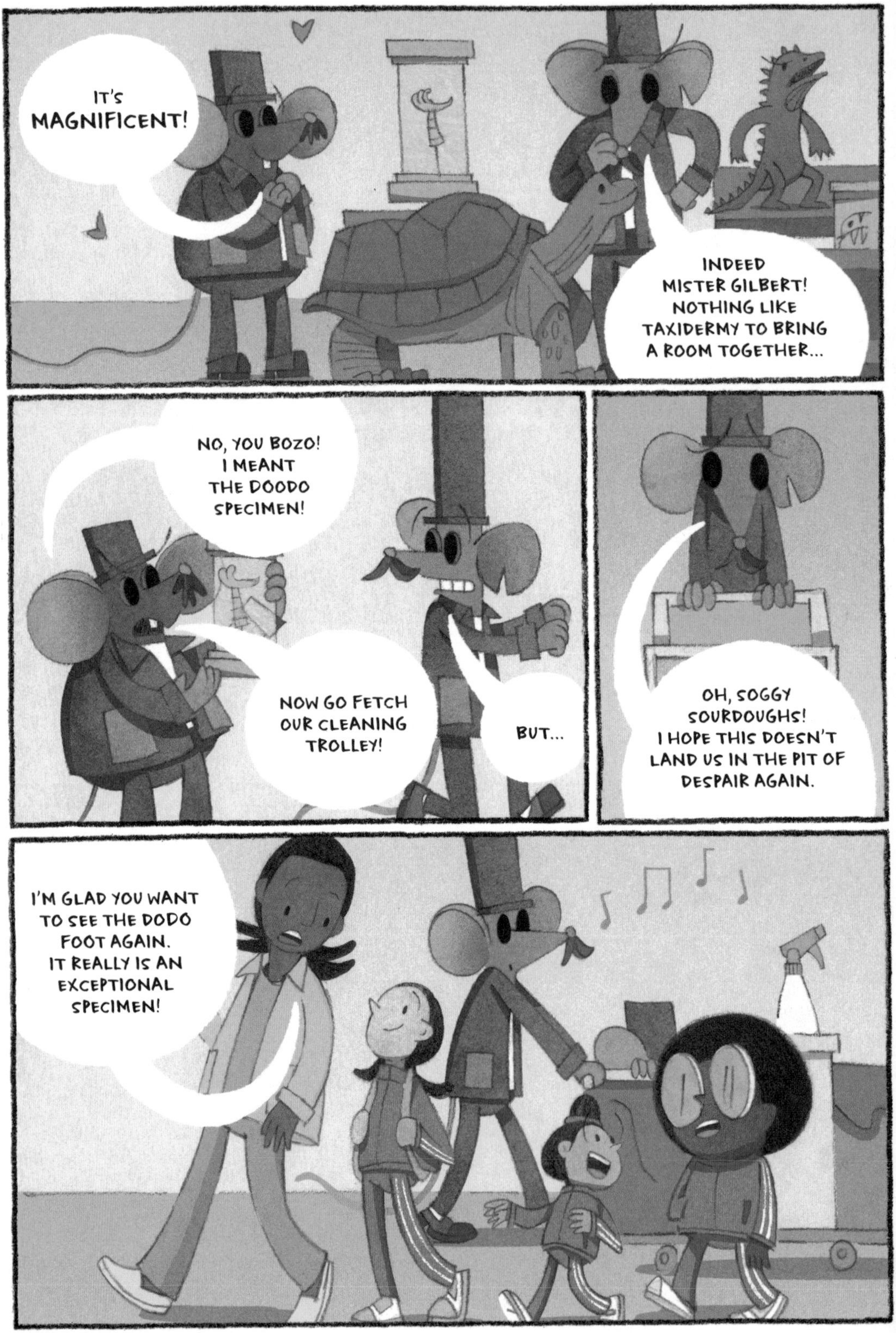
IT'S MAGNIFICENT!
INDEED MISTER GILBERT! NOTHING LIKE TAXIDERMY TO BRING A ROOM TOGETHER...
NO, YOU BOZO! I MEANT THE DODO SPECIMEN!
NOW GO FETCH OUR CLEANING TROLLEY!
BUT...
OH, SOGGY SOURDOUGHS! I HOPE THIS DOESN'T LAND US IN THE PIT OF DESPAIR AGAIN.
I'M GLAD YOU WANT TO SEE THE DODO FOOT AGAIN. IT REALLY IS AN EXCEPTIONAL SPECIMEN!

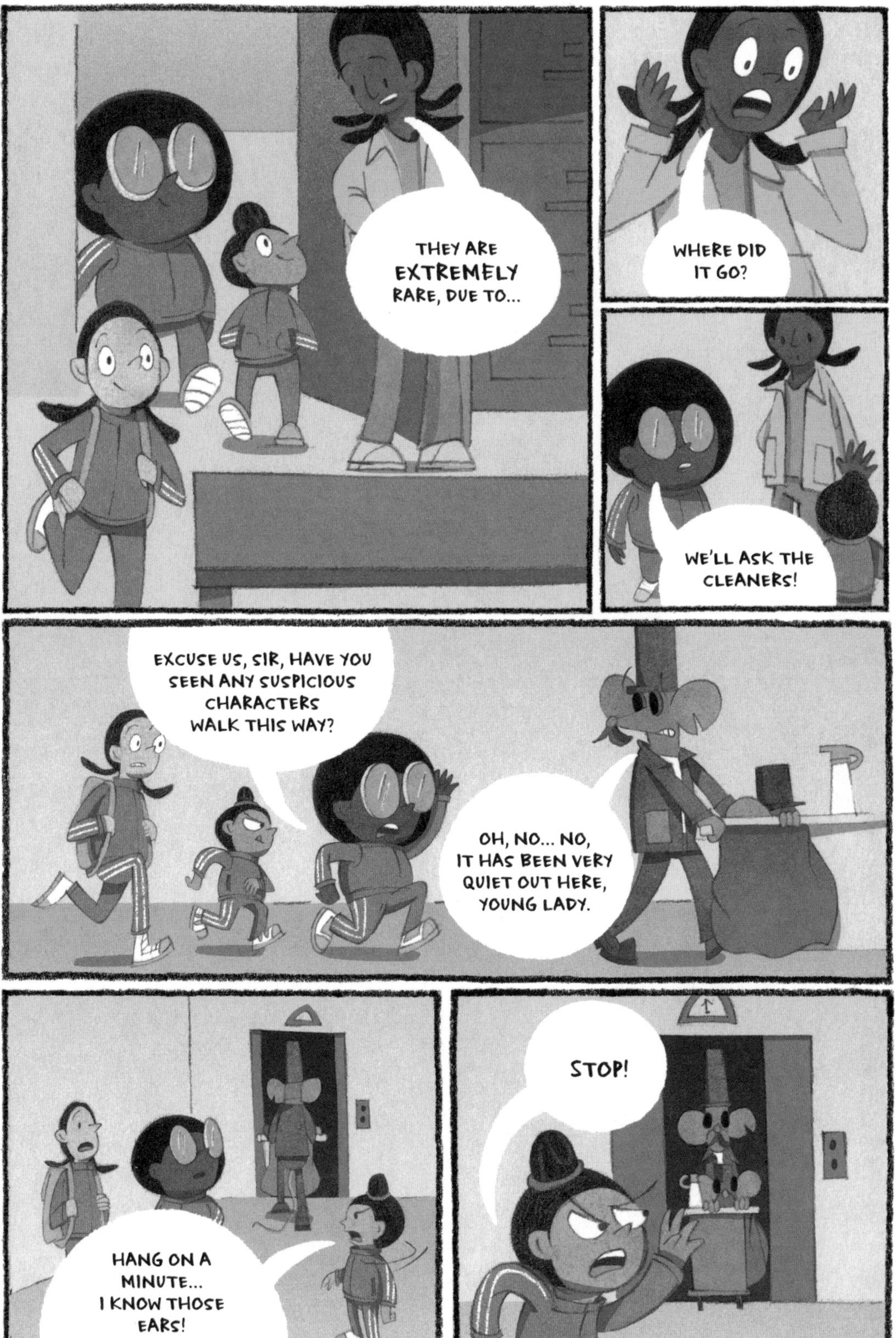
THEY ARE EXTREMELY RARE, DUE TO...
WHERE DID IT GO?
WE'LL ASK THE CLEANERS!
EXCUSE US, SIR, HAVE YOU SEEN ANY SUSPICIOUS CHARACTERS WALK THIS WAY?
OH, NO... NO, IT HAS BEEN VERY QUIET OUT HERE, YOUNG LADY.
HANG ON A MINUTE... I KNOW THOSE EARS!
STOP!

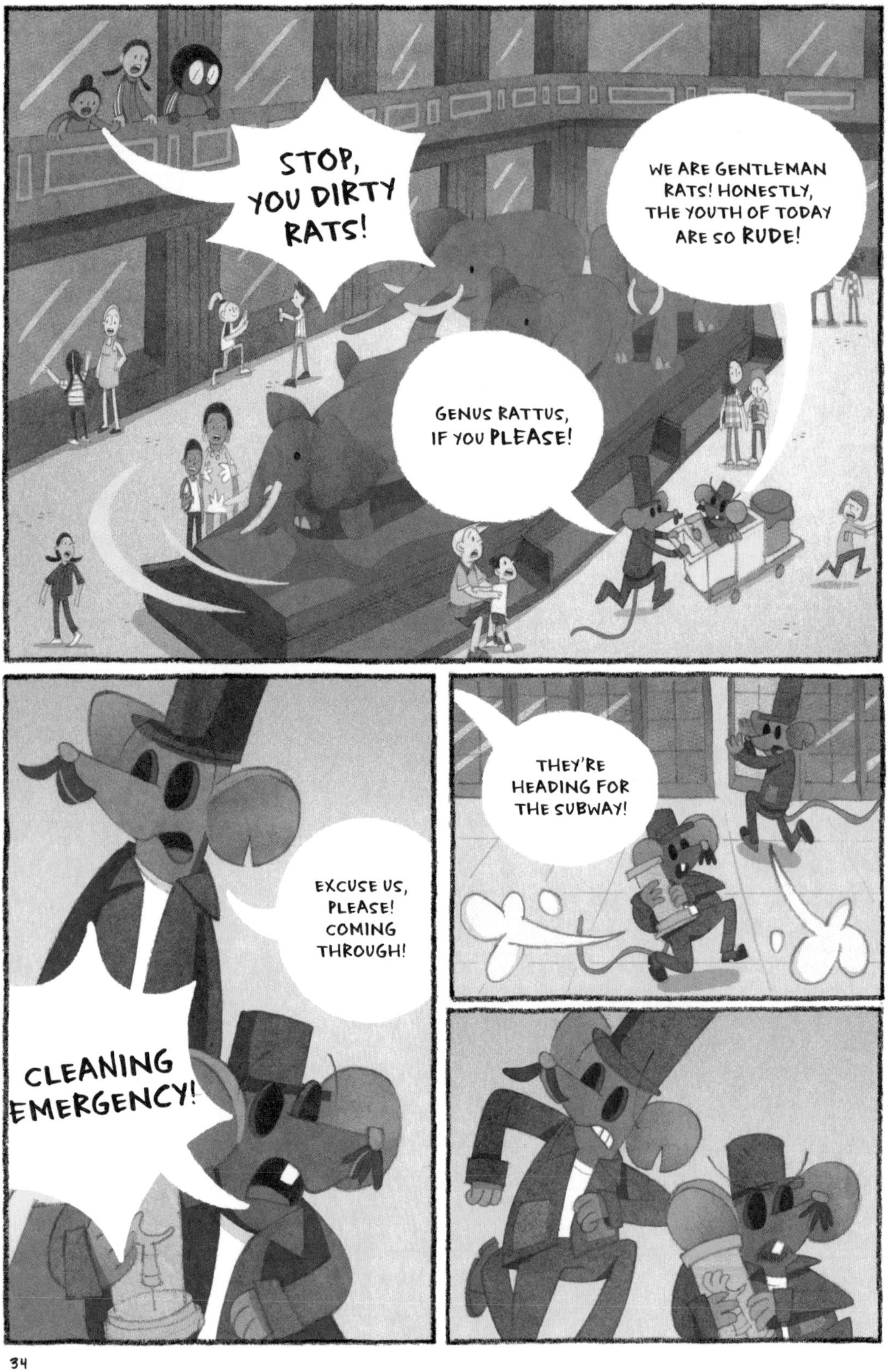
STOP, YOU DIRTY RATS!
WE ARE GENTLEMAN RATS! HONESTLY, THE YOUTH OF TODAY ARE SO RUDE!
GENUS RATTUS, IF YOU PLEASE!
EXCUSE US, PLEASE! COMING THROUGH!
CLEANING EMERGENCY!
THEY'RE HEADING FOR THE SUBWAY!

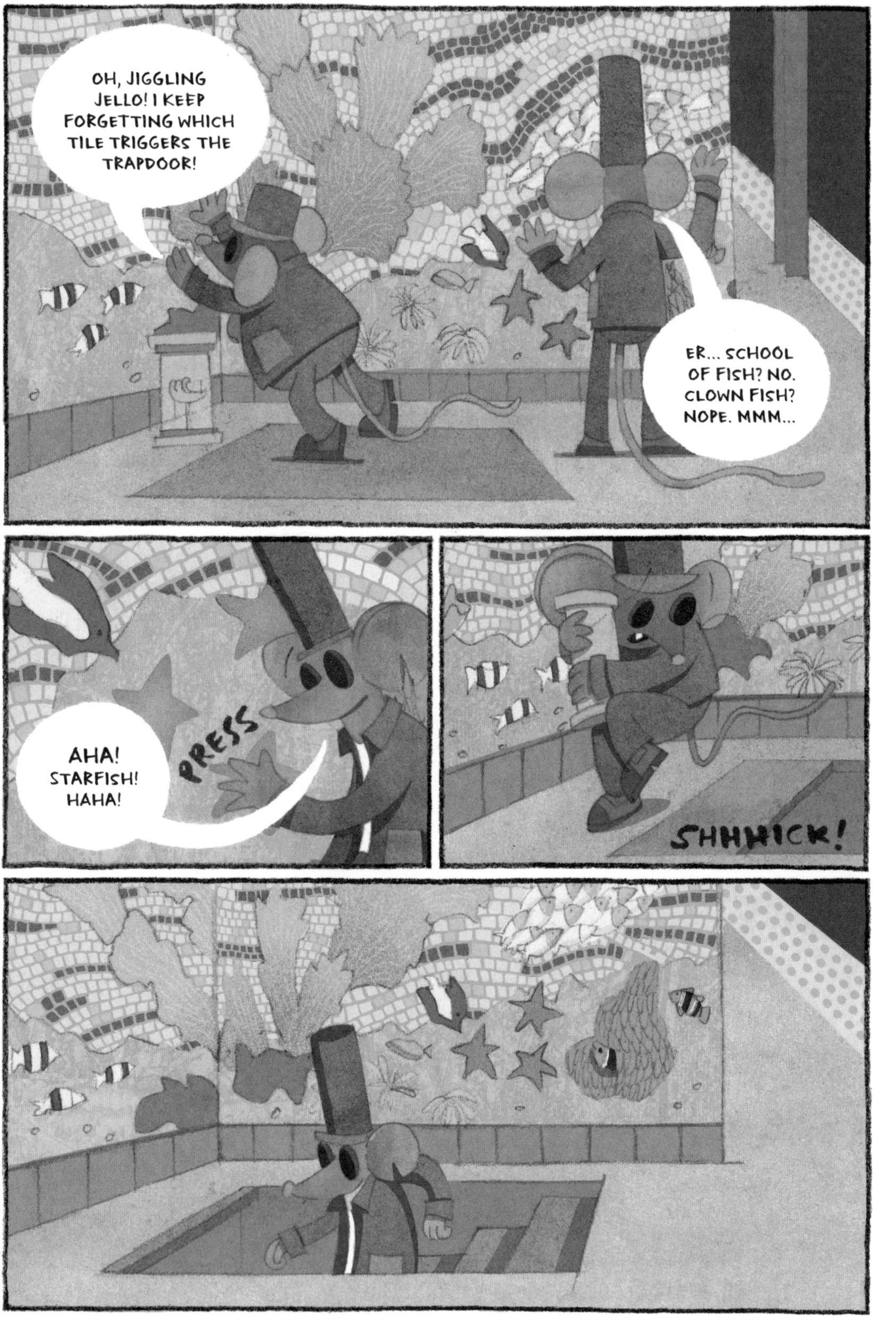
OH, JIGGLING JELLO! I KEEP FORGETTING WHICH TILE TRIGGERS THE TRAPDOOR!
ER... SCHOOL OF FISH? NO. CLOWN FISH? NOPE. MMM...
AHA! STARFISH! HAHA!
PRESS
SHHHICK!

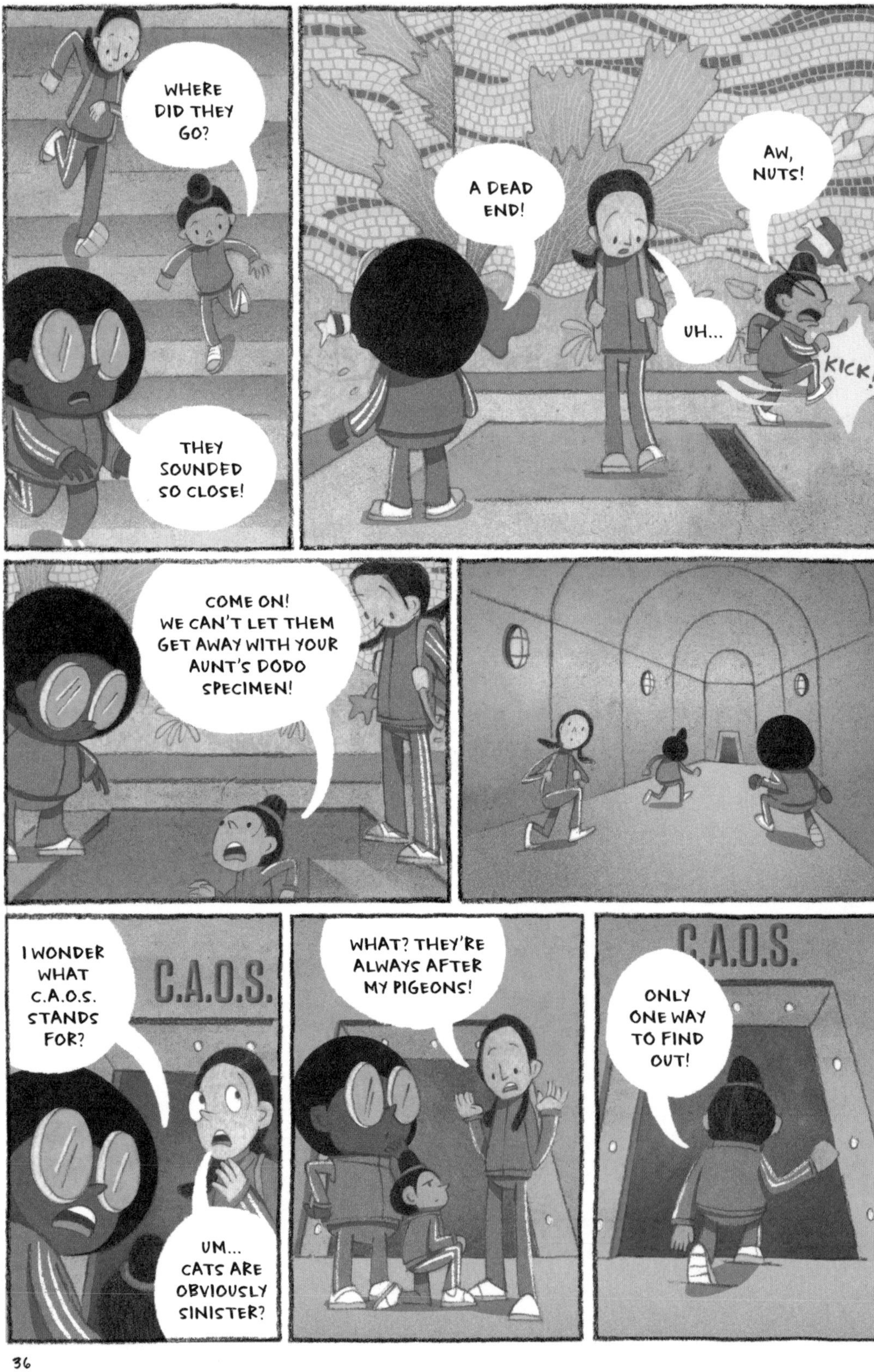
WHERE DID THEY GO?
THEY SOUNDED SO CLOSE!
A DEAD END!
UH...
AW, NUTS!
KICK!
COME ON! WE CAN'T LET THEM GET AWAY WITH YOUR AUNT'S DODO SPECIMEN!
I WONDER WHAT C.A.O.S. STANDS FOR?
C.A.O.S.
UM... CATS ARE OBVIOUSLY SINISTER?
WHAT? THEY'RE ALWAYS AFTER MY PIGEONS!
C.A.O.S.
ONLY ONE WAY TO FIND OUT!

CHAPTER 4
THE LAIR

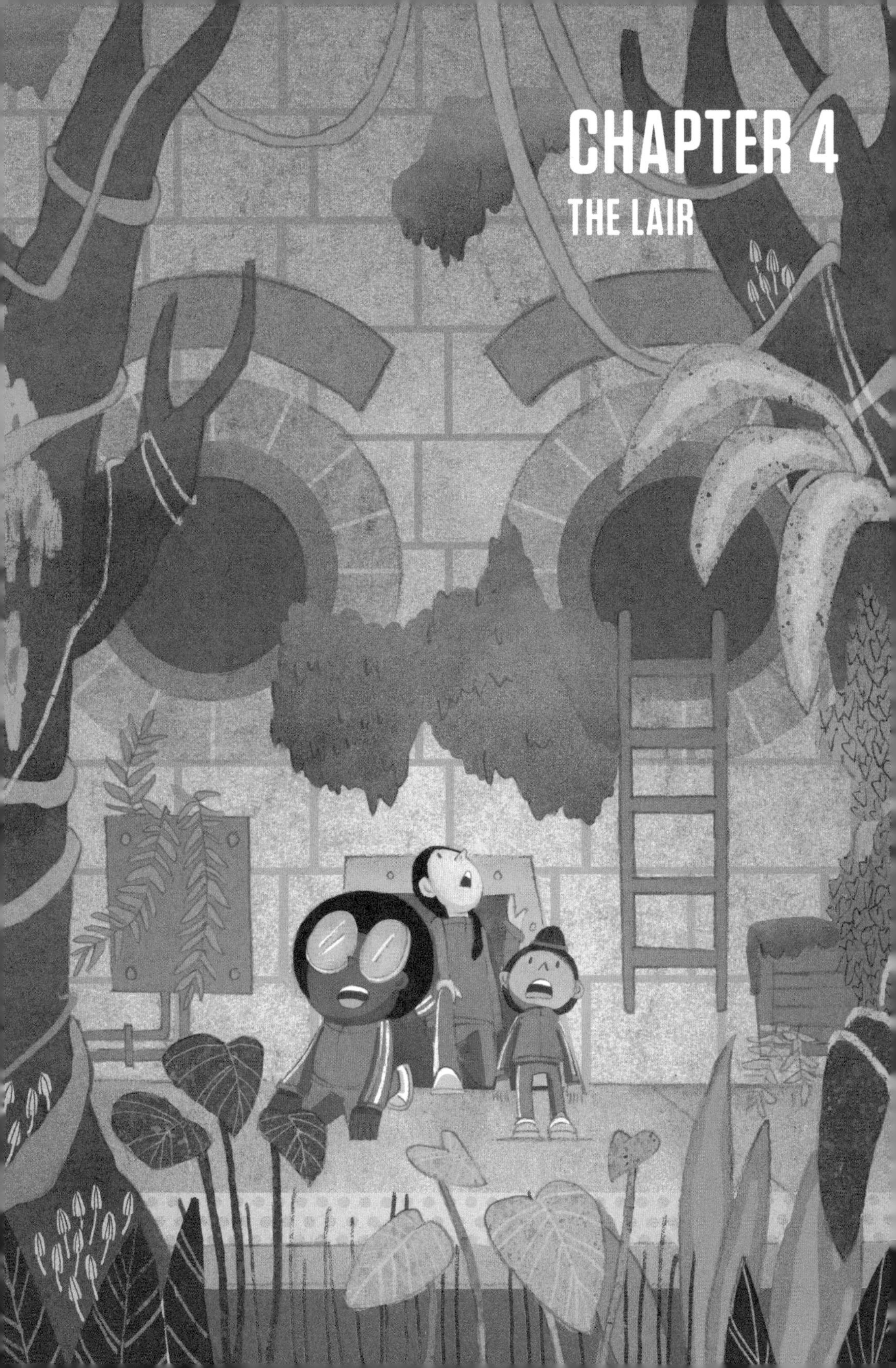

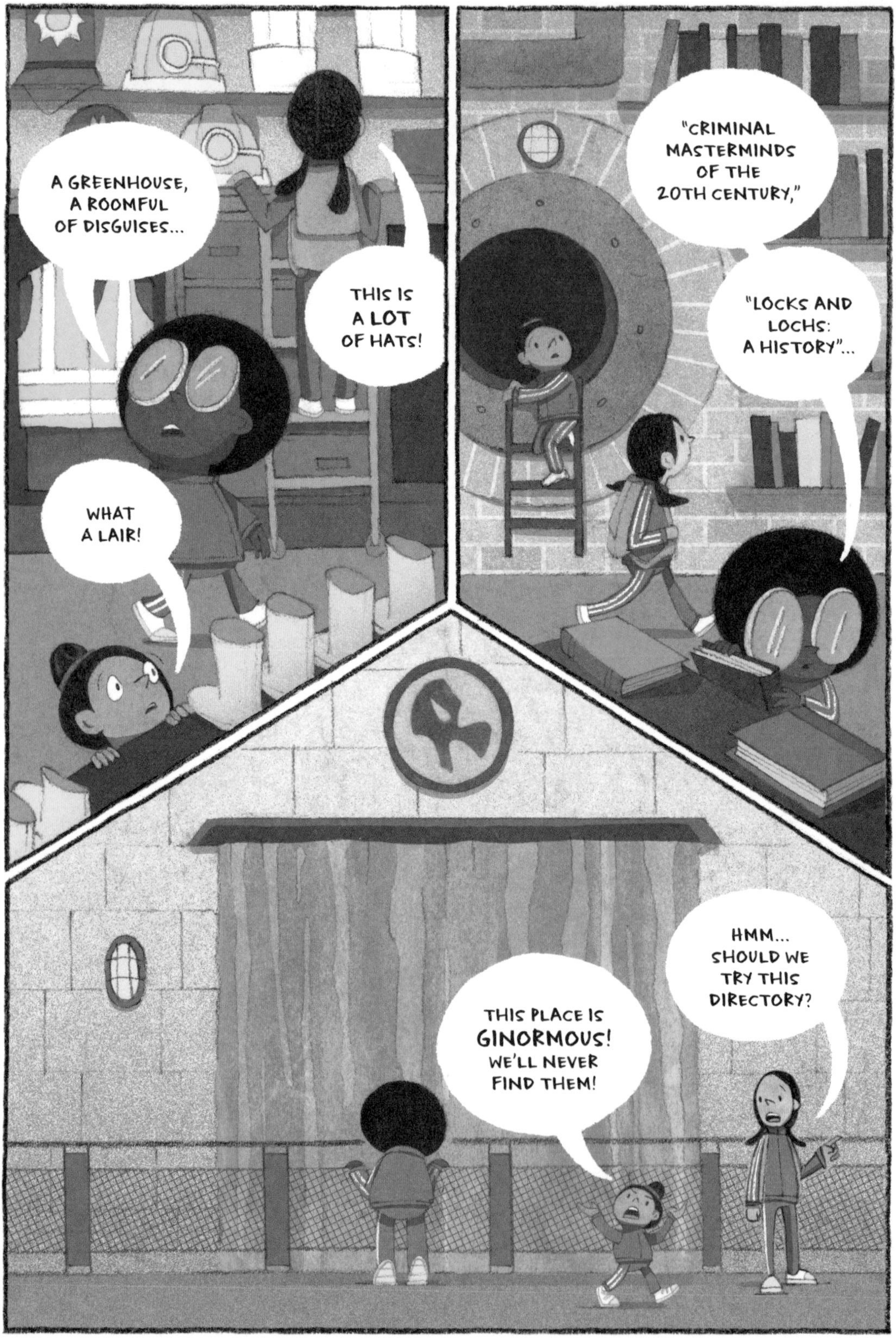

A GREENHOUSE, A ROOMFUL OF DISGUISES...
THIS IS A LOT OF HATS!
WHAT A LAIR!
"CRIMINAL MASTERMINDS OF THE 20TH CENTURY,"
"LOCKS AND LOCHS: A HISTORY"...
HMM... SHOULD WE TRY THIS DIRECTORY?
THIS PLACE IS GINORMOUS! WE'LL NEVER FIND THEM!

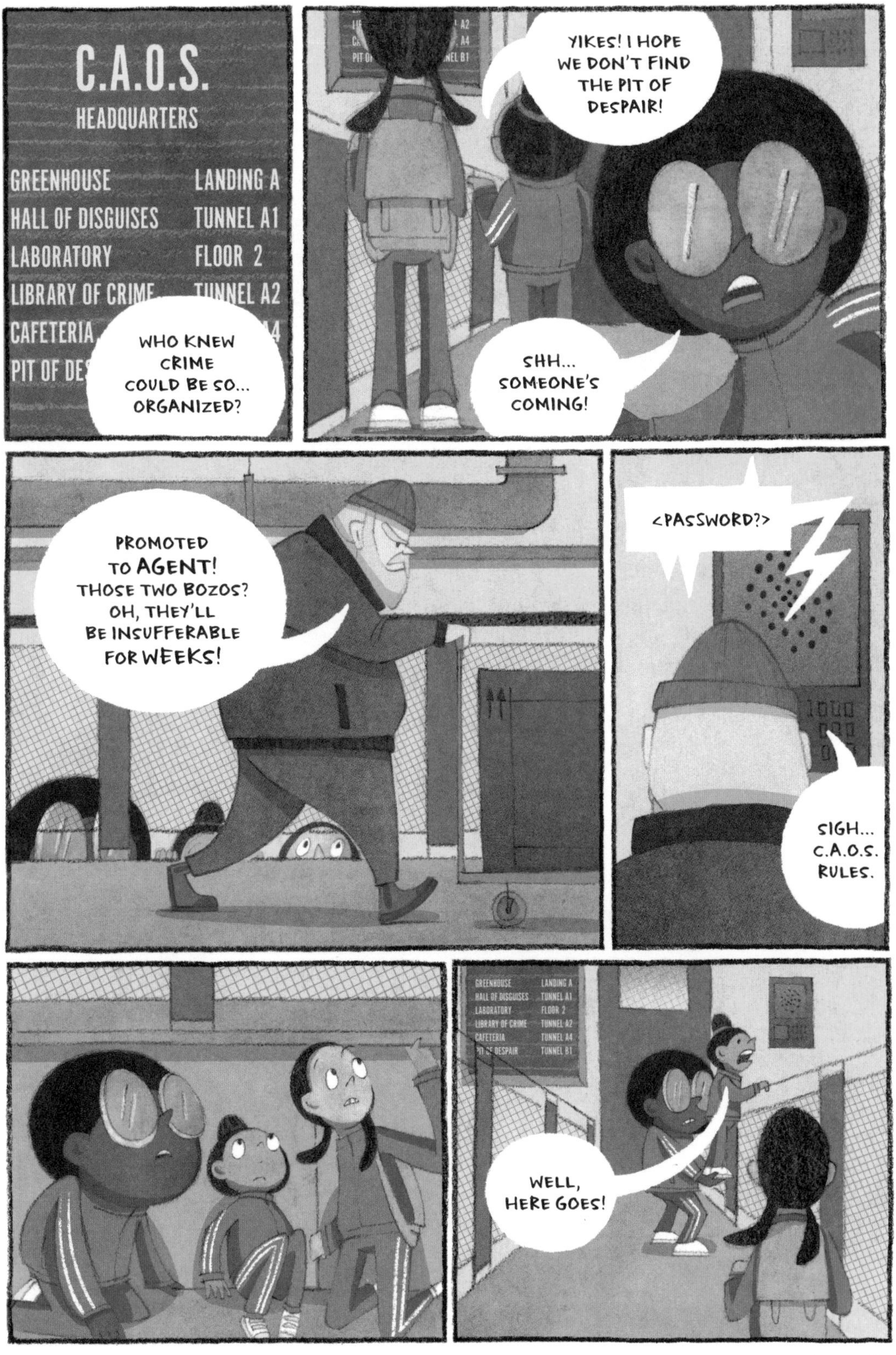
C.A.O.S.
HEADQUARTERS
GREENHOUSE LANDING A
HALL OF DISGUISES TUNNEL A1
LABORATORY FLOOR 2
LIBRARY OF CRIME TUNNEL A2
CAFETERIA
WHO KNEW CRIME COULD BE SO... ORGANIZED?
YIKES! I HOPE WE DON'T FIND THE PIT OF DESPAIR!
SHH... SOMEONE'S COMING!
PROMOTED TO AGENT! THOSE TWO BOZOS? OH, THEY'LL BE INSUFFERABLE FOR WEEKS!
<PASSWORD?>
SIGH... C.A.O.S. RULES.
GREENHOUSE LANDING A
HALL OF DISGUISES TUNNEL A1
LABORATORY FLOOR 2
LIBRARY OF CRIME TUNNEL A2
CAFETERIA TUNNEL A4
TUNNEL B1
WELL, HERE GOES!

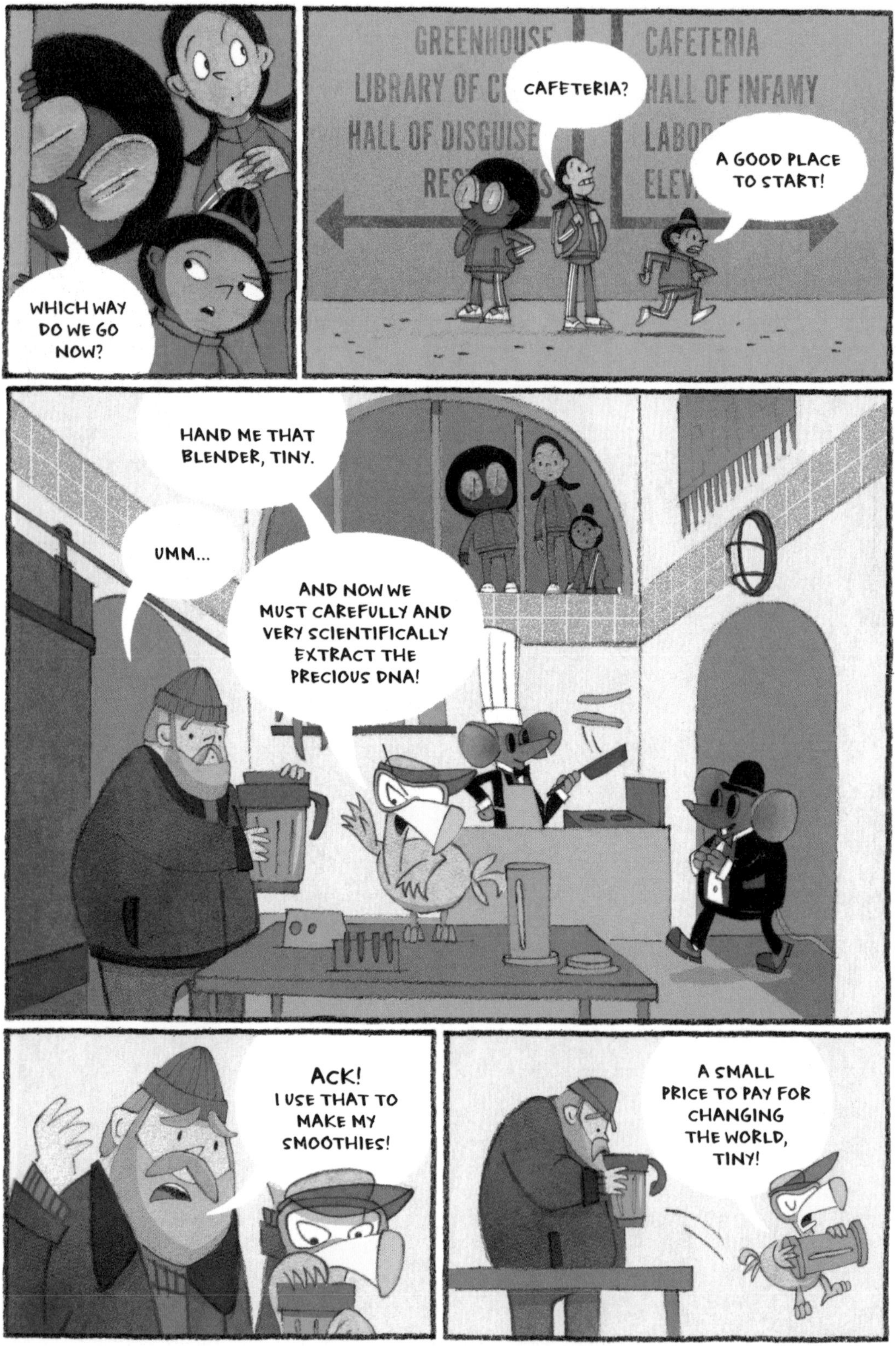
WHICH WAY DO WE GO NOW?
GREENHOUSE
LIBRARY OF C
HALL OF DISGUISE
RES
CAFETERIA
HALL OF INFAMY
LABO
ELEV
CAFETERIA?
A GOOD PLACE TO START!
HAND ME THAT BLENDER, TINY.
UMM...
AND NOW WE MUST CAREFULLY AND VERY SCIENTIFICALLY EXTRACT THE PRECIOUS DNA!
ACK! I USE THAT TO MAKE MY SMOOTHIES!
A SMALL PRICE TO PAY FOR CHANGING THE WORLD, TINY!

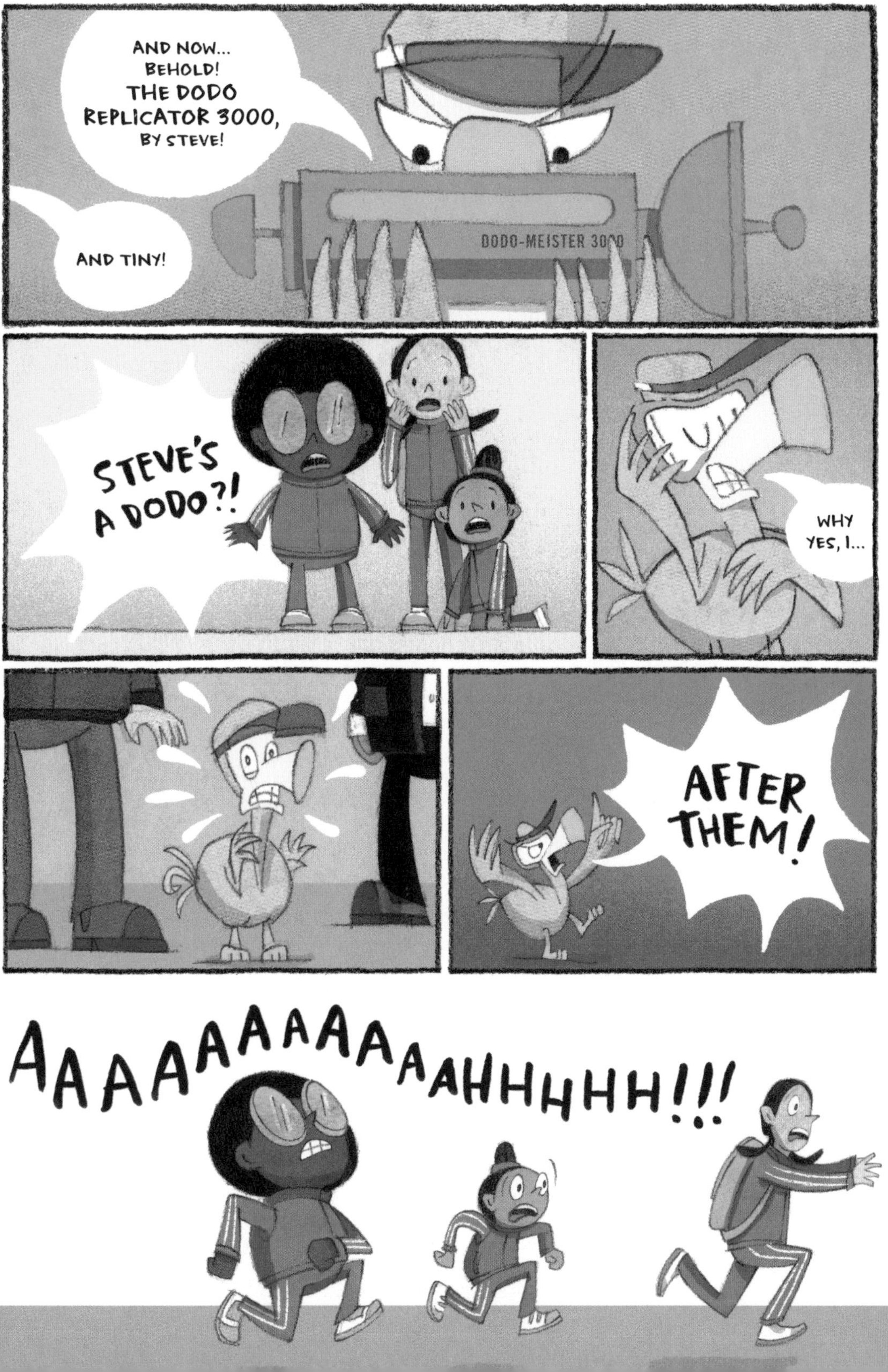
AND NOW... BEHOLD! THE DODO REPLICATOR 3000, BY STEVE!
AND TINY!
DODO-MEISTER 3000
STEVE'S A DODO?!
WHY YES, I...
AFTER THEM!
AAAAAAAAAAAHHHHHH!!!

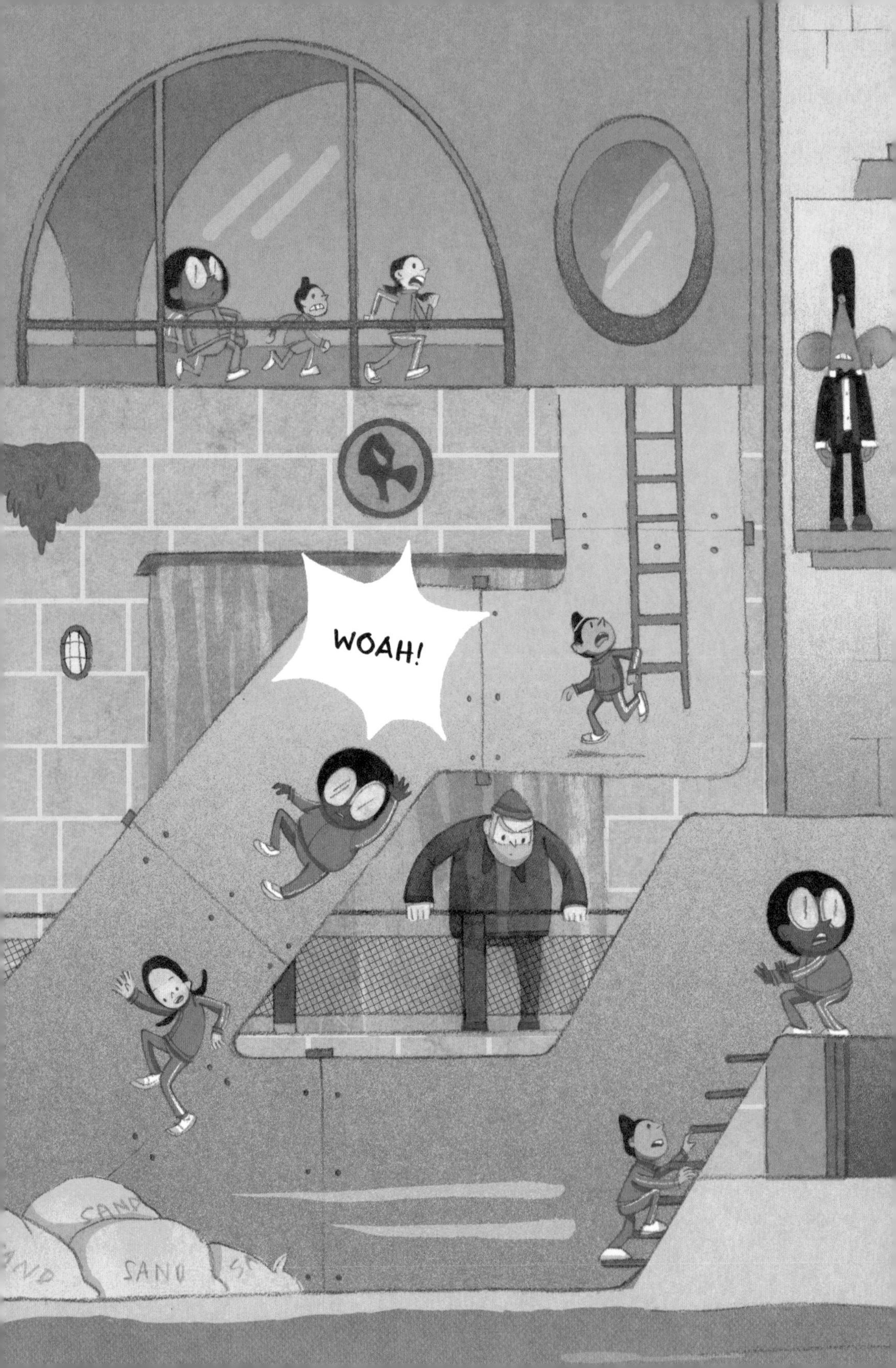
WOAH!
SAND
SAND

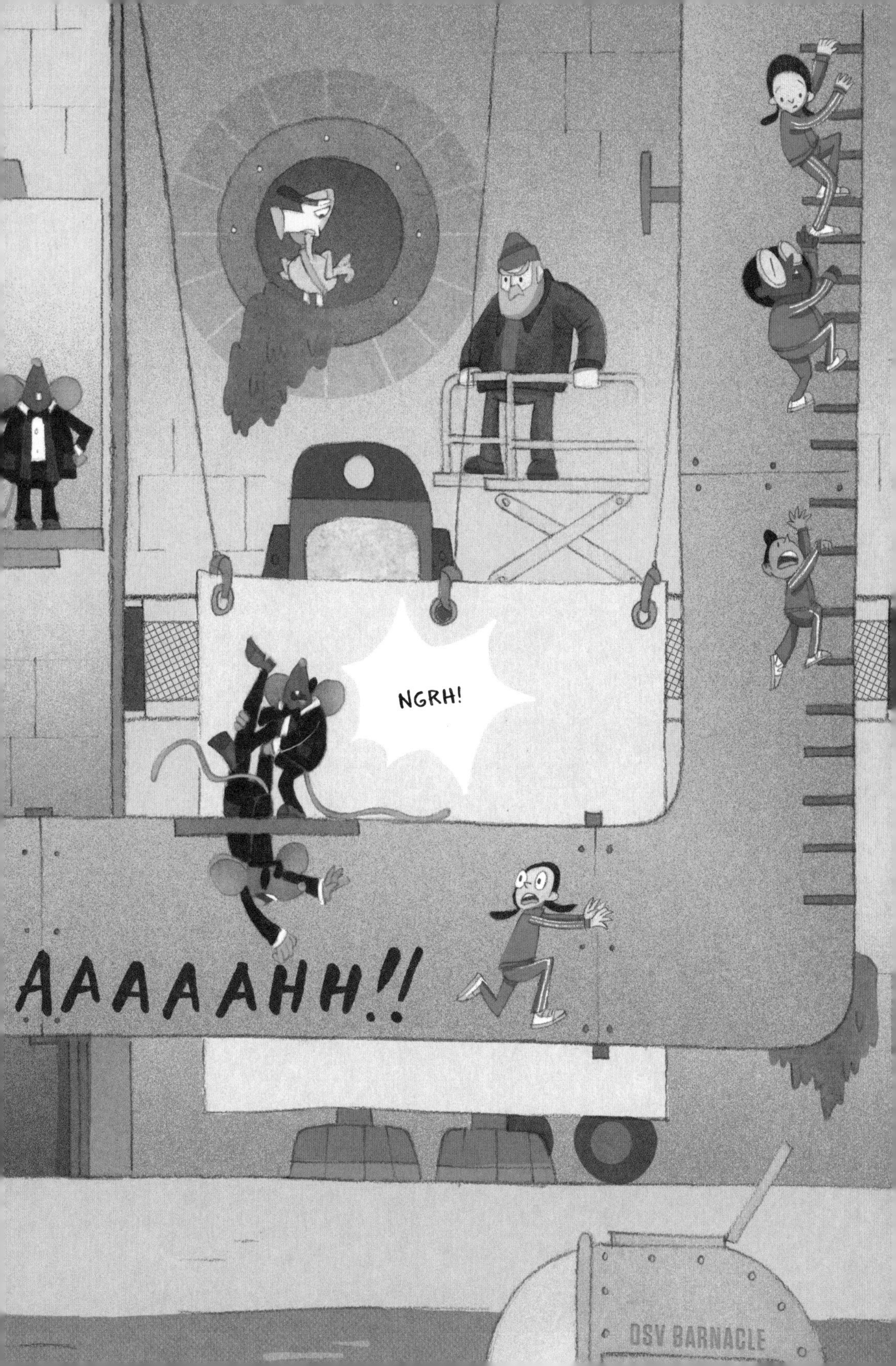
NGRH!
AAAAAHH!!
DSV BARNACLE

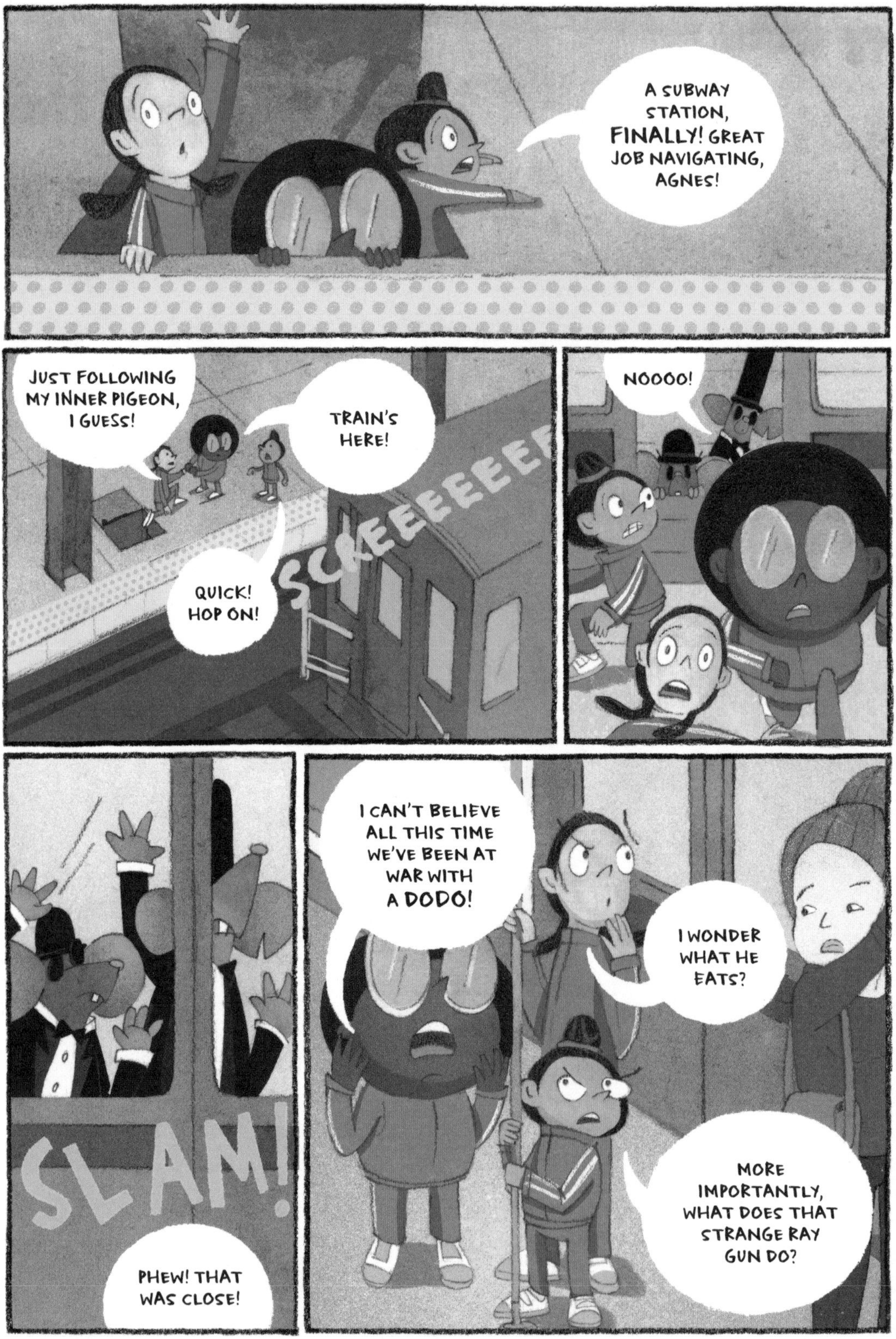
A SUBWAY STATION, FINALLY! GREAT JOB NAVIGATING, AGNES!
JUST FOLLOWING MY INNER PIGEON, I GUESS!
TRAIN'S HERE!
SCREEEEEEE
QUICK! HOP ON!
NOOOO!
SLAM!
PHEW! THAT WAS CLOSE!
I CAN'T BELIEVE ALL THIS TIME WE'VE BEEN AT WAR WITH A DODO!
I WONDER WHAT HE EATS?
MORE IMPORTANTLY, WHAT DOES THAT STRANGE RAY GUN DO?

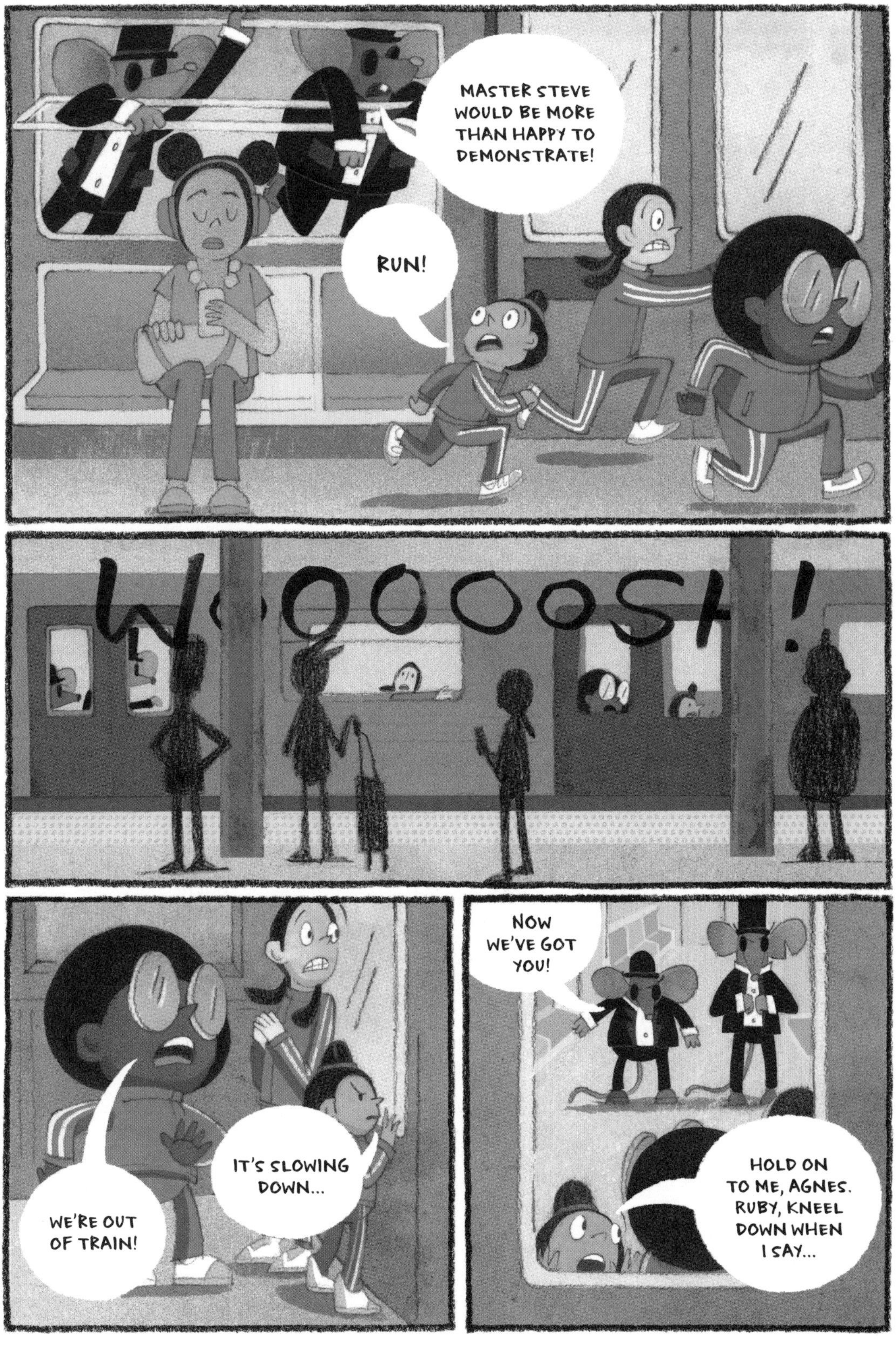
MASTER STEVE WOULD BE MORE THAN HAPPY TO DEMONSTRATE!
RUN!
WOOOOOSH!
WE'RE OUT OF TRAIN!
IT'S SLOWING DOWN...
NOW WE'VE GOT YOU!
HOLD ON TO ME, AGNES. RUBY, KNEEL DOWN WHEN I SAY...

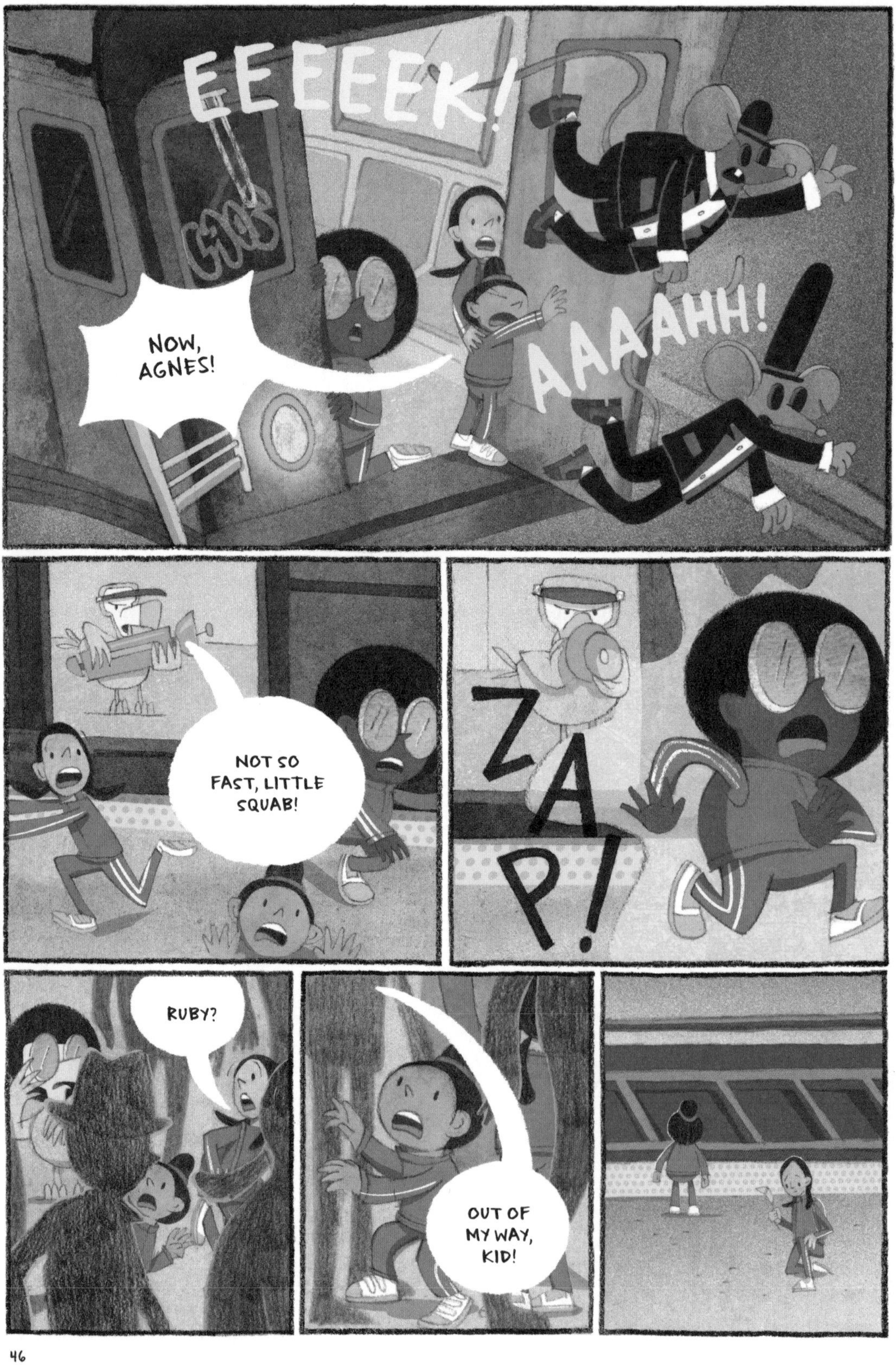
EEEEEK!
NOW, AGNES!
AAAAHH!
NOT SO FAST, LITTLE SQUAB!
ZAP!
RUBY?
OUT OF MY WAY, KID!

CHAPTER 5

OPERATION BIRD BRAIN

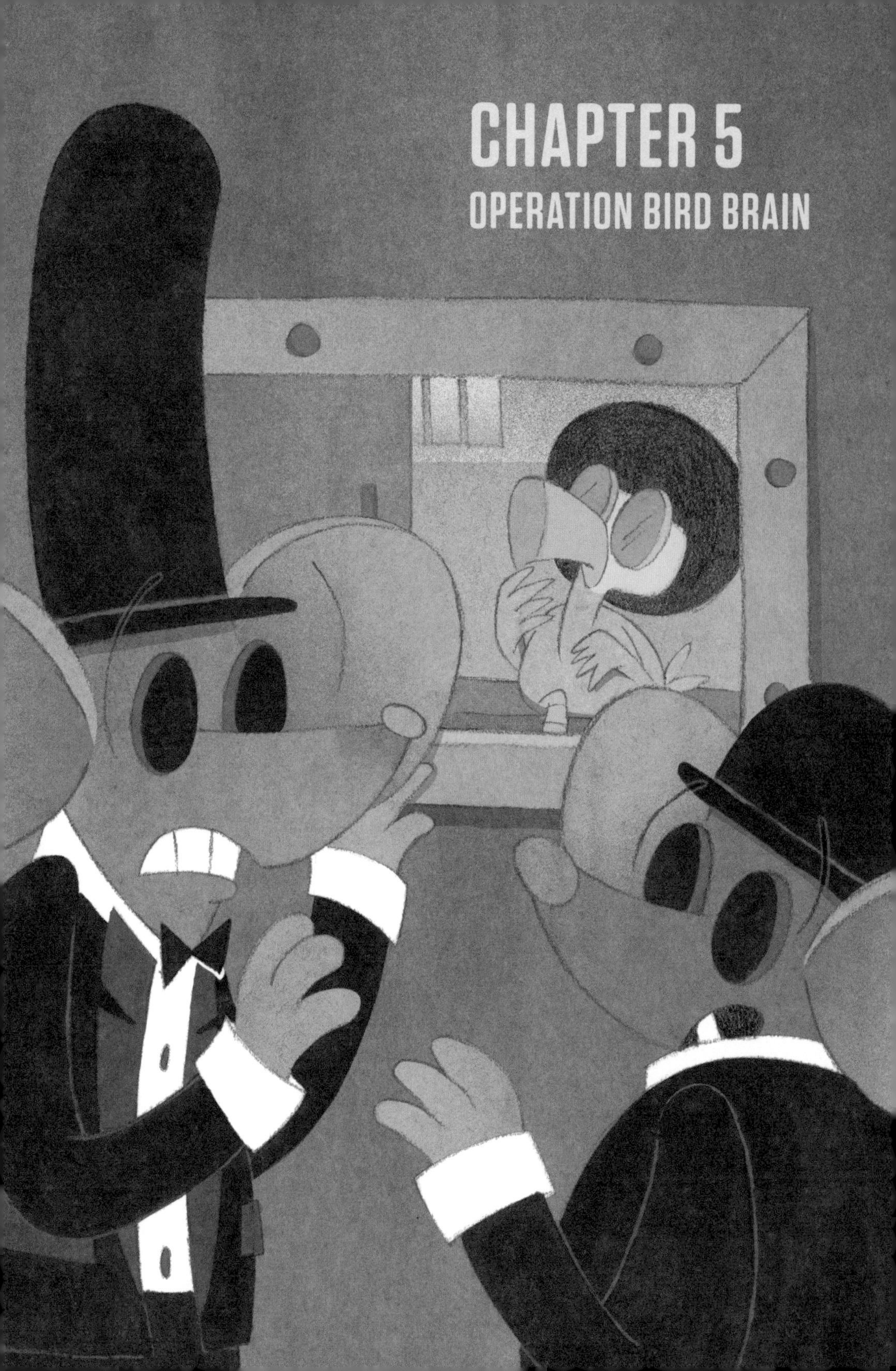

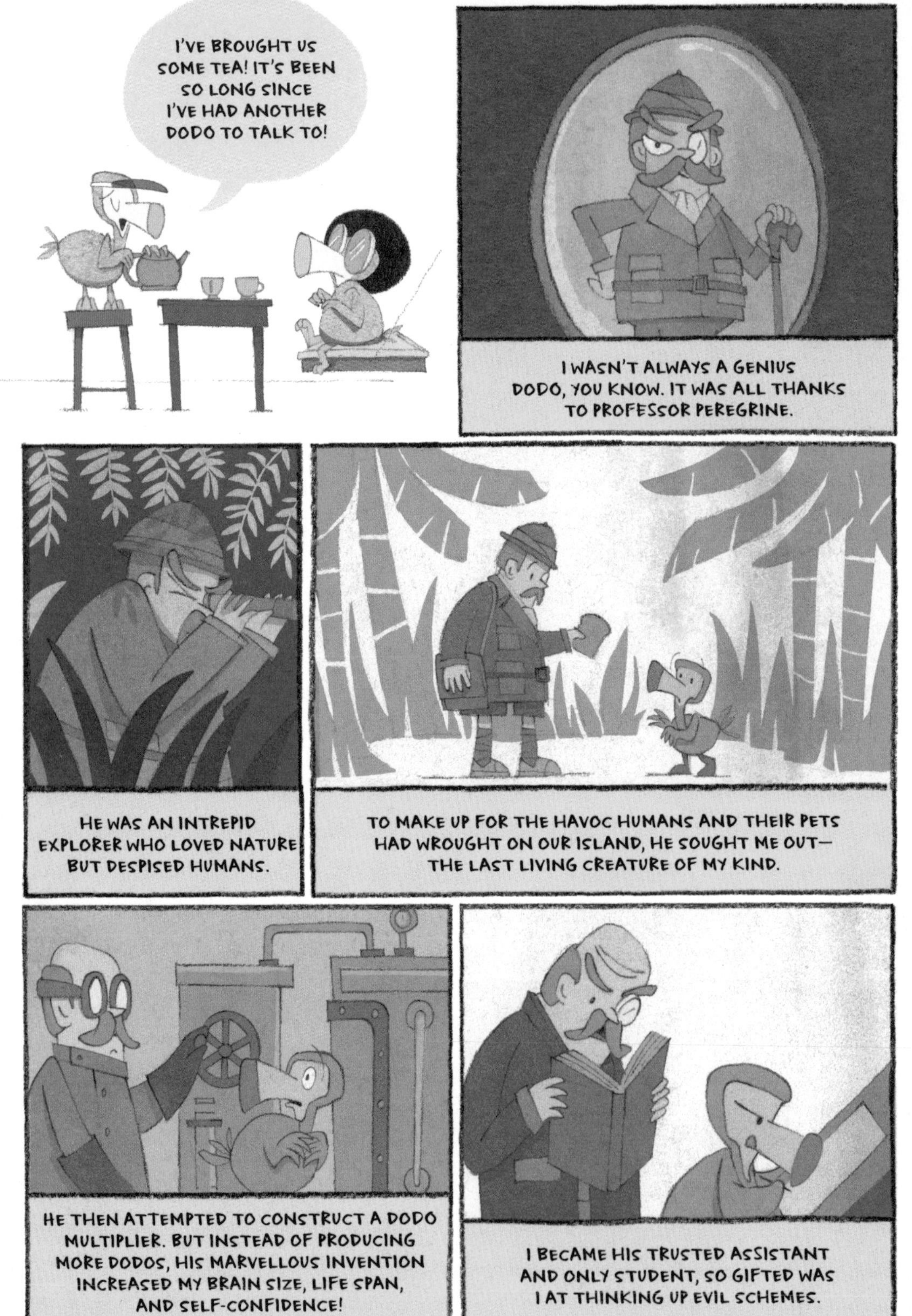
I'VE BROUGHT US SOME TEA! IT'S BEEN SO LONG SINCE I'VE HAD ANOTHER DODO TO TALK TO!
I WASN'T ALWAYS A GENIUS DODO, YOU KNOW. IT WAS ALL THANKS TO PROFESSOR PEREGRINE.
HE WAS AN INTREPID EXPLORER WHO LOVED NATURE BUT DESPISED HUMANS.
TO MAKE UP FOR THE HAVOC HUMANS AND THEIR PETS HAD WROUGHT ON OUR ISLAND, HE SOUGHT ME OUT—THE LAST LIVING CREATURE OF MY KIND.
HE THEN ATTEMPTED TO CONSTRUCT A DODO MULTIPLIER. BUT INSTEAD OF PRODUCING MORE DODOS, HIS MARVELLOUS INVENTION INCREASED MY BRAIN SIZE, LIFE SPAN, AND SELF-CONFIDENCE!
I BECAME HIS TRUSTED ASSISTANT AND ONLY STUDENT, SO GIFTED WAS I AT THINKING UP EVIL SCHEMES.

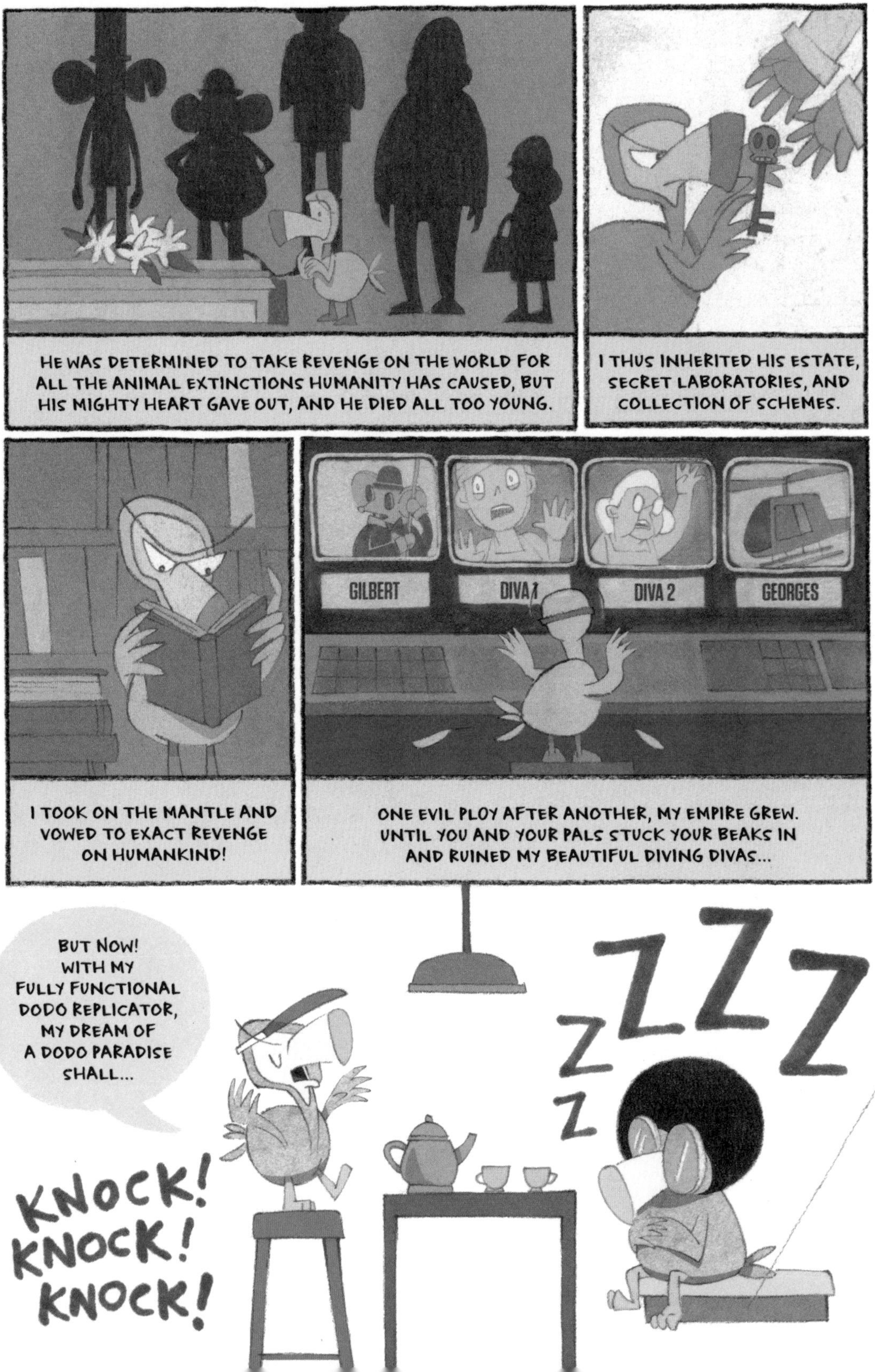
HE WAS DETERMINED TO TAKE REVENGE ON THE WORLD FOR ALL THE ANIMAL EXTINCTIONS HUMANITY HAS CAUSED, BUT HIS MIGHTY HEART GAVE OUT, AND HE DIED ALL TOO YOUNG.
I THUS INHERITED HIS ESTATE, SECRET LABORATORIES, AND COLLECTION OF SCHEMES.
I TOOK ON THE MANTLE AND VOWED TO EXACT REVENGE ON HUMANKIND!
GILBERT
DIVA
DIVA 2
GEORGES
ONE EVIL PLOY AFTER ANOTHER, MY EMPIRE GREW. UNTIL YOU AND YOUR PALS STUCK YOUR BEAKS IN AND RUINED MY BEAUTIFUL DIVING DIVAS...
BUT NOW! WITH MY FULLY FUNCTIONAL DODO REPLICATOR, MY DREAM OF A DODO PARADISE SHALL...
ZZZZZ
KNOCK! KNOCK! KNOCK!

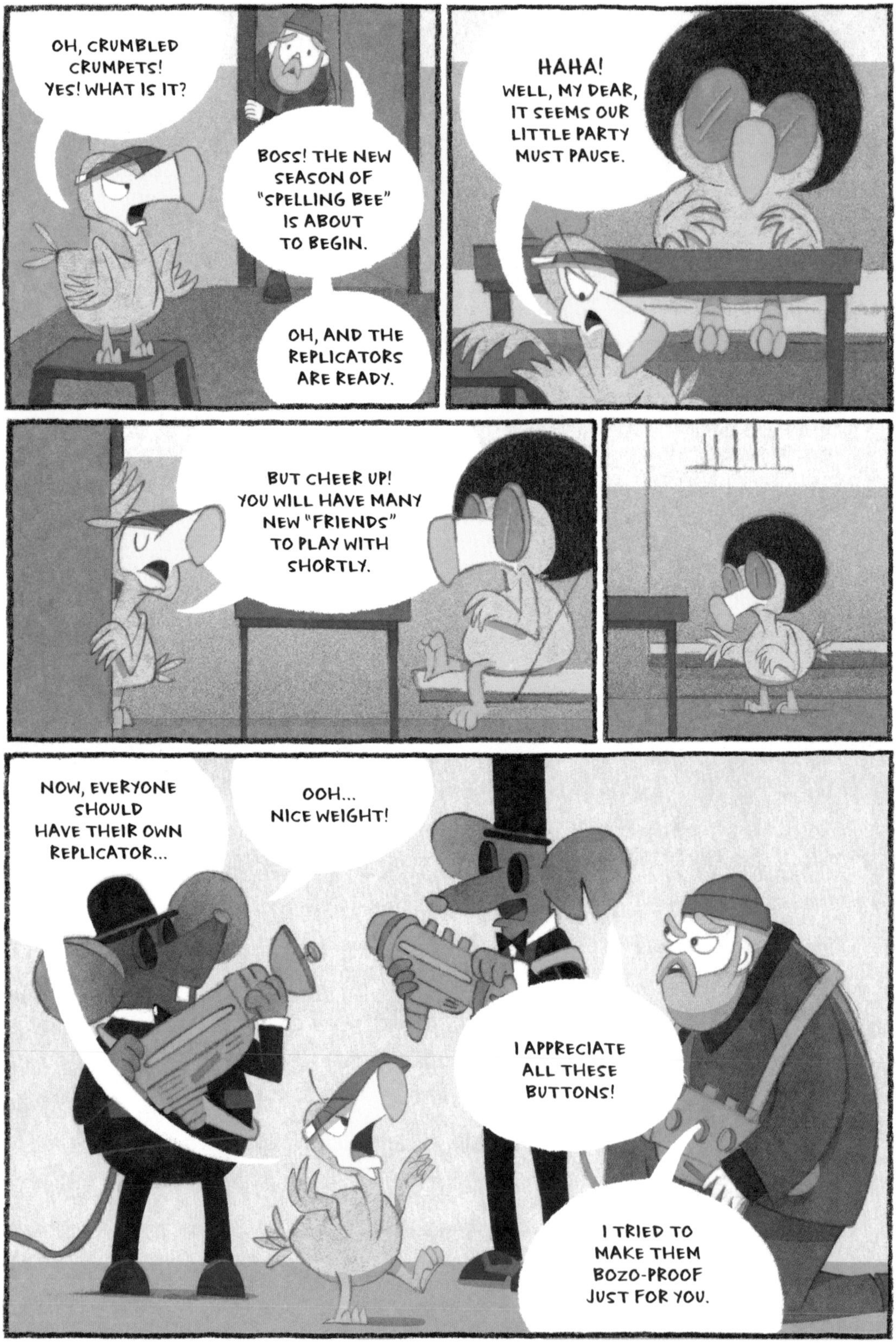
OH, CRUMBLED CRUMPETS! YES! WHAT IS IT?
BOSS! THE NEW SEASON OF "SPELLING BEE" IS ABOUT TO BEGIN.
OH, AND THE REPLICATORS ARE READY.
HAHA! WELL, MY DEAR, IT SEEMS OUR LITTLE PARTY MUST PAUSE.
BUT CHEER UP! YOU WILL HAVE MANY NEW "FRIENDS" TO PLAY WITH SHORTLY.
NOW, EVERYONE SHOULD HAVE THEIR OWN REPLICATOR...
OOH... NICE WEIGHT!
I APPRECIATE ALL THESE BUTTONS!
I TRIED TO MAKE THEM BOZO-PROOF JUST FOR YOU.

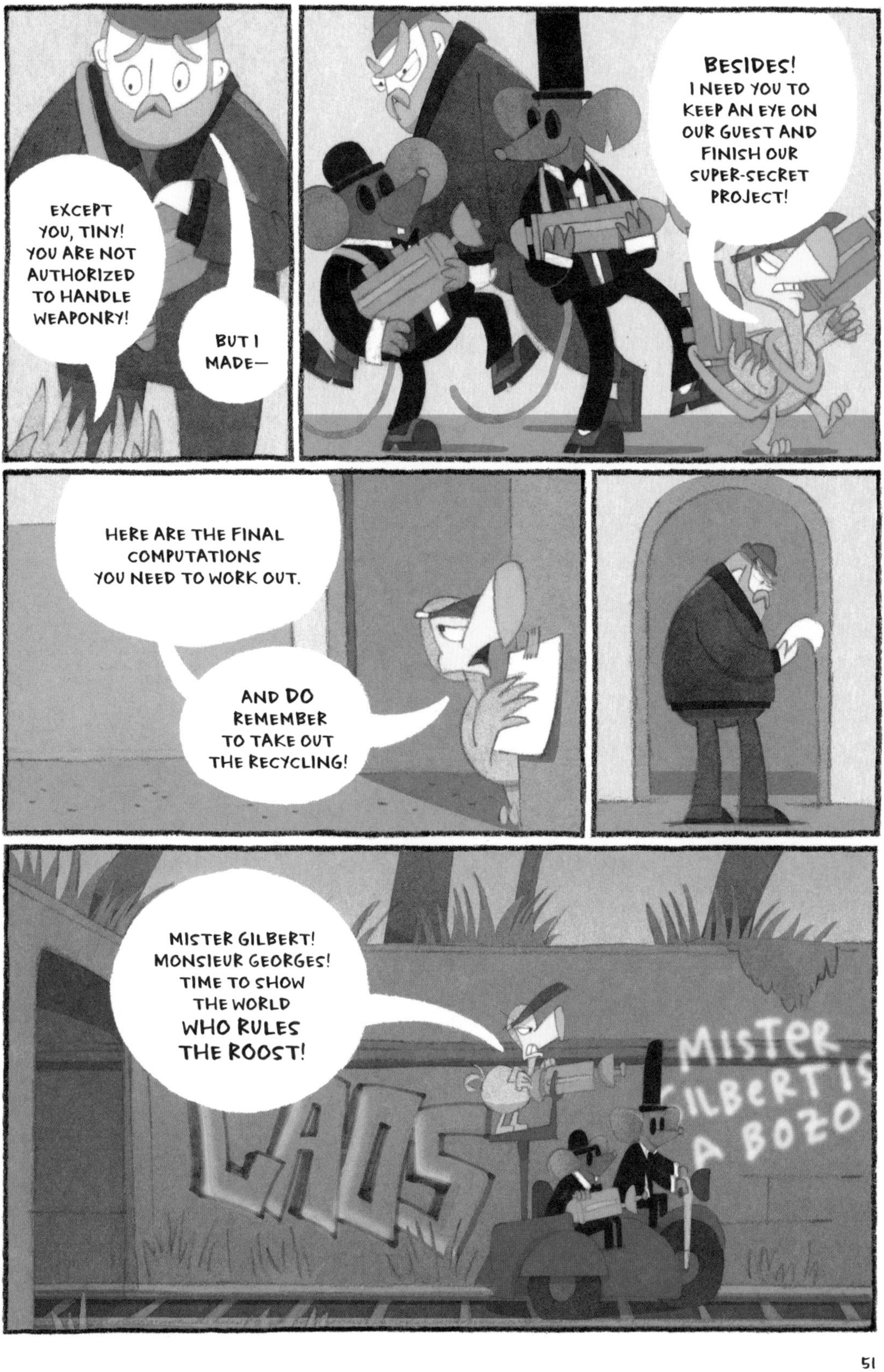
EXCEPT YOU, TINY! YOU ARE NOT AUTHORIZED TO HANDLE WEAPONRY!
BUT I MADE—
BESIDES! I NEED YOU TO KEEP AN EYE ON OUR GUEST AND FINISH OUR SUPER-SECRET PROJECT!
HERE ARE THE FINAL COMPUTATIONS YOU NEED TO WORK OUT.
AND DO REMEMBER TO TAKE OUT THE RECYCLING!
MISTER GILBERT! MONSIEUR GEORGES! TIME TO SHOW THE WORLD WHO RULES THE ROOST!
CAOS
MISTER GILBERT IS A BOZO

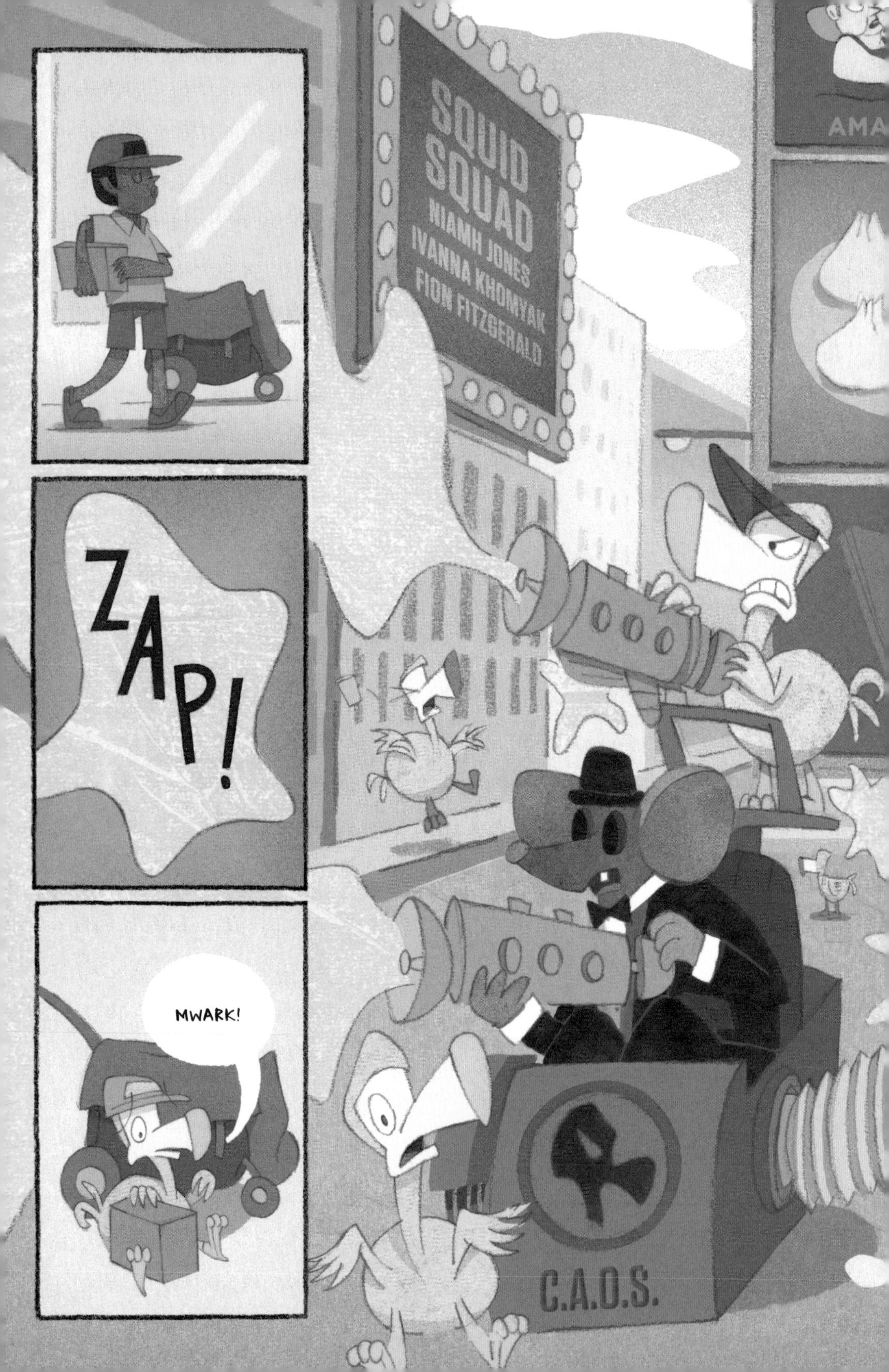

SQUID SQUAD
NIAMH JONES
IVANNA KHOMYAK
FION FITZGERALD
ZAP!
MWARK!
C.A.O.S.

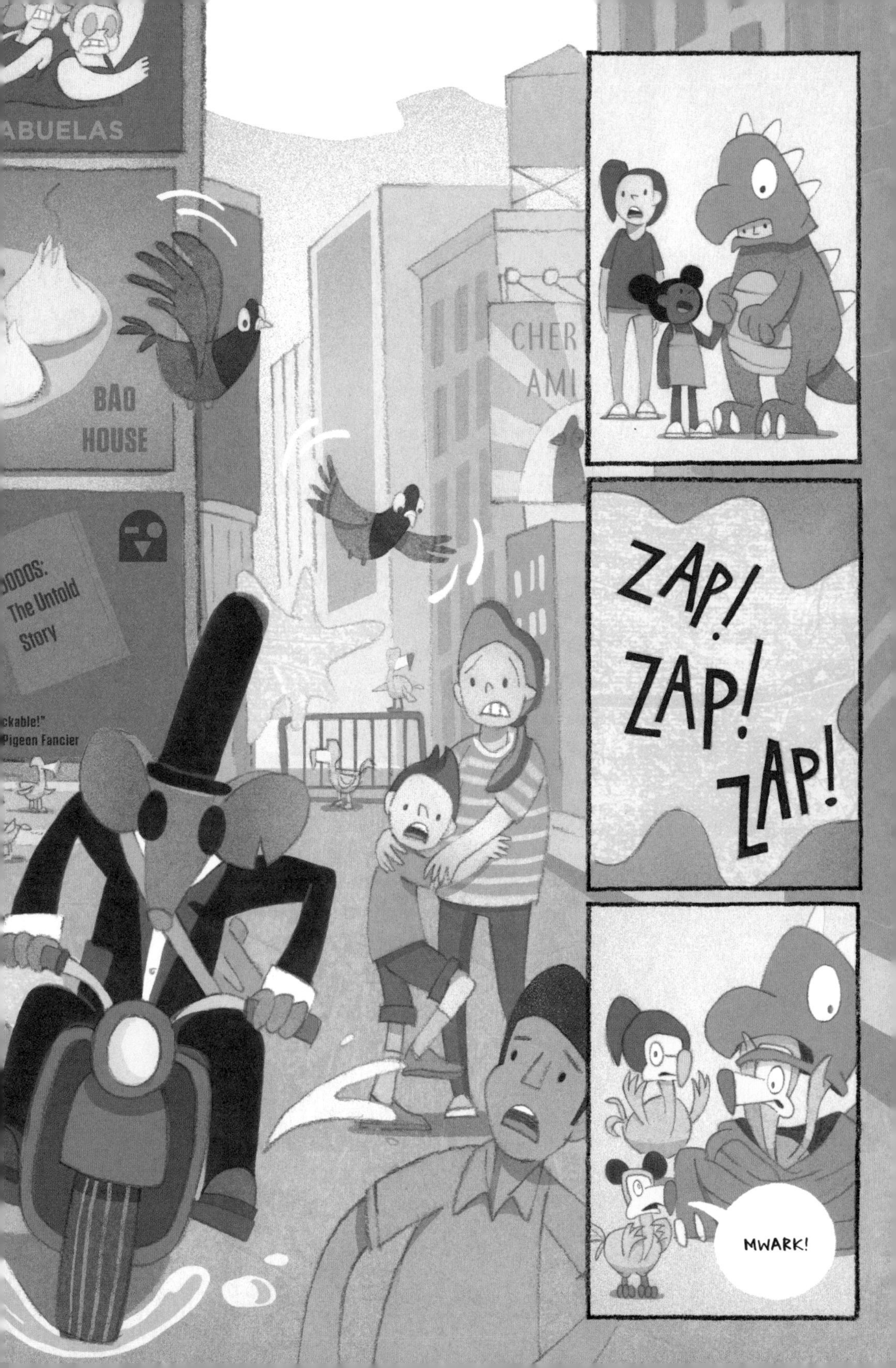
ABUELAS
BAO HOUSE
DODOS: The Untold Story
ckable!"
Pigeon Fancier
CHER AMI
ZAP! ZAP! ZAP!
MWARK!

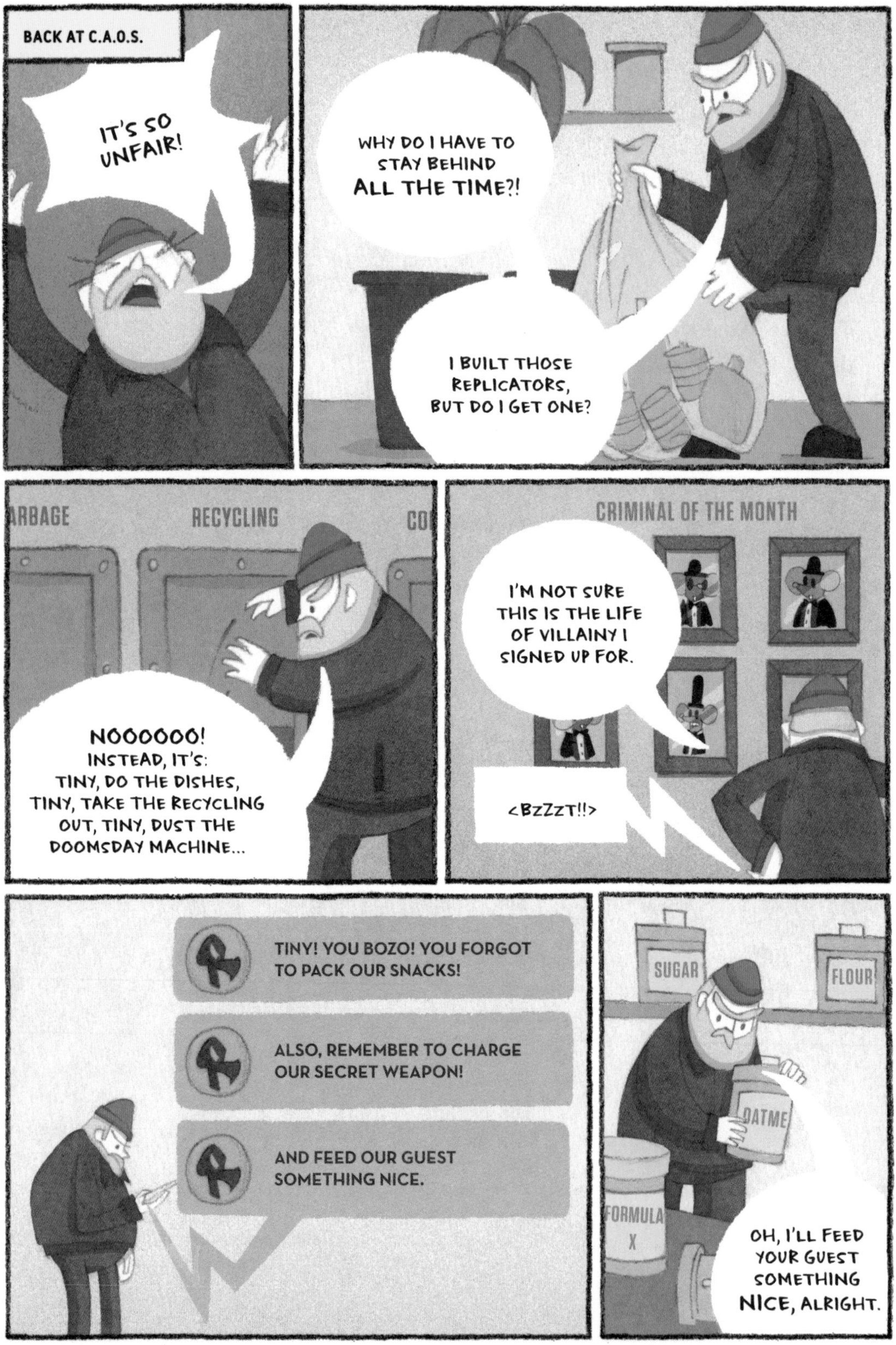
BACK AT C.A.O.S.
IT'S SO UNFAIR!
WHY DO I HAVE TO STAY BEHIND ALL THE TIME?!
I BUILT THOSE REPLICATORS, BUT DO I GET ONE?
RECYCLING
NOOOOOO! INSTEAD, IT'S: TINY, DO THE DISHES, TINY, TAKE THE RECYCLING OUT, TINY, DUST THE DOOMSDAY MACHINE...
CRIMINAL OF THE MONTH
I'M NOT SURE THIS IS THE LIFE OF VILLAINY I SIGNED UP FOR.
<BzZzT!!>
TINY! YOU BOZO! YOU FORGOT TO PACK OUR SNACKS!
ALSO, REMEMBER TO CHARGE OUR SECRET WEAPON!
AND FEED OUR GUEST SOMETHING NICE.
SUGAR
FLOUR
DATME
FORMULA X
OH, I'LL FEED YOUR GUEST SOMETHING NICE, ALRIGHT.

CHAPTER 6
THE CURE

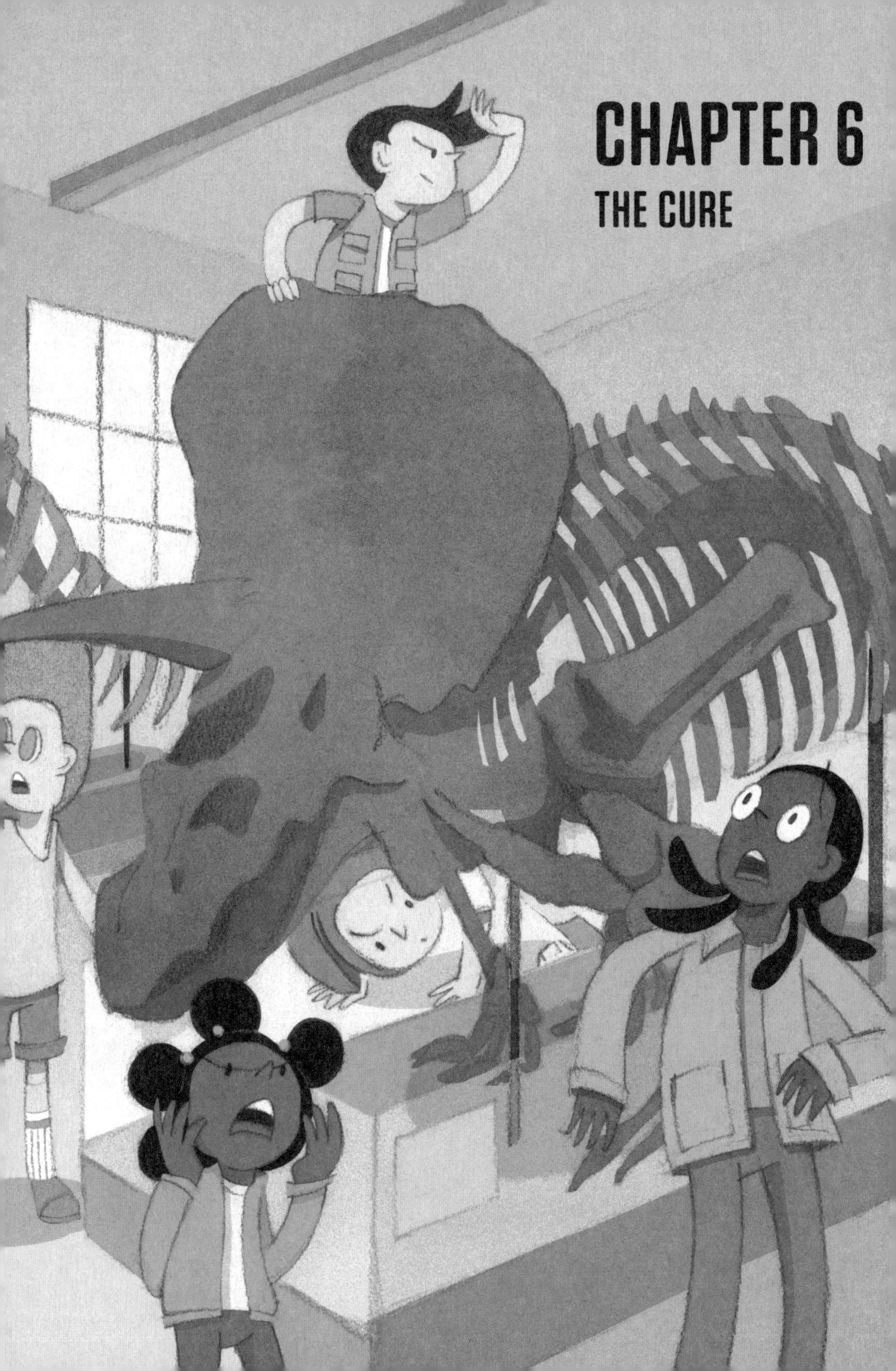

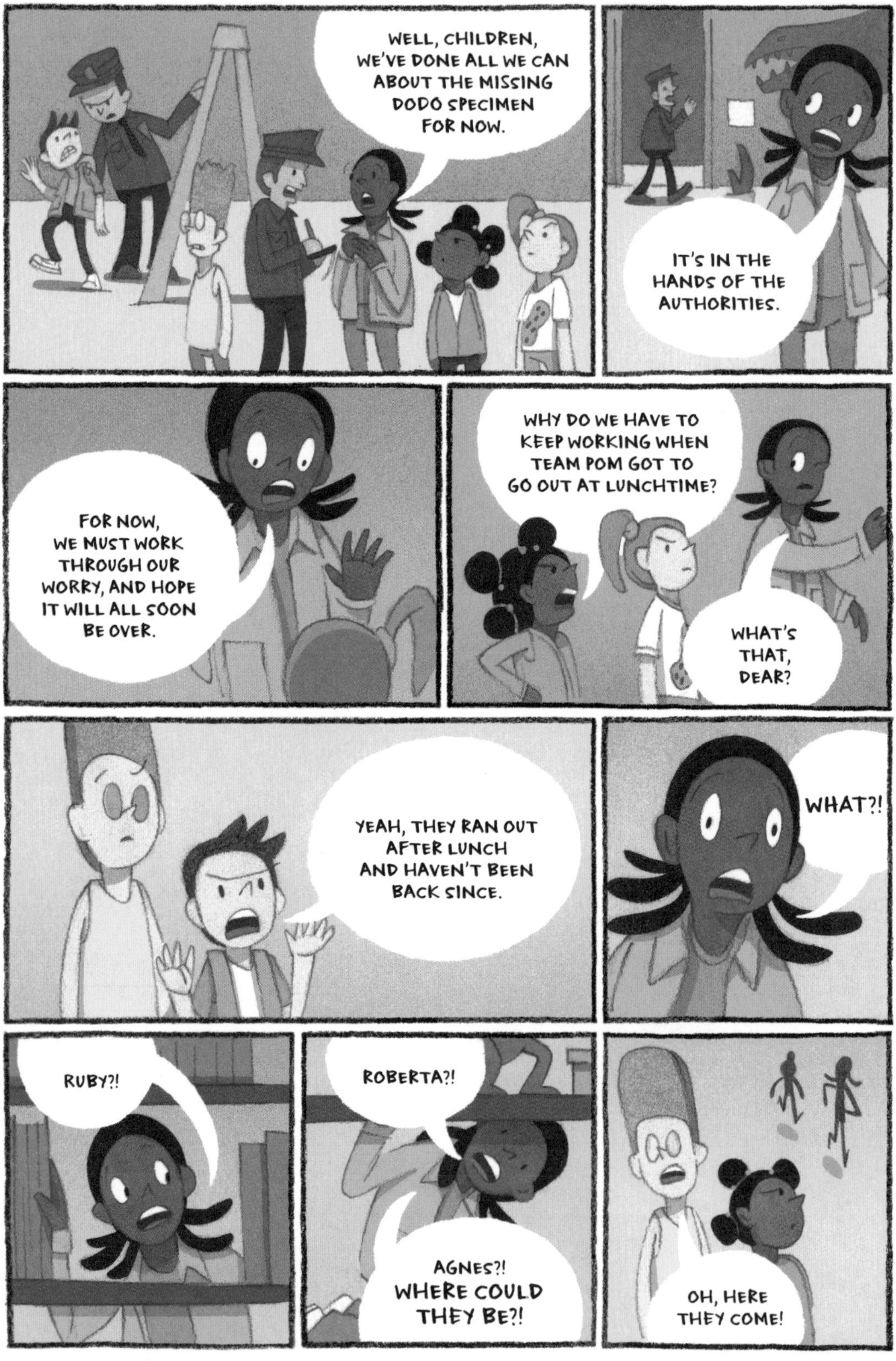
WELL, CHILDREN, WE'VE DONE ALL WE CAN ABOUT THE MISSING DODO SPECIMEN FOR NOW.
IT'S IN THE HANDS OF THE AUTHORITIES.
FOR NOW, WE MUST WORK THROUGH OUR WORRY, AND HOPE IT WILL ALL SOON BE OVER.
WHY DO WE HAVE TO KEEP WORKING WHEN TEAM POM GOT TO GO OUT AT LUNCHTIME?
WHAT'S THAT, DEAR?
YEAH, THEY RAN OUT AFTER LUNCH AND HAVEN'T BEEN BACK SINCE.
WHAT?!
RUBY?!
ROBERTA?!
AGNES?! WHERE COULD THEY BE?!
OH, HERE THEY COME!

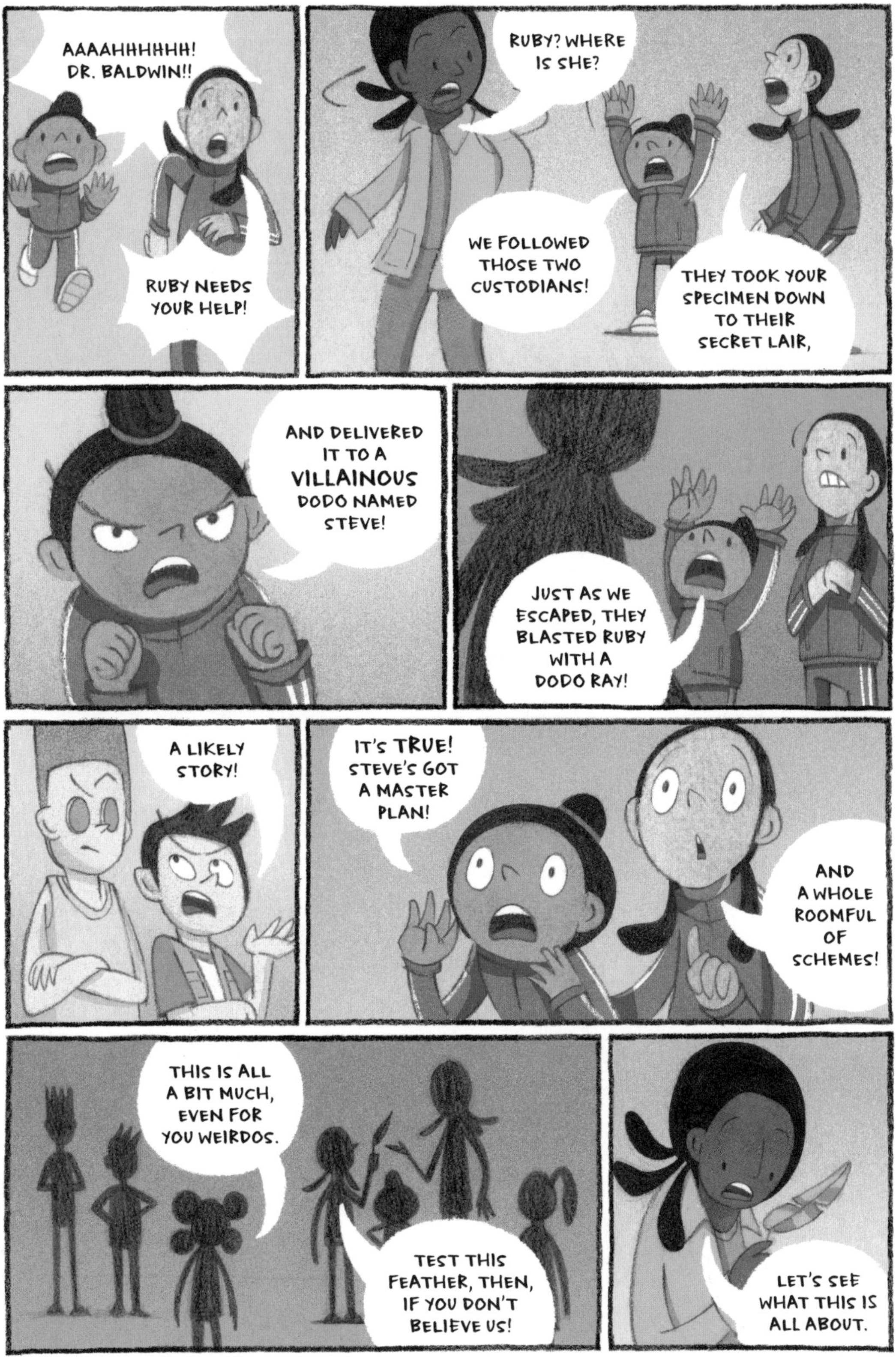
AAAAHHHHHH! DR. BALDWIN!!
RUBY NEEDS YOUR HELP!
RUBY? WHERE IS SHE?
WE FOLLOWED THOSE TWO CUSTODIANS!
THEY TOOK YOUR SPECIMEN DOWN TO THEIR SECRET LAIR,
AND DELIVERED IT TO A VILLAINOUS DODO NAMED STEVE!
JUST AS WE ESCAPED, THEY BLASTED RUBY WITH A DODO RAY!
A LIKELY STORY!
IT'S TRUE! STEVE'S GOT A MASTER PLAN!
AND A WHOLE ROOMFUL OF SCHEMES!
THIS IS ALL A BIT MUCH, EVEN FOR YOU WEIRDOS.
TEST THIS FEATHER, THEN, IF YOU DON'T BELIEVE US!
LET'S SEE WHAT THIS IS ALL ABOUT.

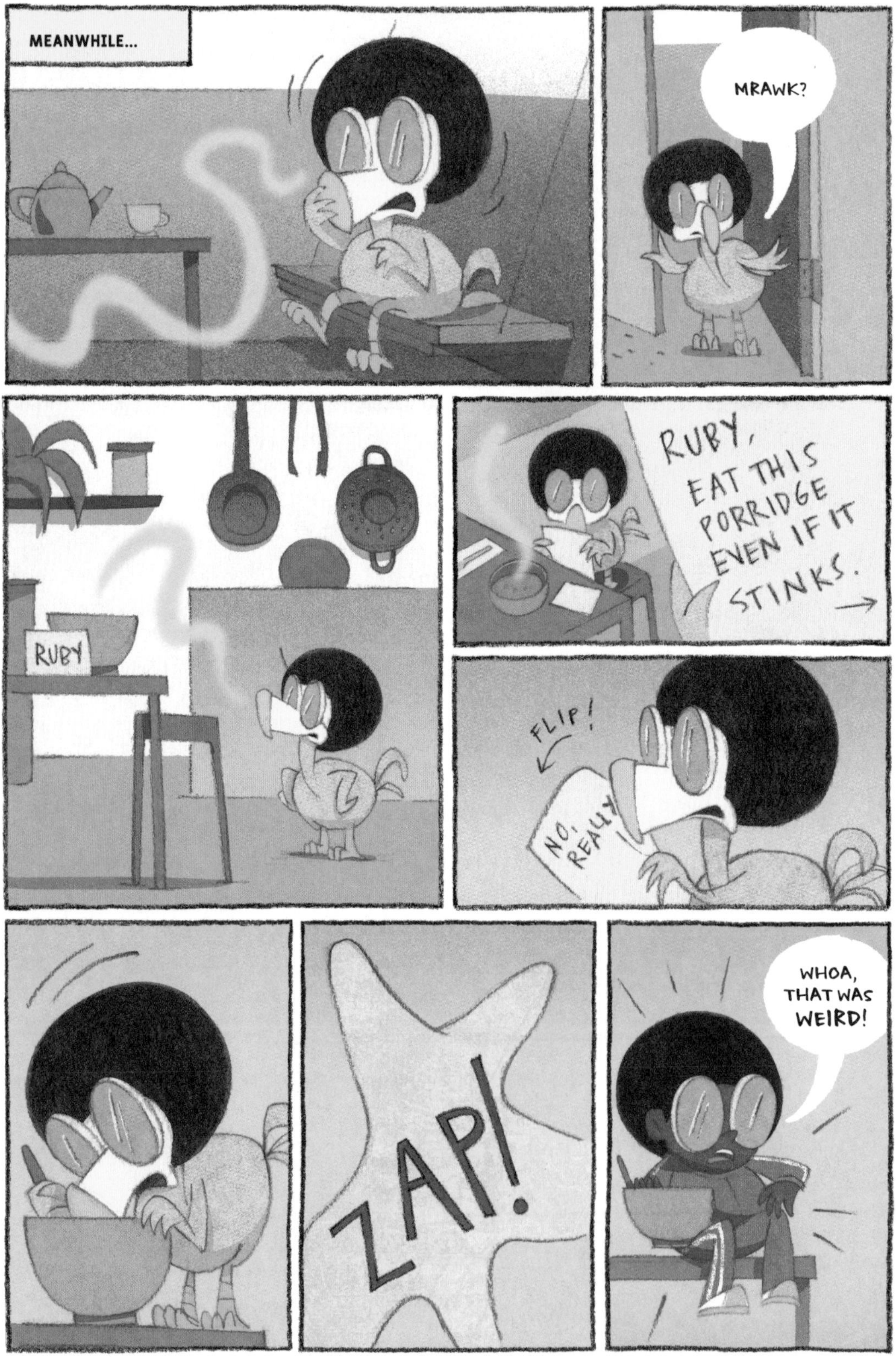
MEANWHILE...
MRAWK?
RUBY
RUBY, EAT THIS PORRIDGE EVEN IF IT STINKS.
FLIP!
NO, REALLY
ZAP!
WHOA, THAT WAS WEIRD!

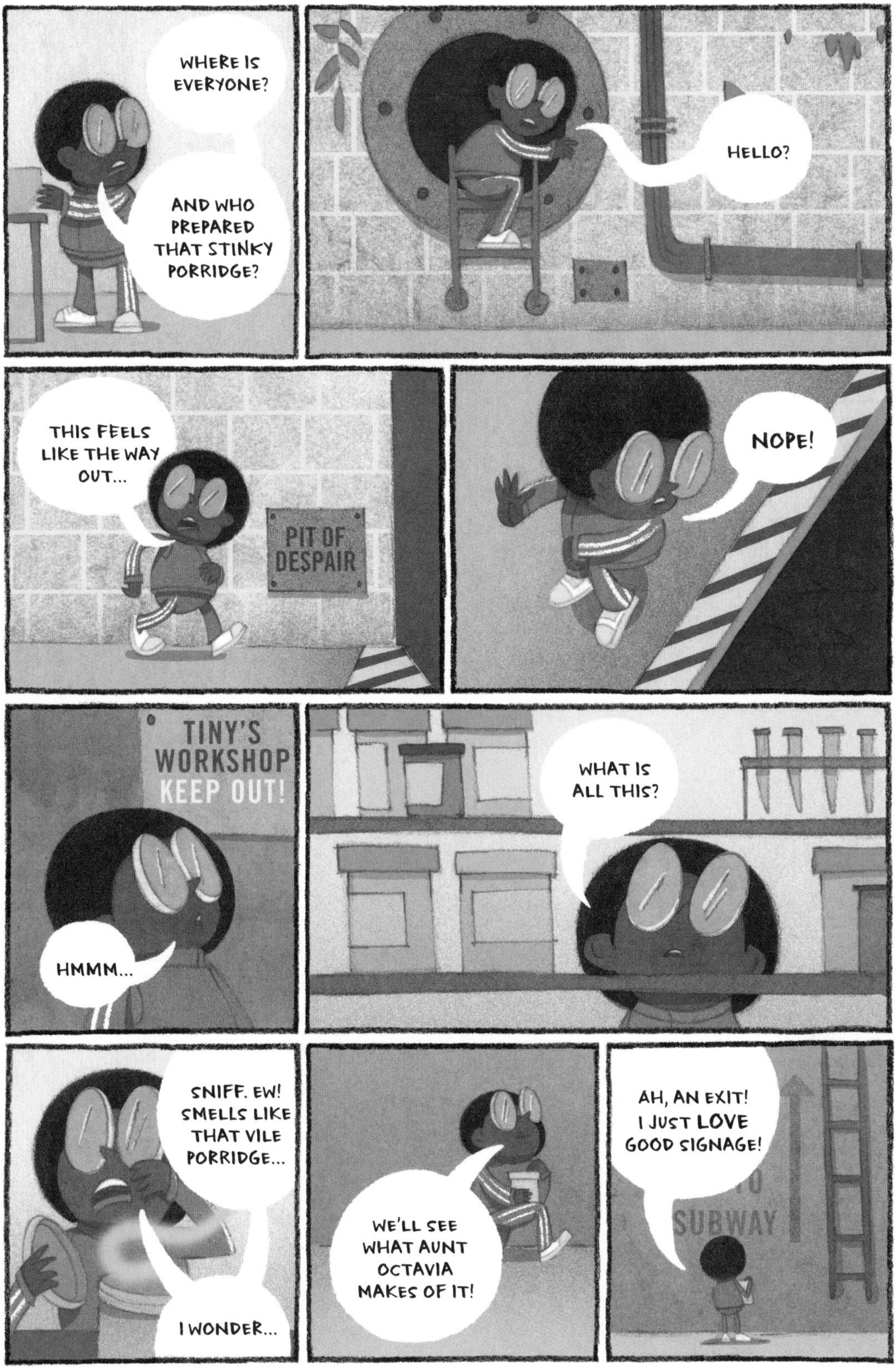
WHERE IS EVERYONE?
AND WHO PREPARED THAT STINKY PORRIDGE?
HELLO?
THIS FEELS LIKE THE WAY OUT...
PIT OF DESPAIR
NOPE!
TINY'S WORKSHOP KEEP OUT!
HMMM...
WHAT IS ALL THIS?
SNIFF. EW! SMELLS LIKE THAT VILE PORRIDGE...
I WONDER...
WE'LL SEE WHAT AUNT OCTAVIA MAKES OF IT!
AH, AN EXIT! I JUST LOVE GOOD SIGNAGE!
SUBWAY

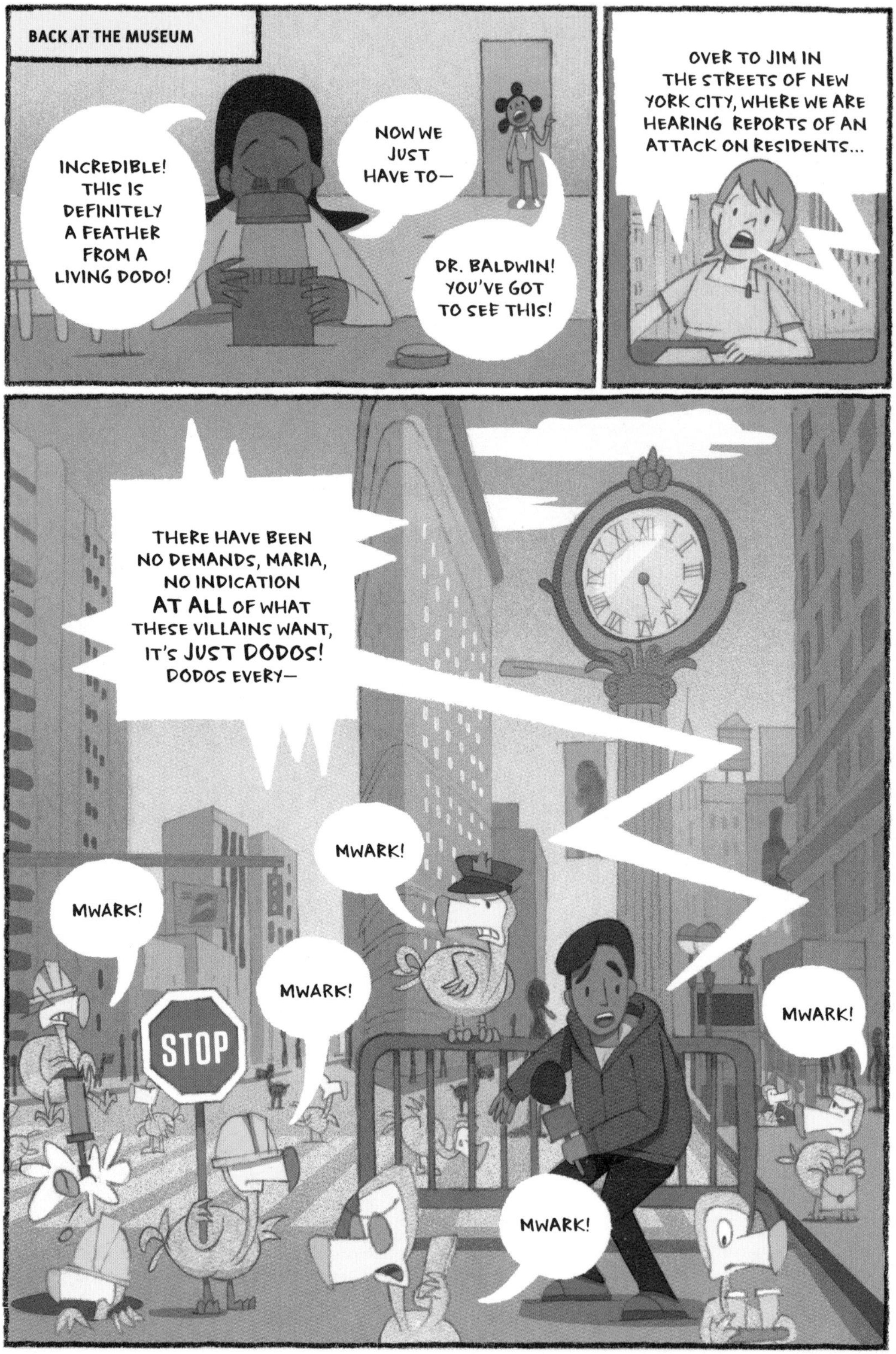
BACK AT THE MUSEUM
INCREDIBLE! THIS IS DEFINITELY A FEATHER FROM A LIVING DODO!
NOW WE JUST HAVE TO—
DR. BALDWIN! YOU'VE GOT TO SEE THIS!
OVER TO JIM IN THE STREETS OF NEW YORK CITY, WHERE WE ARE HEARING REPORTS OF AN ATTACK ON RESIDENTS...
THERE HAVE BEEN NO DEMANDS, MARIA, NO INDICATION AT ALL OF WHAT THESE VILLAINS WANT, IT'S JUST DODOS! DODOS EVERY—
MWARK!
MWARK!
MWARK!
MWARK!
MWARK!
STOP

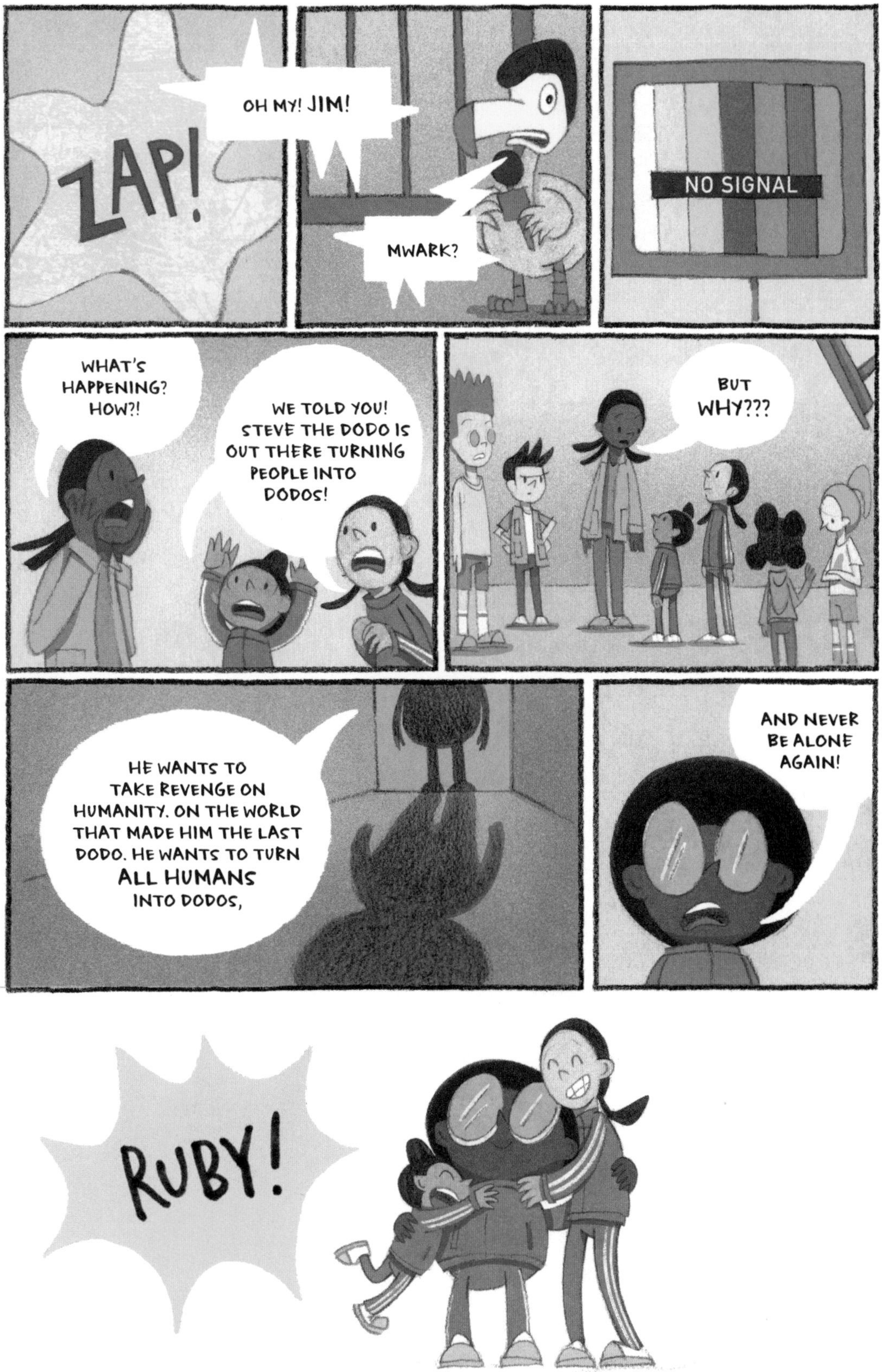
ZAP!
OH MY! JIM!
MWARK?
NO SIGNAL
WHAT'S HAPPENING? HOW?!
WE TOLD YOU! STEVE THE DODO IS OUT THERE TURNING PEOPLE INTO DODOS!
BUT WHY???
HE WANTS TO TAKE REVENGE ON HUMANITY. ON THE WORLD THAT MADE HIM THE LAST DODO. HE WANTS TO TURN ALL HUMANS INTO DODOS,
AND NEVER BE ALONE AGAIN!
RUBY!

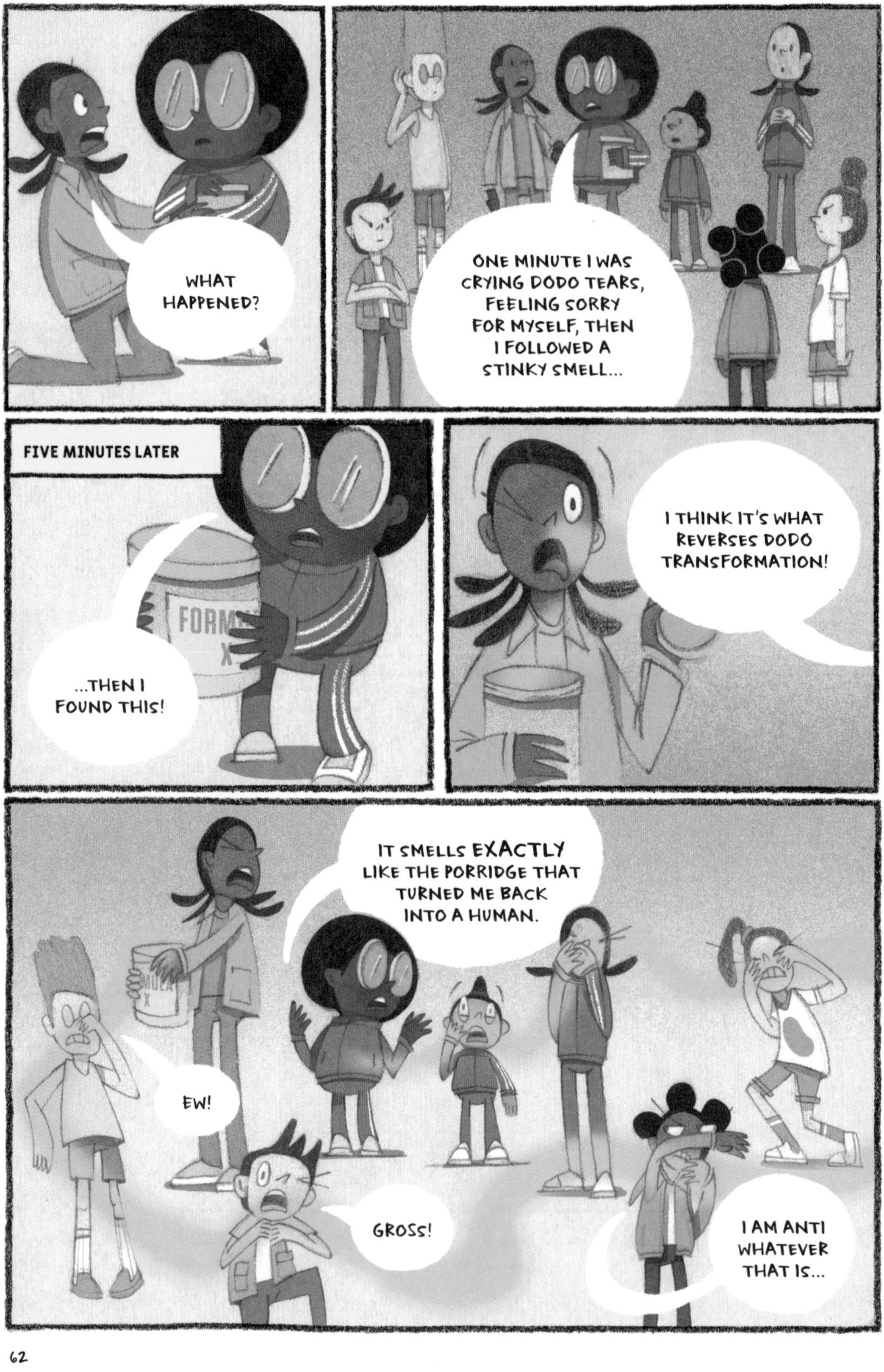

WHAT HAPPENED?
ONE MINUTE I WAS CRYING DODO TEARS, FEELING SORRY FOR MYSELF, THEN I FOLLOWED A STINKY SMELL...
FIVE MINUTES LATER
...THEN I FOUND THIS!
FORMU
X
I THINK IT'S WHAT REVERSES DODO TRANSFORMATION!
IT SMELLS EXACTLY LIKE THE PORRIDGE THAT TURNED ME BACK INTO A HUMAN.
MULA
X
EW!
GROSS!
I AM ANTI WHATEVER THAT IS...

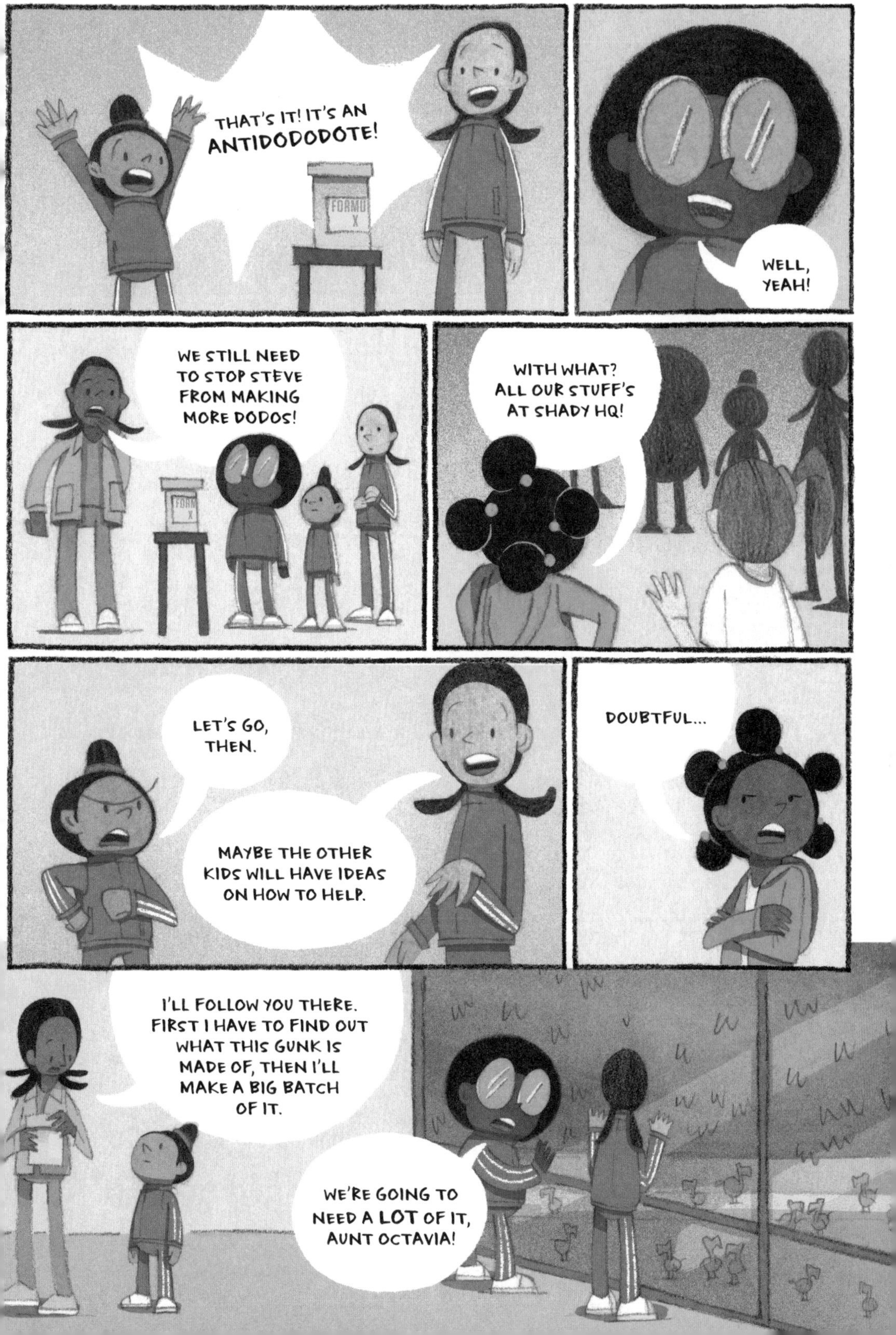
THAT'S IT! IT'S AN ANTIDODODOTE!
FORMU X
WELL, YEAH!
WE STILL NEED TO STOP STEVE FROM MAKING MORE DODOS!
FORMU X
WITH WHAT? ALL OUR STUFF'S AT SHADY HQ!
LET'S GO, THEN.
MAYBE THE OTHER KIDS WILL HAVE IDEAS ON HOW TO HELP.
DOUBTFUL...
I'LL FOLLOW YOU THERE. FIRST I HAVE TO FIND OUT WHAT THIS GUNK IS MADE OF, THEN I'LL MAKE A BIG BATCH OF IT.
WE'RE GOING TO NEED A LOT OF IT, AUNT OCTAVIA!

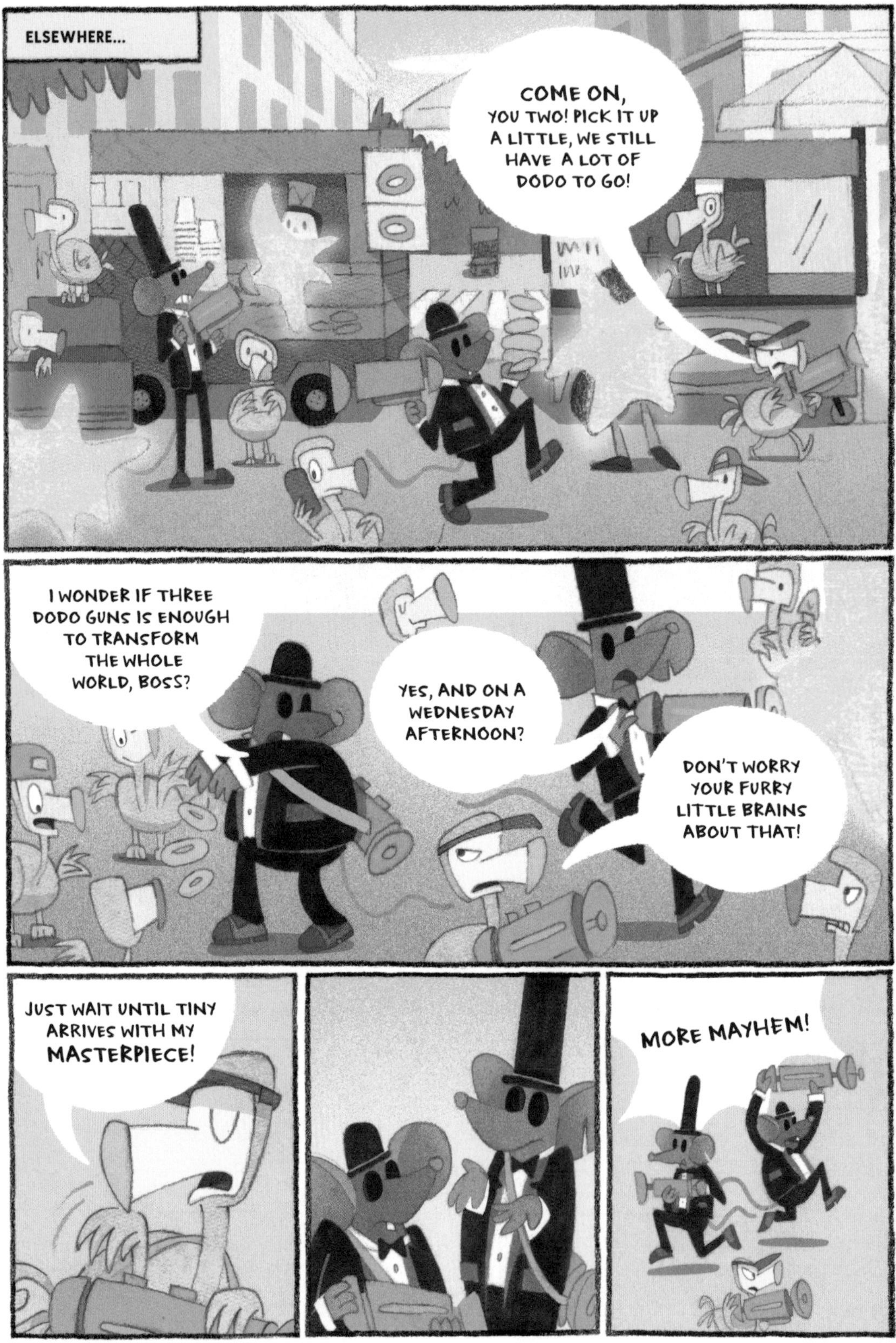
ELSEWHERE...
COME ON, YOU TWO! PICK IT UP A LITTLE, WE STILL HAVE A LOT OF DODO TO GO!
I WONDER IF THREE DODO GUNS IS ENOUGH TO TRANSFORM THE WHOLE WORLD, BOSS?
YES, AND ON A WEDNESDAY AFTERNOON?
DON'T WORRY YOUR FURRY LITTLE BRAINS ABOUT THAT!
JUST WAIT UNTIL TINY ARRIVES WITH MY MASTERPIECE!
MORE MAYHEM!

CHAPTER 7

THE DODO'S LAST STAND

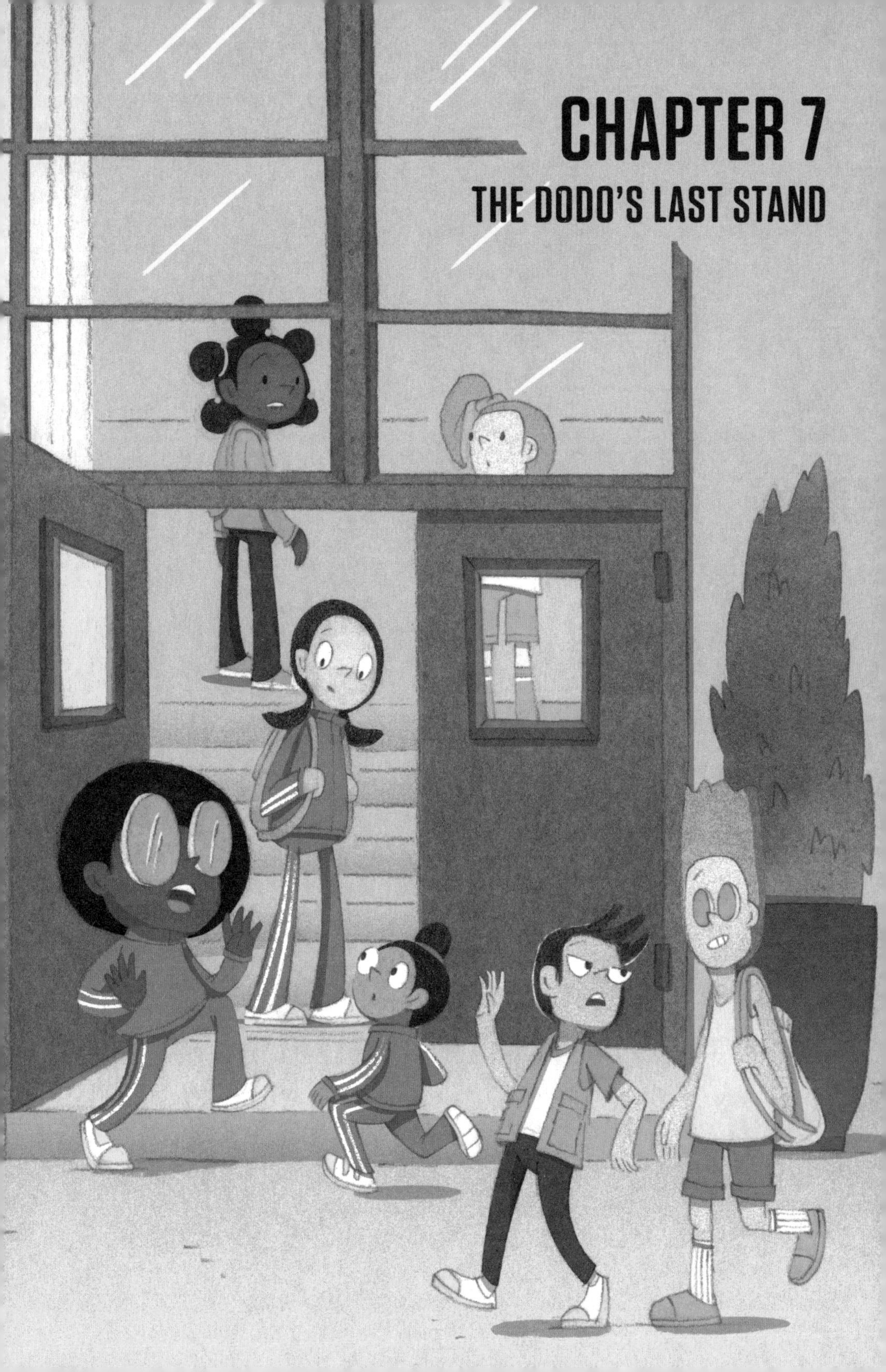

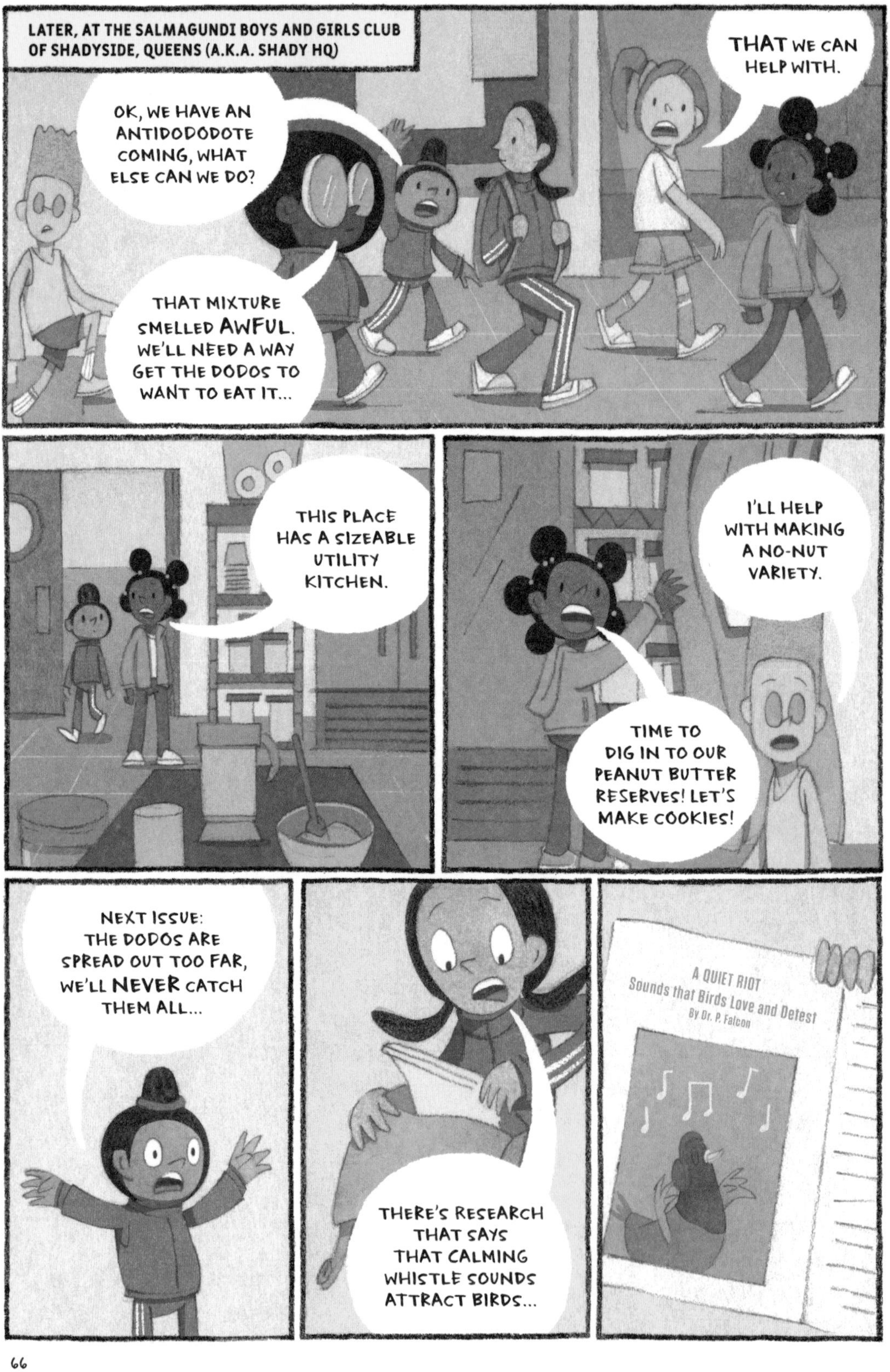
LATER, AT THE SALMAGUNDI BOYS AND GIRLS CLUB OF SHADYSIDE, QUEENS (A.K.A. SHADY HQ)
OK, WE HAVE AN ANTIDODODOTE COMING, WHAT ELSE CAN WE DO?
THAT MIXTURE SMELLED AWFUL. WE'LL NEED A WAY GET THE DODOS TO WANT TO EAT IT...
THAT WE CAN HELP WITH.
THIS PLACE HAS A SIZEABLE UTILITY KITCHEN.
TIME TO DIG IN TO OUR PEANUT BUTTER RESERVES! LET'S MAKE COOKIES!
I'LL HELP WITH MAKING A NO-NUT VARIETY.
NEXT ISSUE: THE DODOS ARE SPREAD OUT TOO FAR, WE'LL NEVER CATCH THEM ALL...
THERE'S RESEARCH THAT SAYS THAT CALMING WHISTLE SOUNDS ATTRACT BIRDS...
A QUIET RIOT
Sounds that Birds Love and Detest
By Dr. P. Falcon

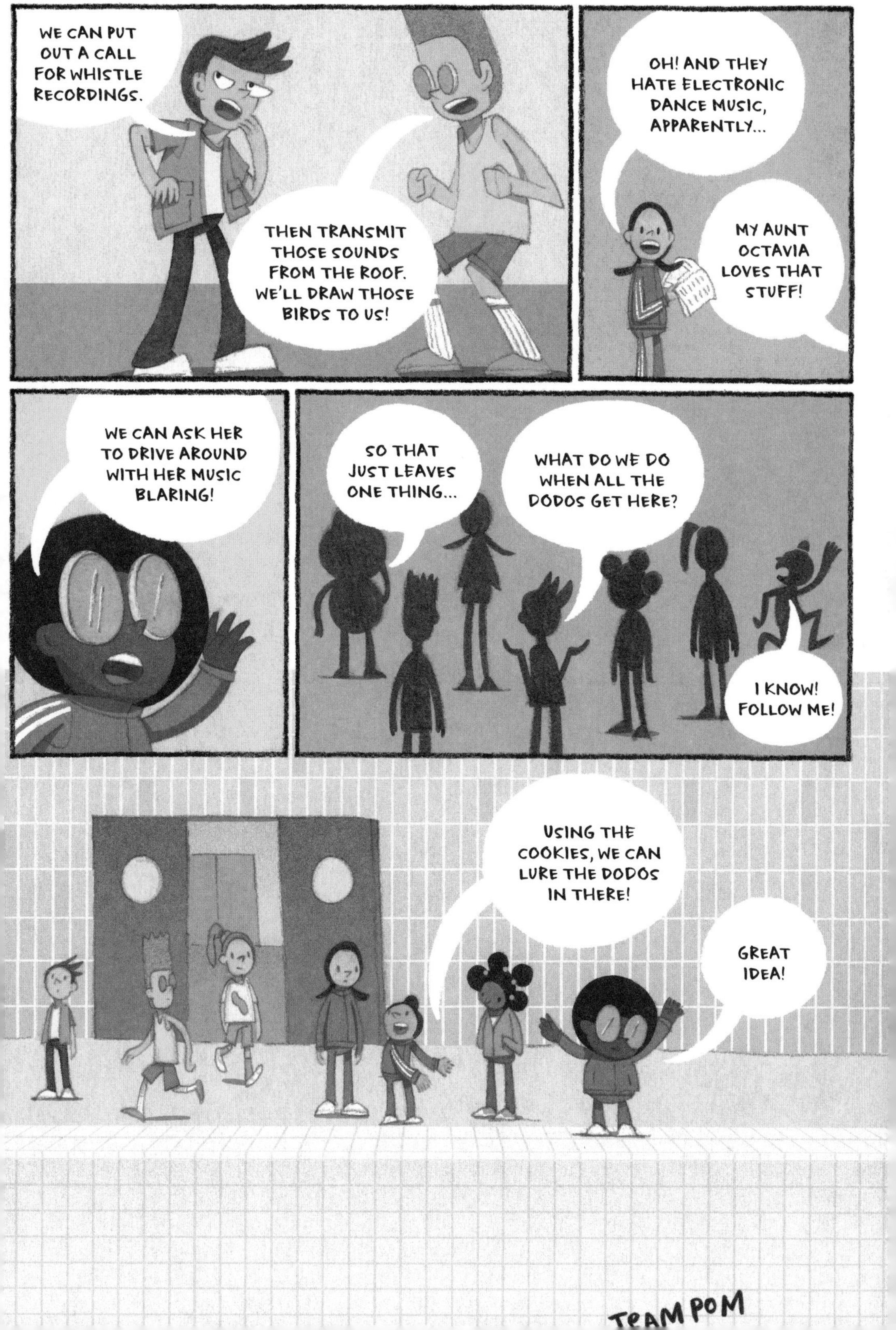
WE CAN PUT OUT A CALL FOR WHISTLE RECORDINGS.
THEN TRANSMIT THOSE SOUNDS FROM THE ROOF. WE'LL DRAW THOSE BIRDS TO US!
OH! AND THEY HATE ELECTRONIC DANCE MUSIC, APPARENTLY...
MY AUNT OCTAVIA LOVES THAT STUFF!
WE CAN ASK HER TO DRIVE AROUND WITH HER MUSIC BLARING!
SO THAT JUST LEAVES ONE THING...
WHAT DO WE DO WHEN ALL THE DODOS GET HERE?
I KNOW! FOLLOW ME!
USING THE COOKIES, WE CAN LURE THE DODOS IN THERE!
GREAT IDEA!
TEAM POM

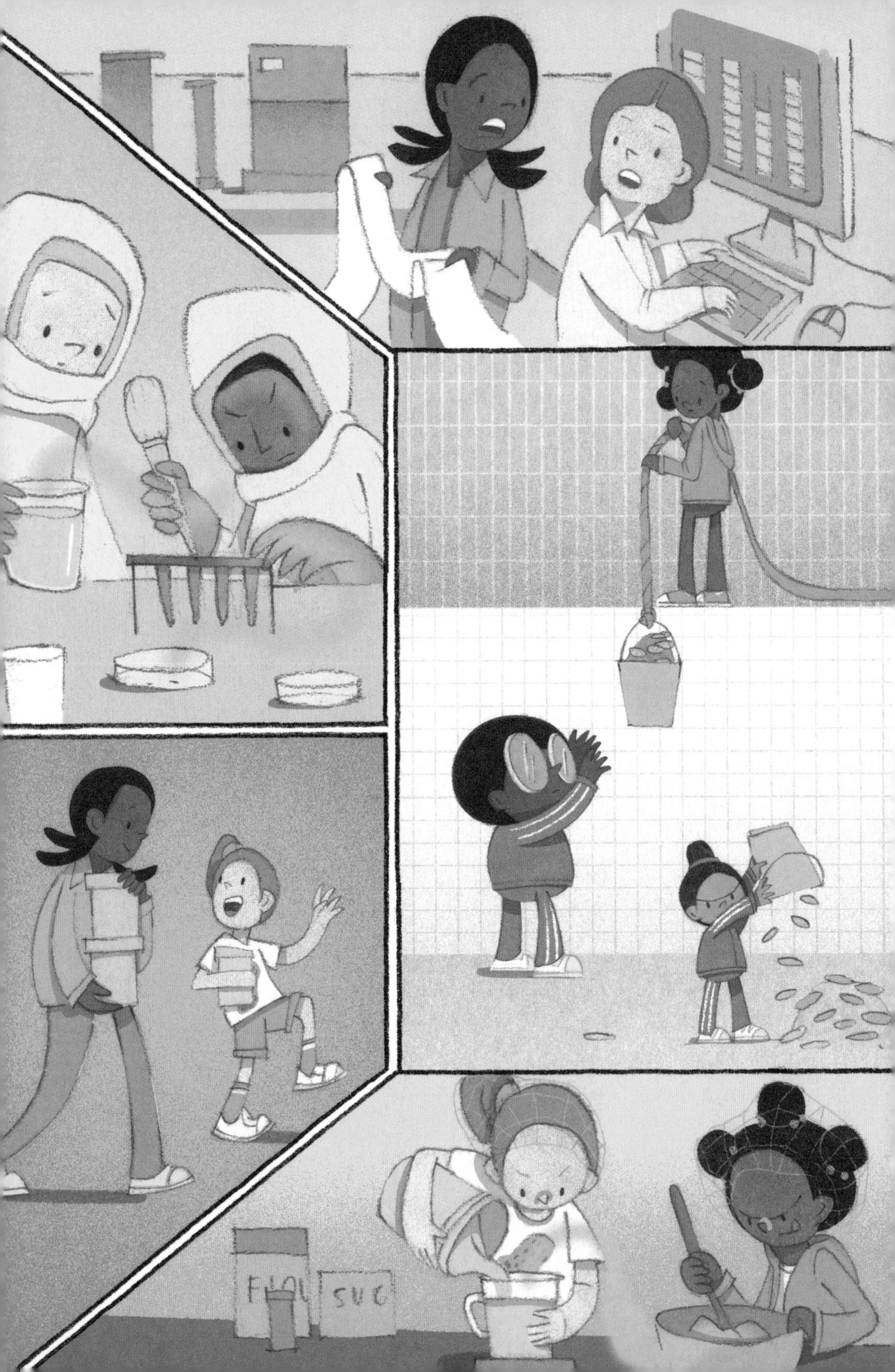
FLOU
SUG

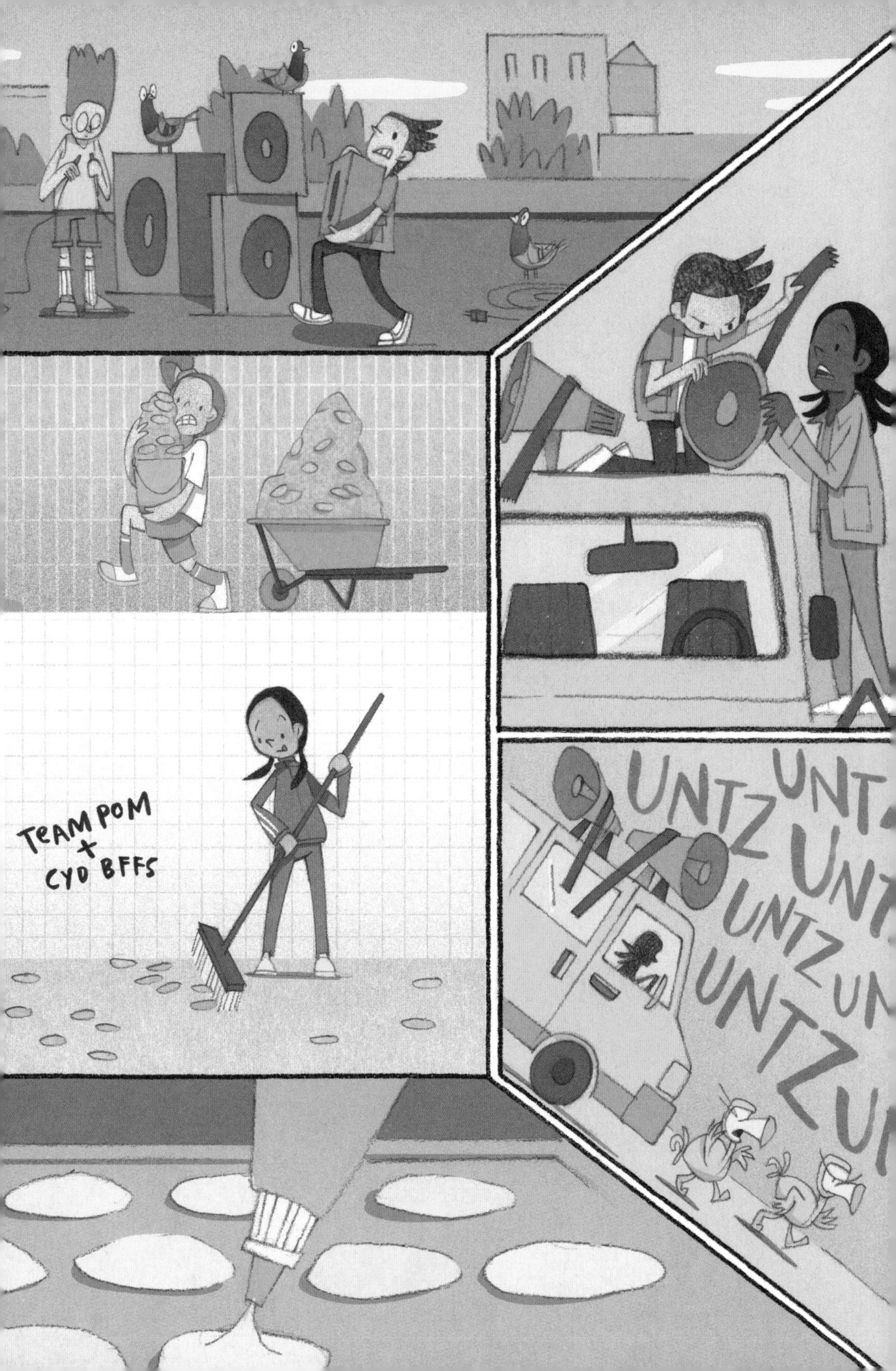
TEAM POM + CYD BFFS
UNTZ UNTZ UNTZ UNTZ UNTZ UNTZ

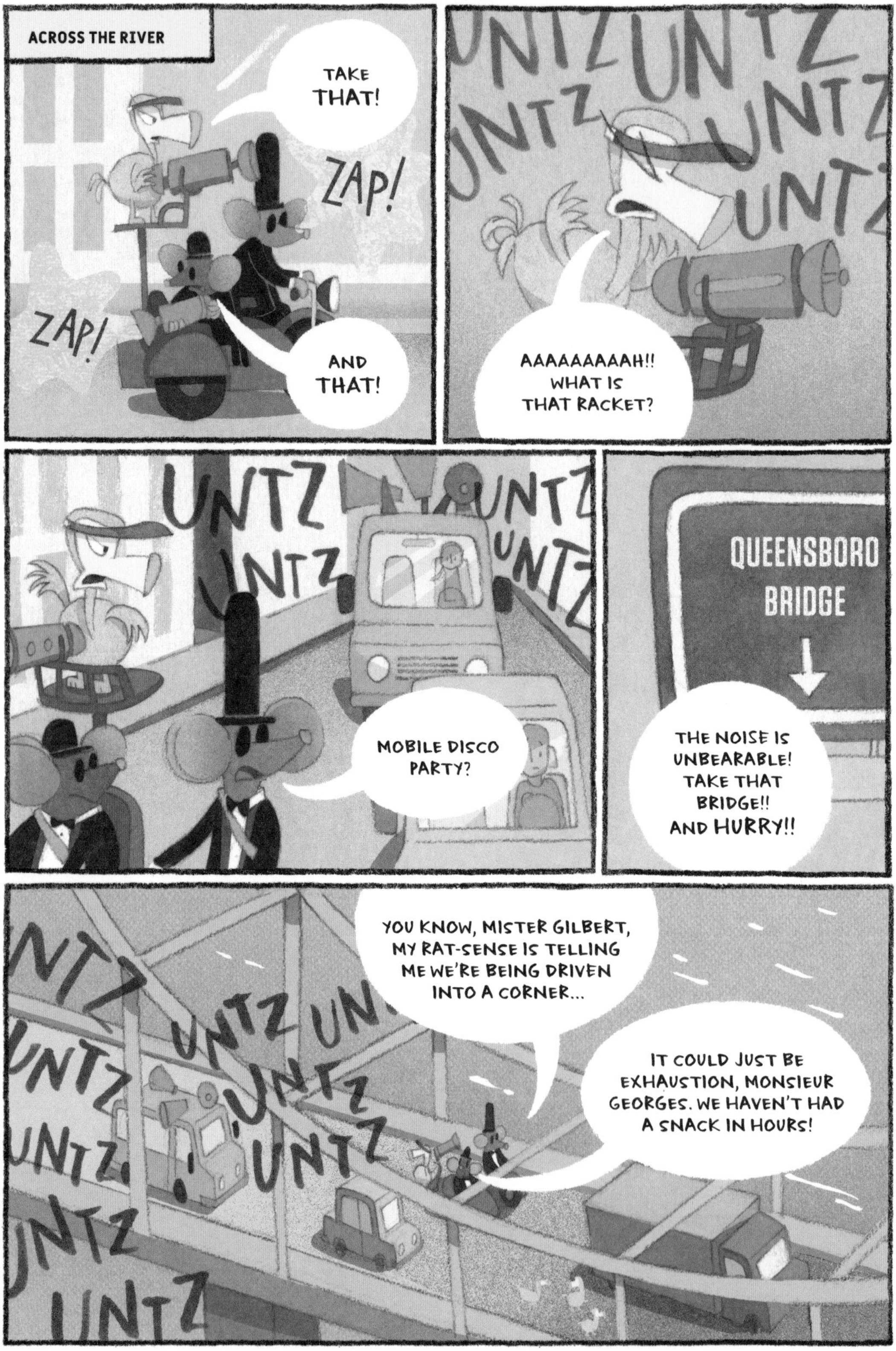
ACROSS THE RIVER
TAKE THAT!
ZAP!
ZAP!
AND THAT!
UNTZ UNTZ UNTZ UNTZ UNTZ
AAAAAAAAAH!! WHAT IS THAT RACKET?
UNTZ UNTZ UNTZ UNTZ
MOBILE DISCO PARTY?
QUEENSBORO BRIDGE
THE NOISE IS UNBEARABLE! TAKE THAT BRIDGE!! AND HURRY!!
YOU KNOW, MISTER GILBERT, MY RAT-SENSE IS TELLING ME WE'RE BEING DRIVEN INTO A CORNER...
IT COULD JUST BE EXHAUSTION, MONSIEUR GEORGES. WE HAVEN'T HAD A SNACK IN HOURS!
UNTZ UNTZ UNTZ UNTZ UNTZ UNTZ UNTZ UNTZ

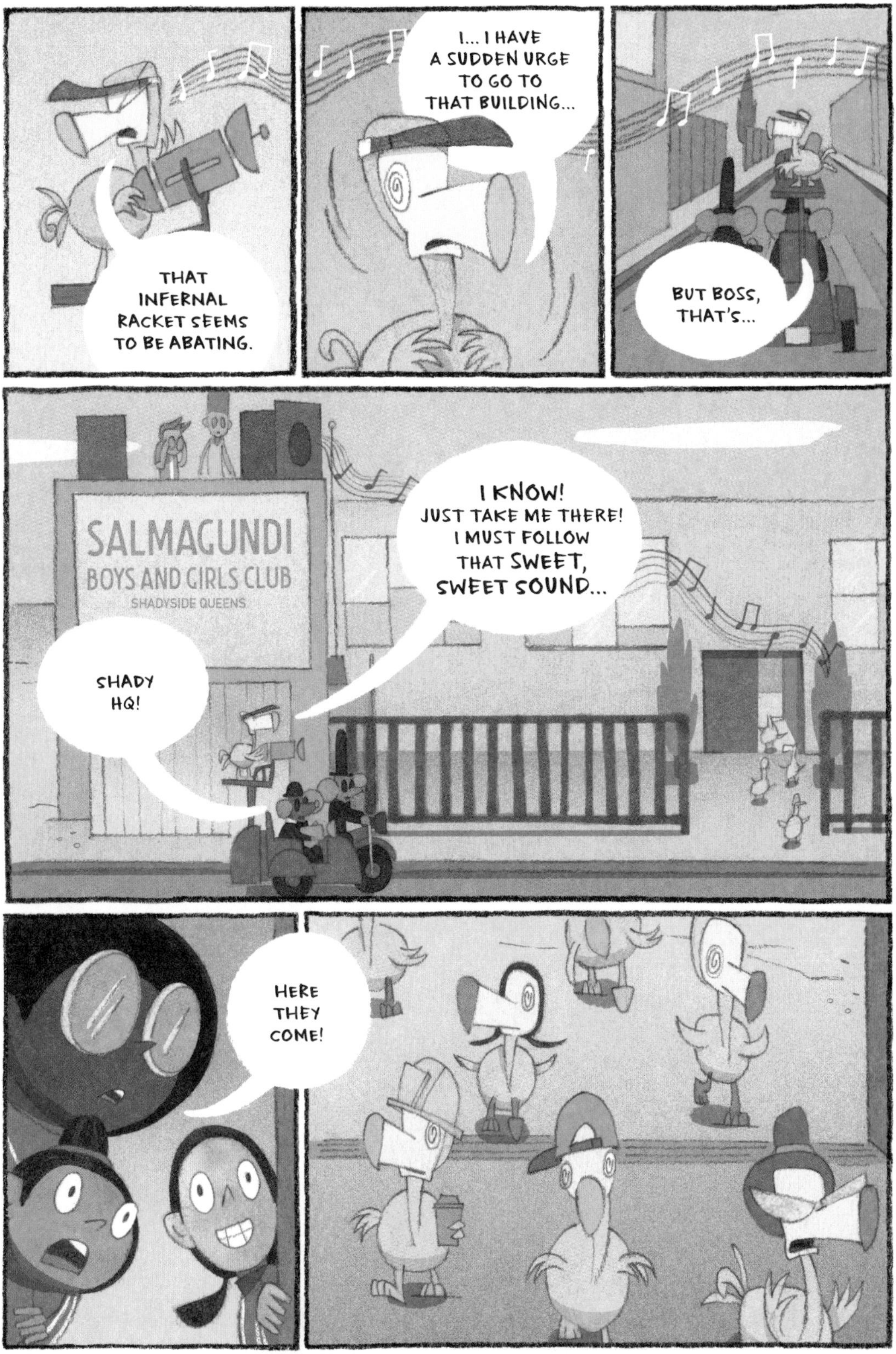
THAT INFERNAL RACKET SEEMS TO BE ABATING.
I... I HAVE A SUDDEN URGE TO GO TO THAT BUILDING...
BUT BOSS, THAT'S...
SALMAGUNDI BOYS AND GIRLS CLUB
SHADYSIDE QUEENS
SHADY HQ!
I KNOW! JUST TAKE ME THERE! I MUST FOLLOW THAT SWEET, SWEET SOUND...
HERE THEY COME!

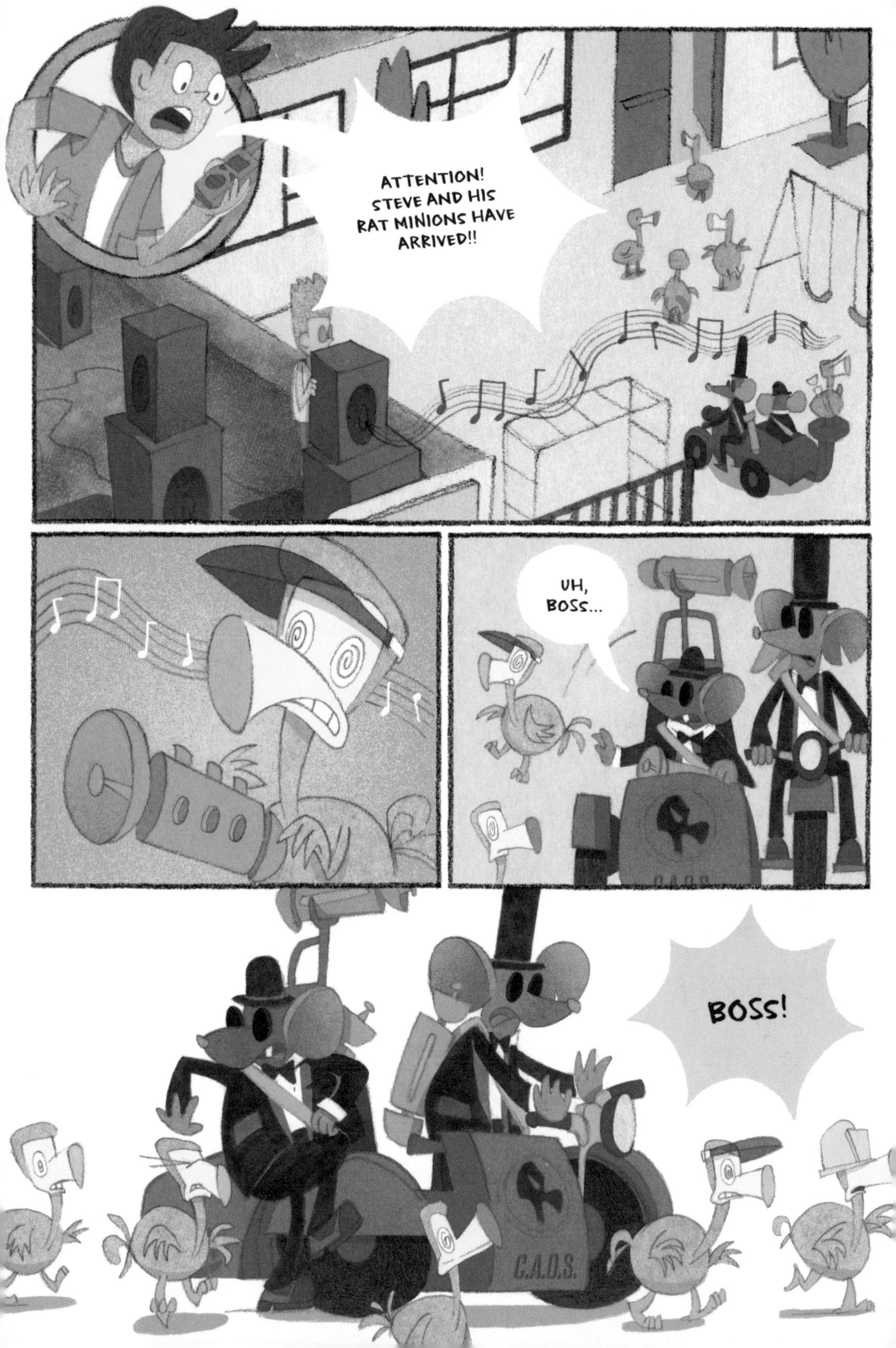
ATTENTION! STEVE AND HIS RAT MINIONS HAVE ARRIVED!!
UH, BOSS...
BOSS!
C.A.O.S.

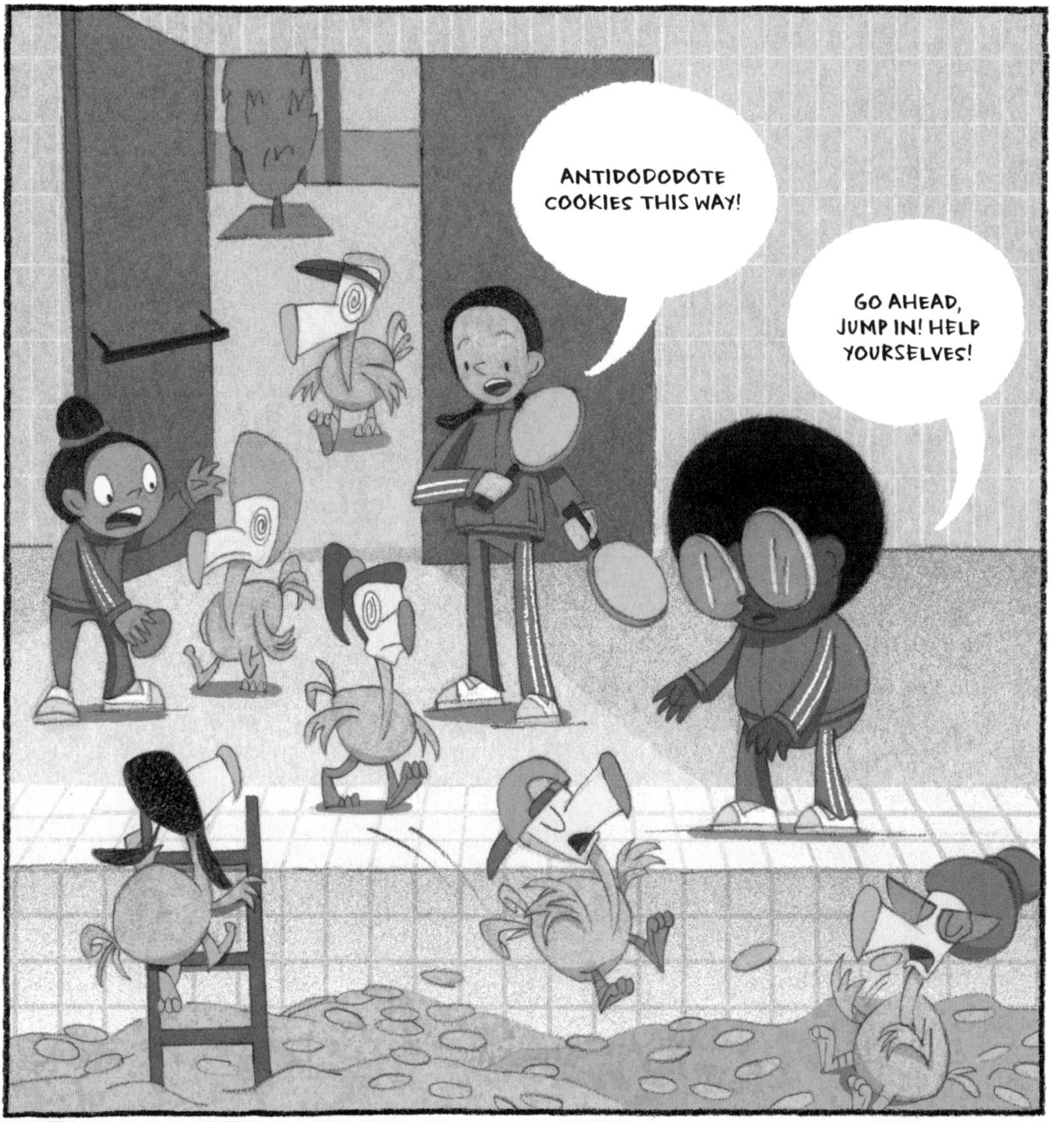
ANTIDODODOTE COOKIES THIS WAY!
GO AHEAD, JUMP IN! HELP YOURSELVES!

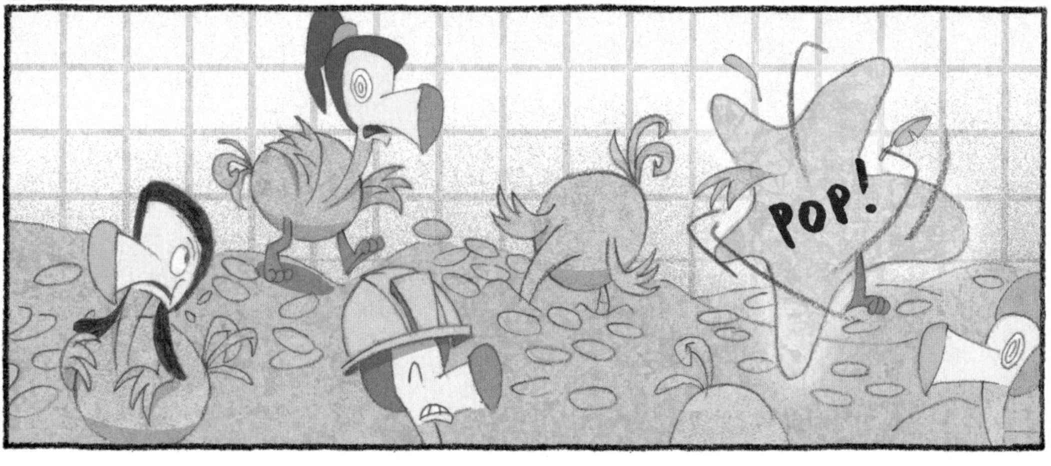
POP!

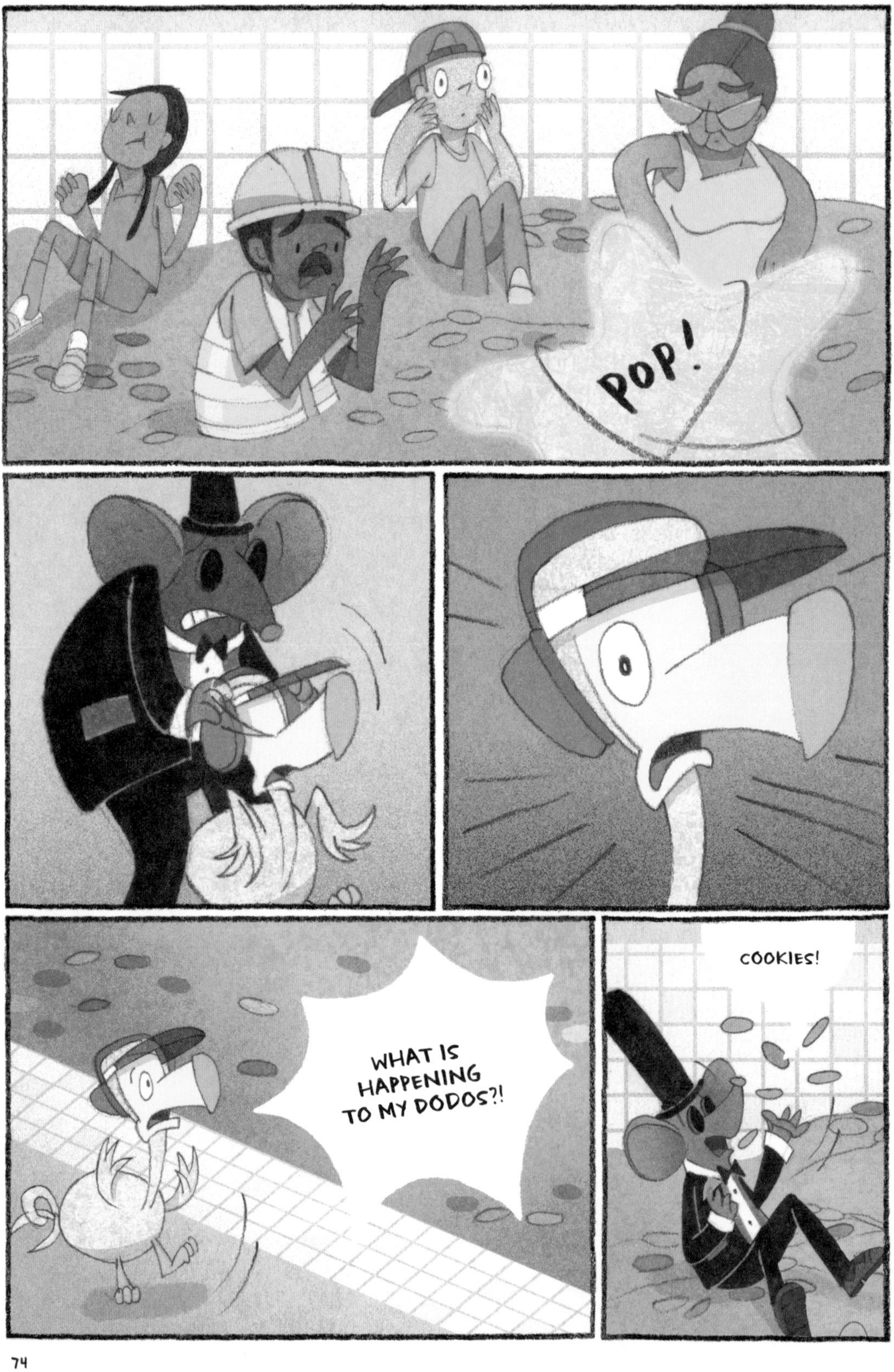
POP!
WHAT IS HAPPENING TO MY DODOS?!
COOKIES!

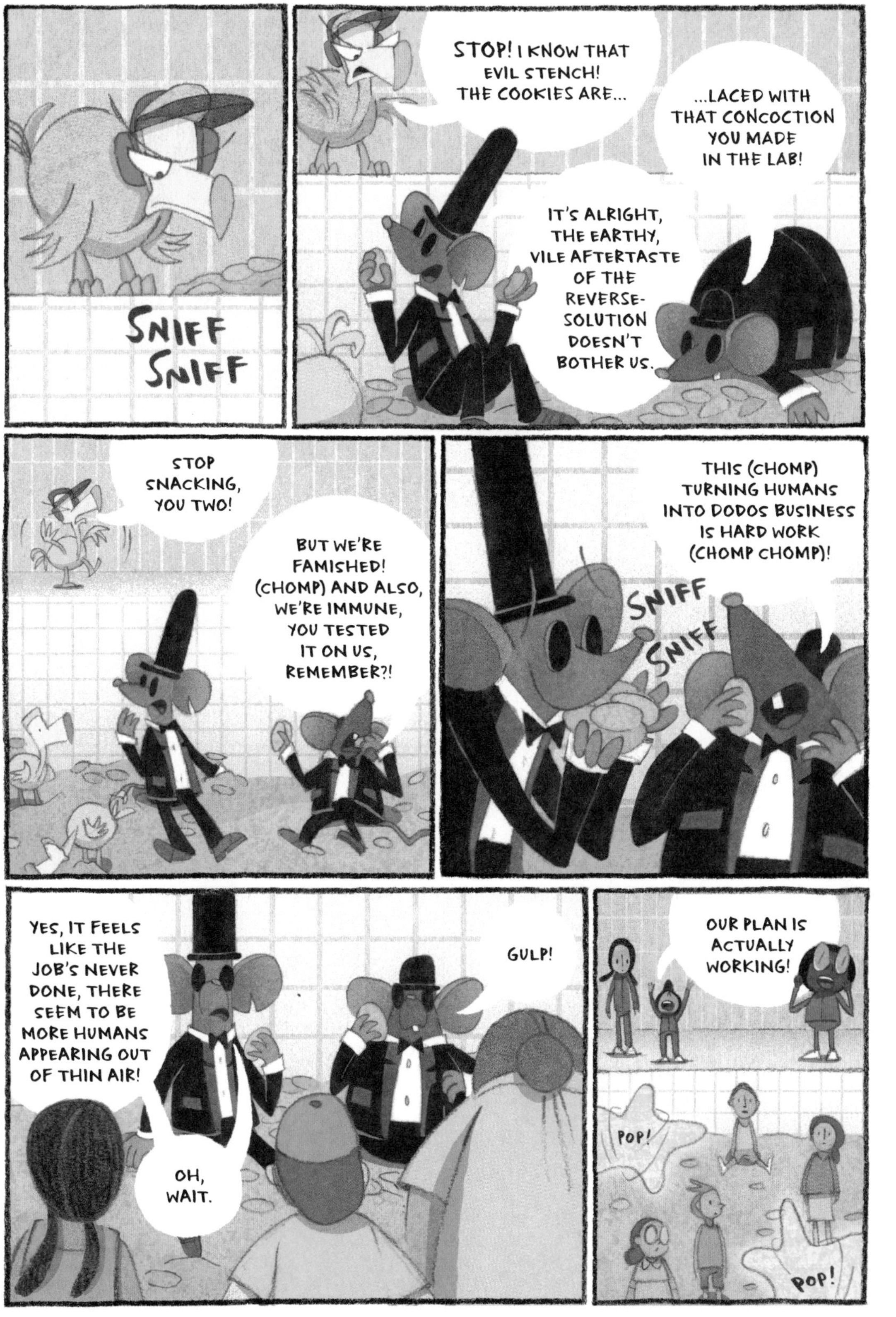
SNIFF SNIFF
STOP! I KNOW THAT EVIL STENCH! THE COOKIES ARE...
...LACED WITH THAT CONCOCTION YOU MADE IN THE LAB!
IT'S ALRIGHT, THE EARTHY, VILE AFTERTASTE OF THE REVERSE-SOLUTION DOESN'T BOTHER US.
STOP SNACKING, YOU TWO!
BUT WE'RE FAMISHED! (CHOMP) AND ALSO, WE'RE IMMUNE, YOU TESTED IT ON US, REMEMBER?!
THIS (CHOMP) TURNING HUMANS INTO DODOS BUSINESS IS HARD WORK (CHOMP CHOMP)!
SNIFF SNIFF
YES, IT FEELS LIKE THE JOB'S NEVER DONE, THERE SEEM TO BE MORE HUMANS APPEARING OUT OF THIN AIR!
GULP!
OH, WAIT.
OUR PLAN IS ACTUALLY WORKING!
POP!
POP!

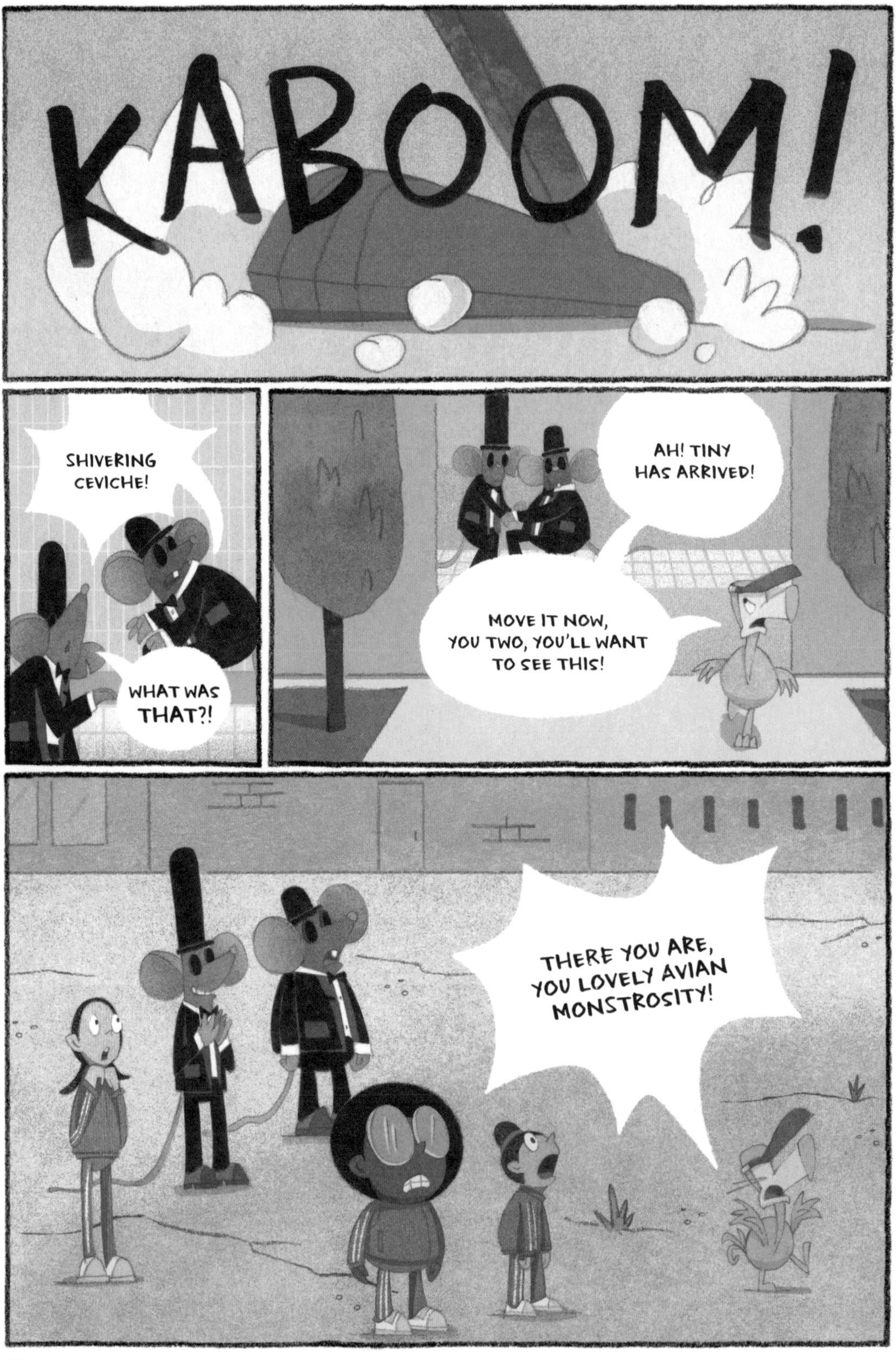
KABOOM!
SHIVERING CEVICHE!
WHAT WAS THAT?!
AH! TINY HAS ARRIVED!
MOVE IT NOW, YOU TWO, YOU'LL WANT TO SEE THIS!
THERE YOU ARE, YOU LOVELY AVIAN MONSTROSITY!

CHAPTER 8
DOOMSDAY

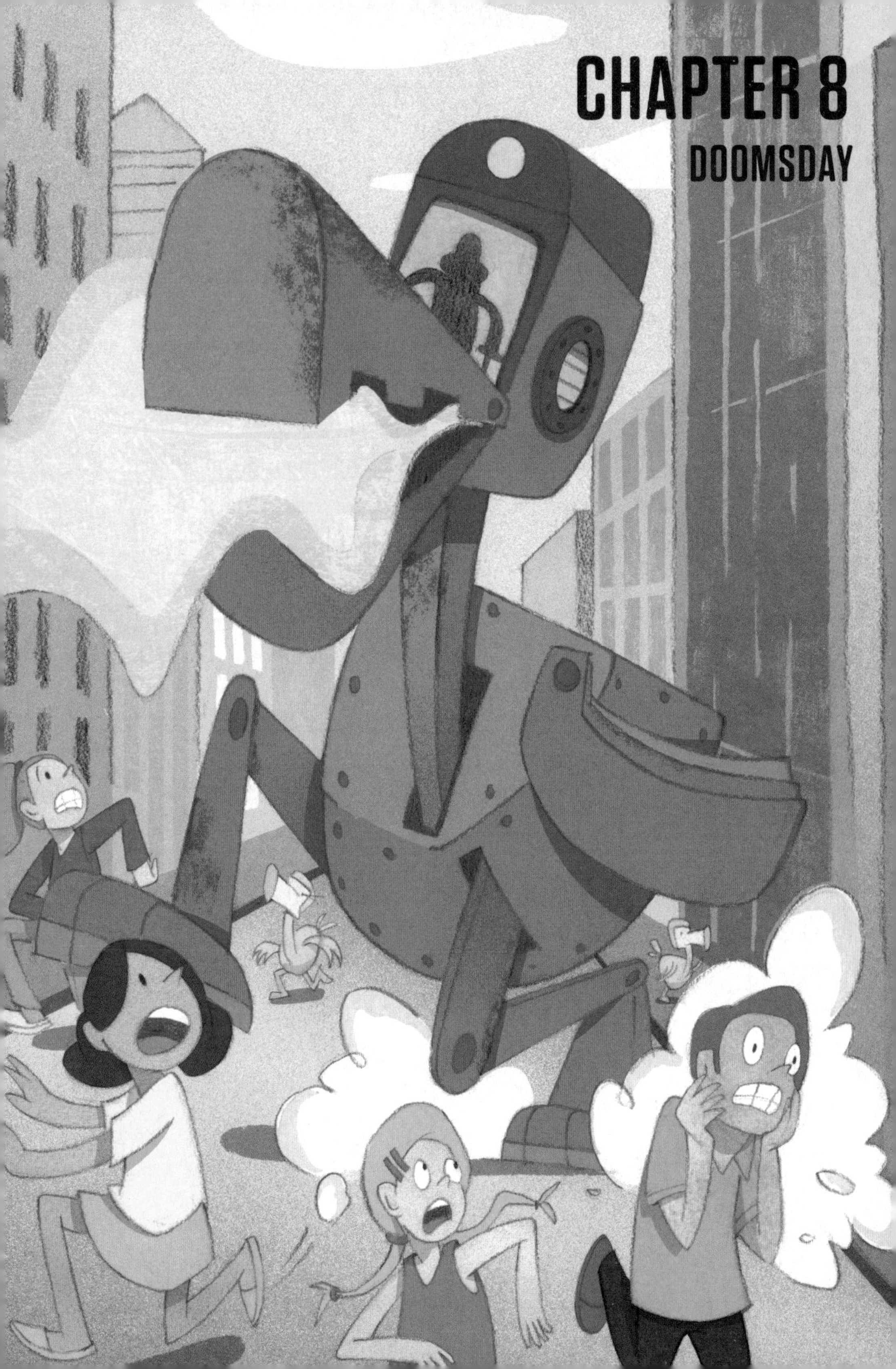

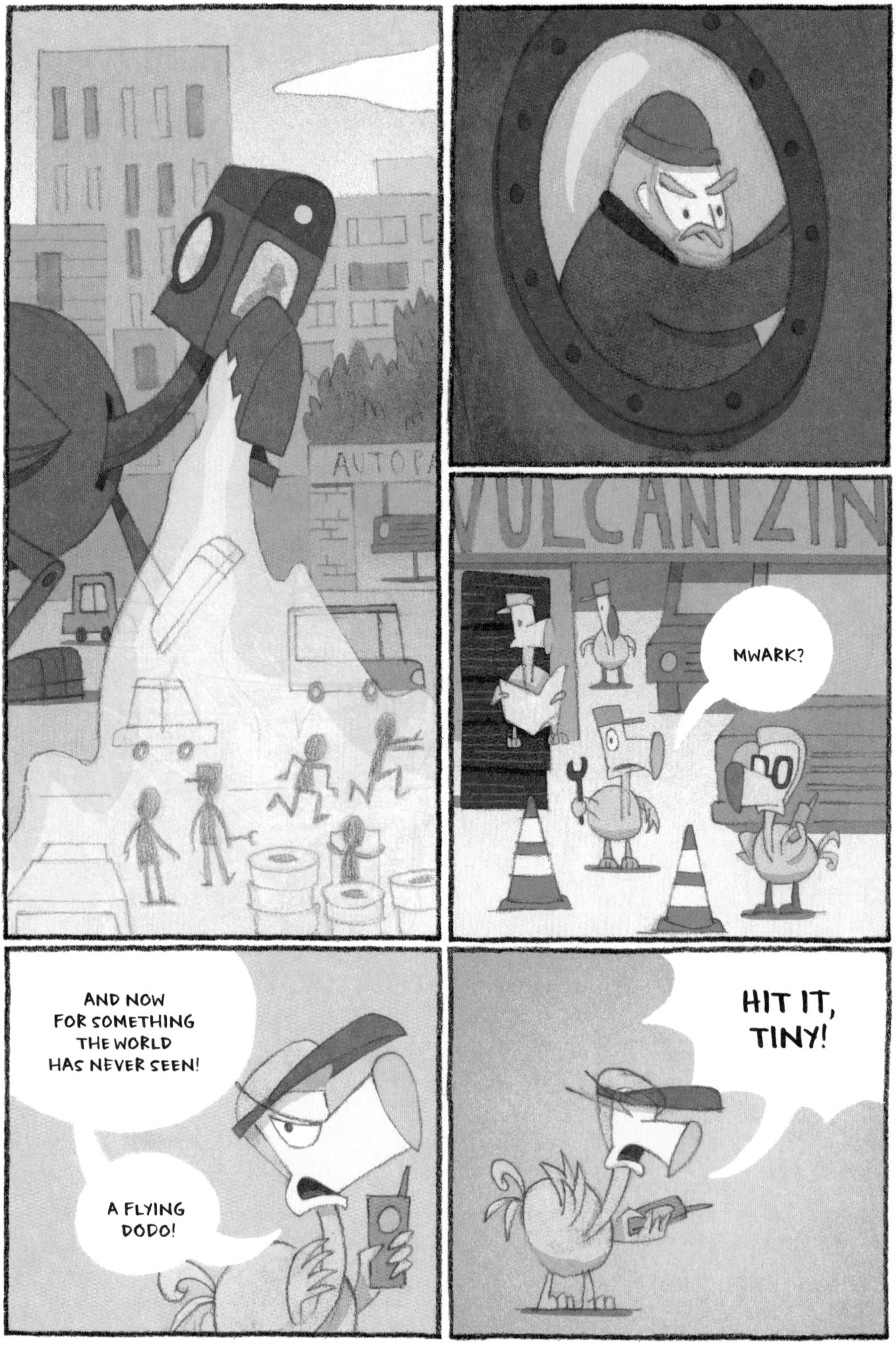
AUTOPA
VULCANIZIN
MWARK?
AND NOW FOR SOMETHING THE WORLD HAS NEVER SEEN!
A FLYING DODO!
HIT IT, TINY!

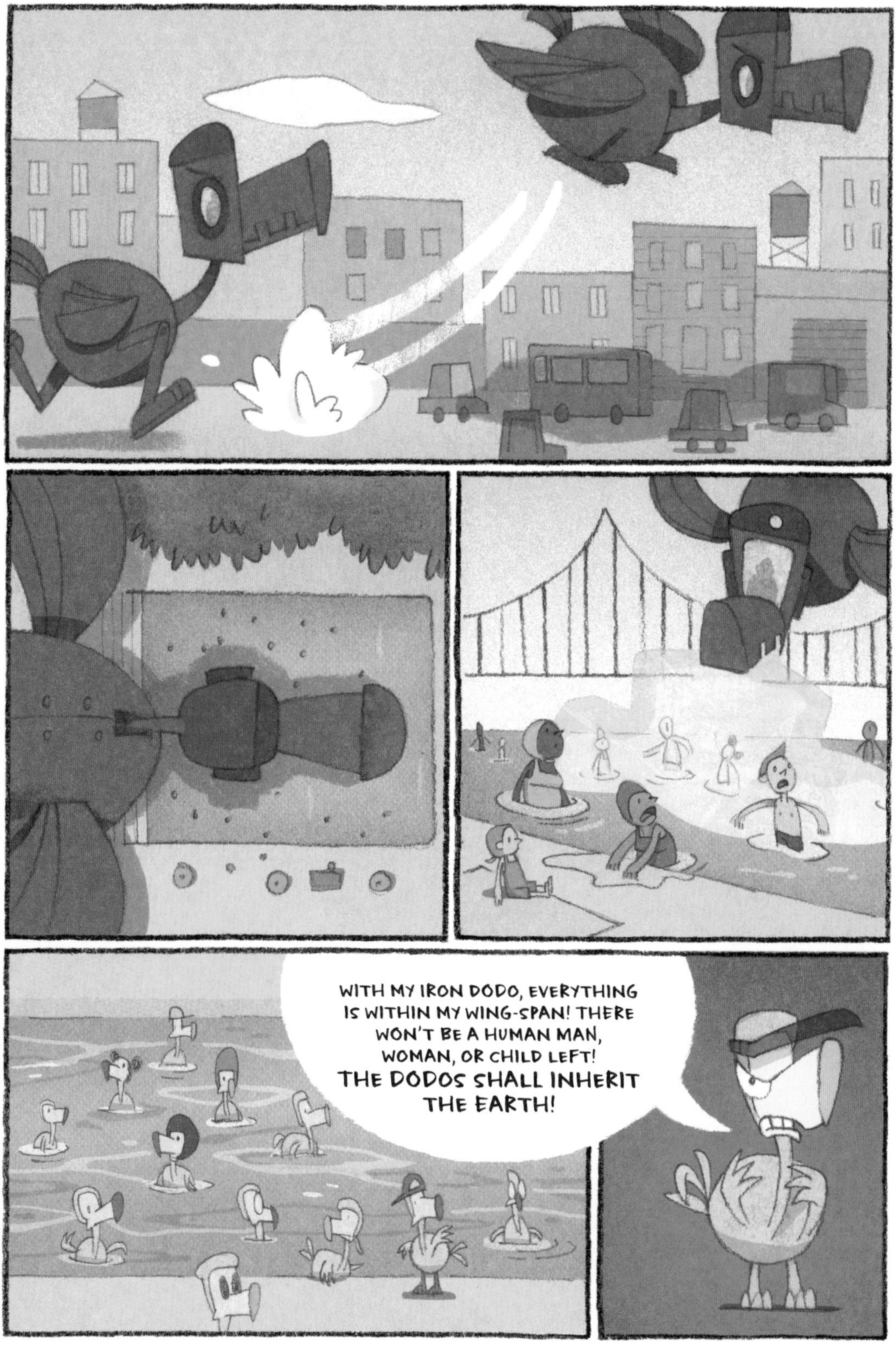
WITH MY IRON DODO, EVERYTHING IS WITHIN MY WING-SPAN! THERE WON'T BE A HUMAN MAN, WOMAN, OR CHILD LEFT! THE DODOS SHALL INHERIT THE EARTH!

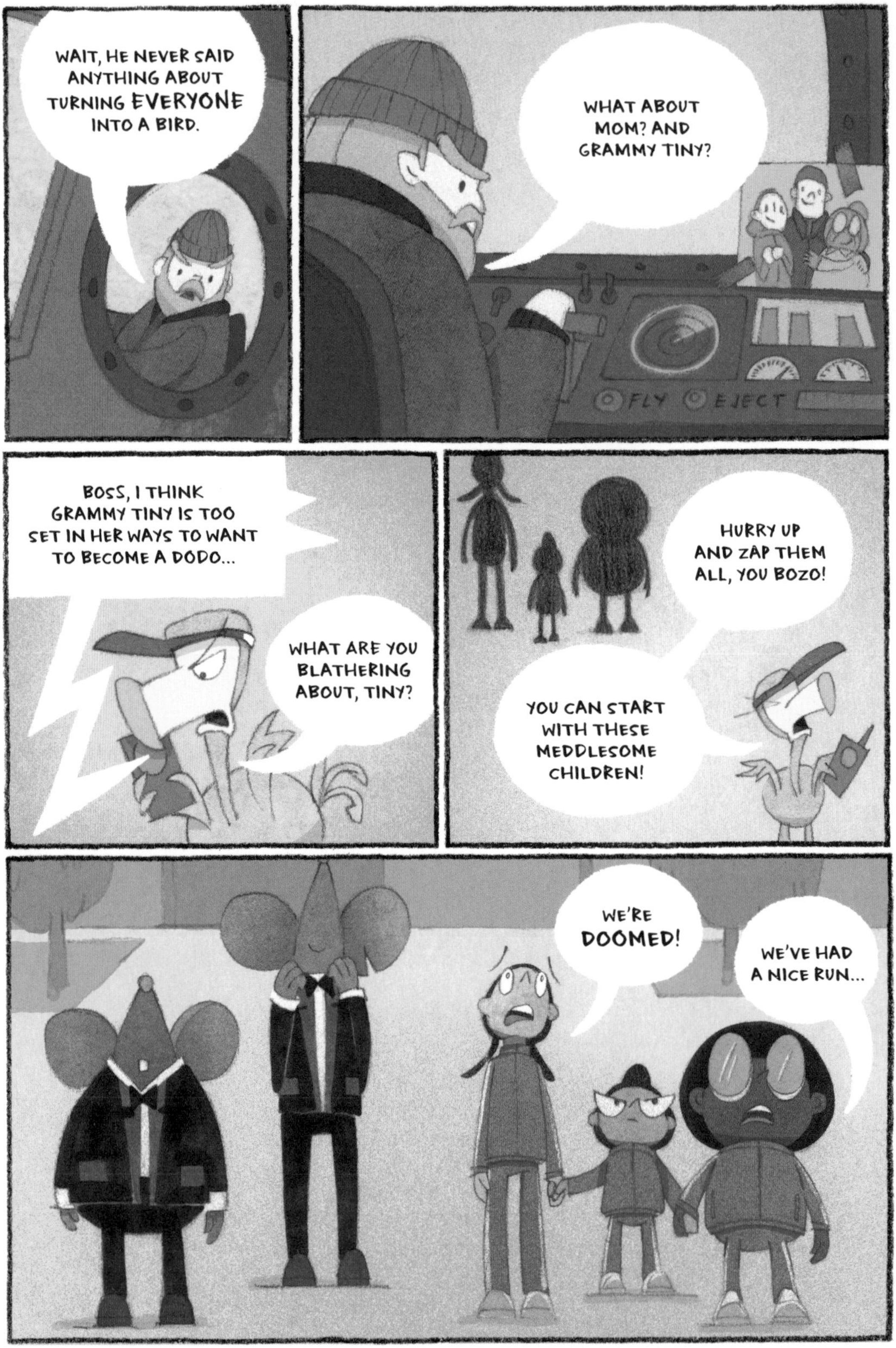

WAIT, HE NEVER SAID ANYTHING ABOUT TURNING EVERYONE INTO A BIRD.
WHAT ABOUT MOM? AND GRAMMY TINY?
FLY
EJECT
BOSS, I THINK GRAMMY TINY IS TOO SET IN HER WAYS TO WANT TO BECOME A DODO...
WHAT ARE YOU BLATHERING ABOUT, TINY?
HURRY UP AND ZAP THEM ALL, YOU BOZO!
YOU CAN START WITH THESE MEDDLESOME CHILDREN!
WE'RE DOOMED!
WE'VE HAD A NICE RUN...

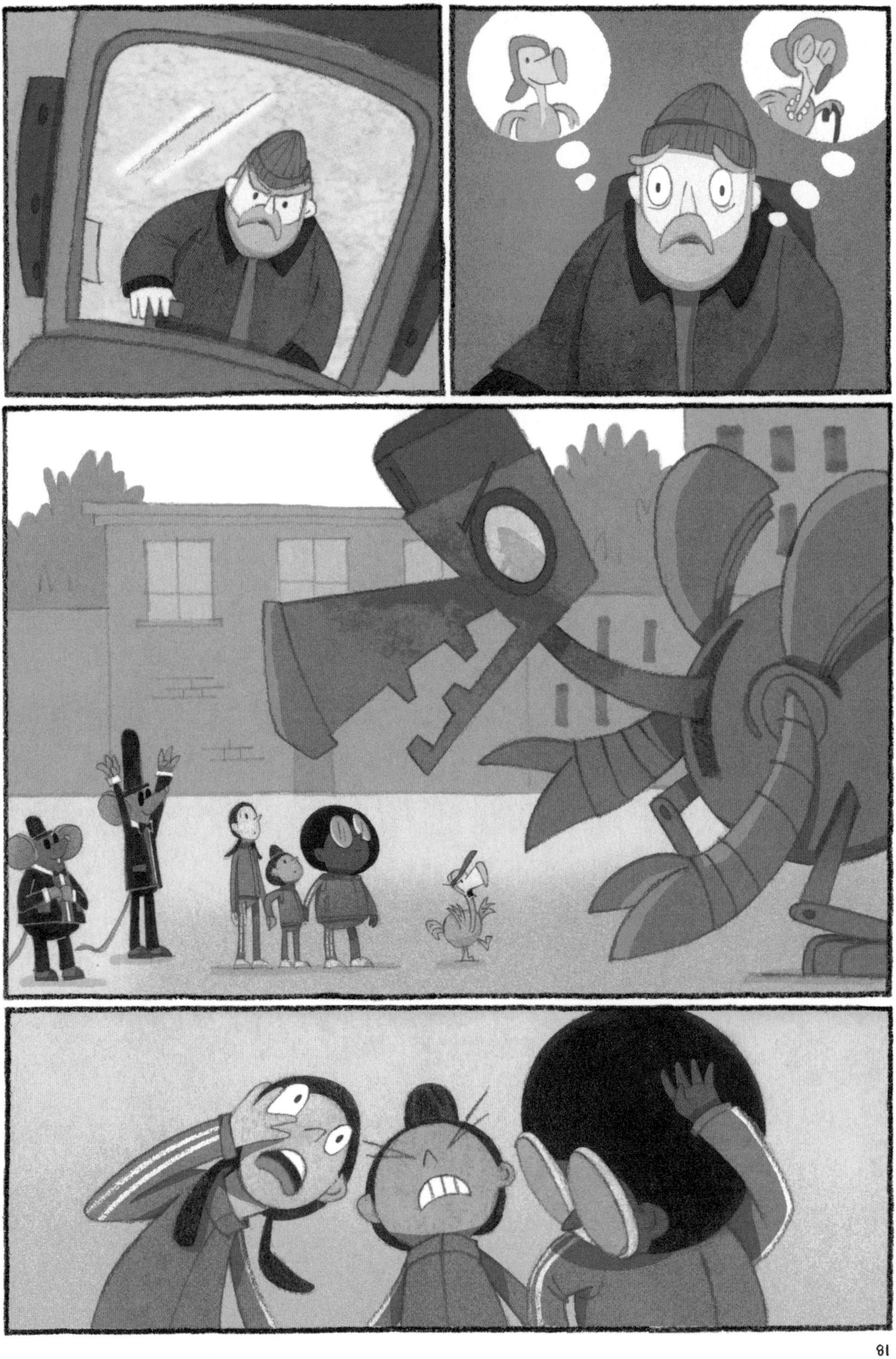

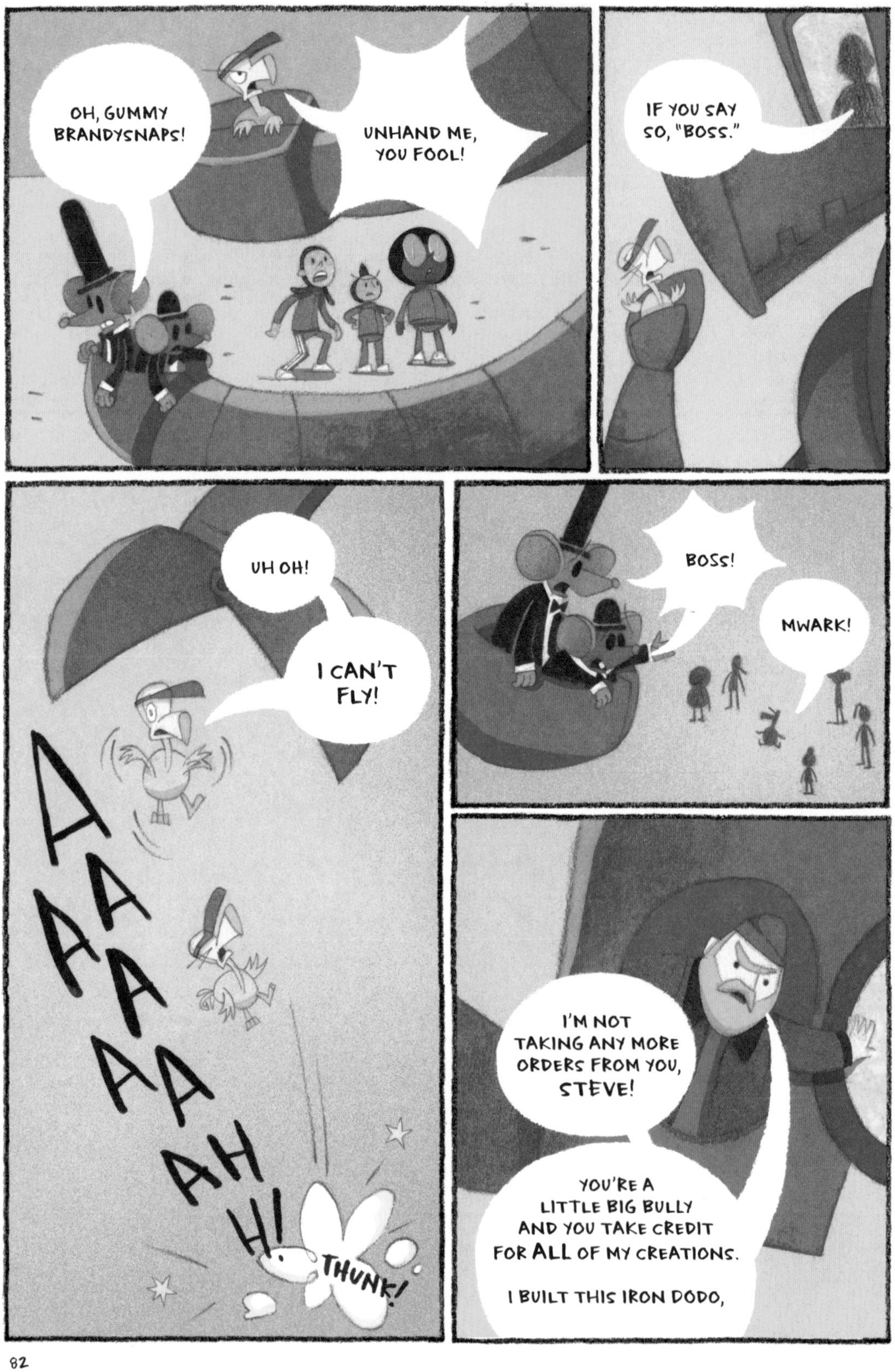

OH, GUMMY BRANDYSNAPS!
UNHAND ME, YOU FOOL!
IF YOU SAY SO, "BOSS."
UH OH!
I CAN'T FLY!
AAAAAAAAAHH!
THUNK!
BOSS!
MWARK!
I'M NOT TAKING ANY MORE ORDERS FROM YOU, STEVE!
YOU'RE A LITTLE BIG BULLY AND YOU TAKE CREDIT FOR ALL OF MY CREATIONS.
I BUILT THIS IRON DODO,

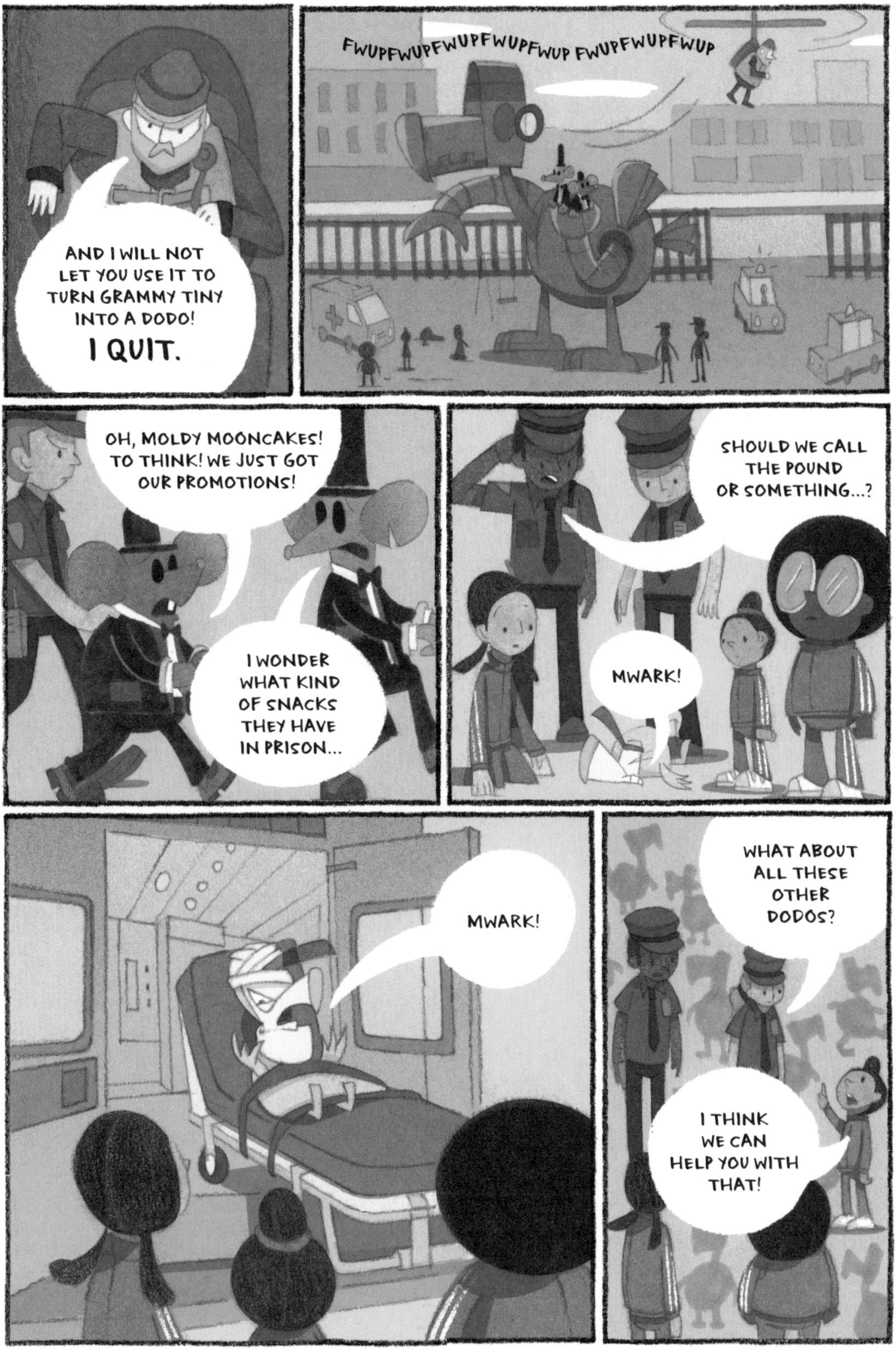
AND I WILL NOT LET YOU USE IT TO TURN GRAMMY TINY INTO A DODO!
I QUIT.
FWUPFWUPFWUPFWUPFWUP FWUPFWUPFWUP
OH, MOLDY MOONCAKES! TO THINK! WE JUST GOT OUR PROMOTIONS!
I WONDER WHAT KIND OF SNACKS THEY HAVE IN PRISON...
SHOULD WE CALL THE POUND OR SOMETHING...?
MWARK!
MWARK!
WHAT ABOUT ALL THESE OTHER DODOS?
I THINK WE CAN HELP YOU WITH THAT!

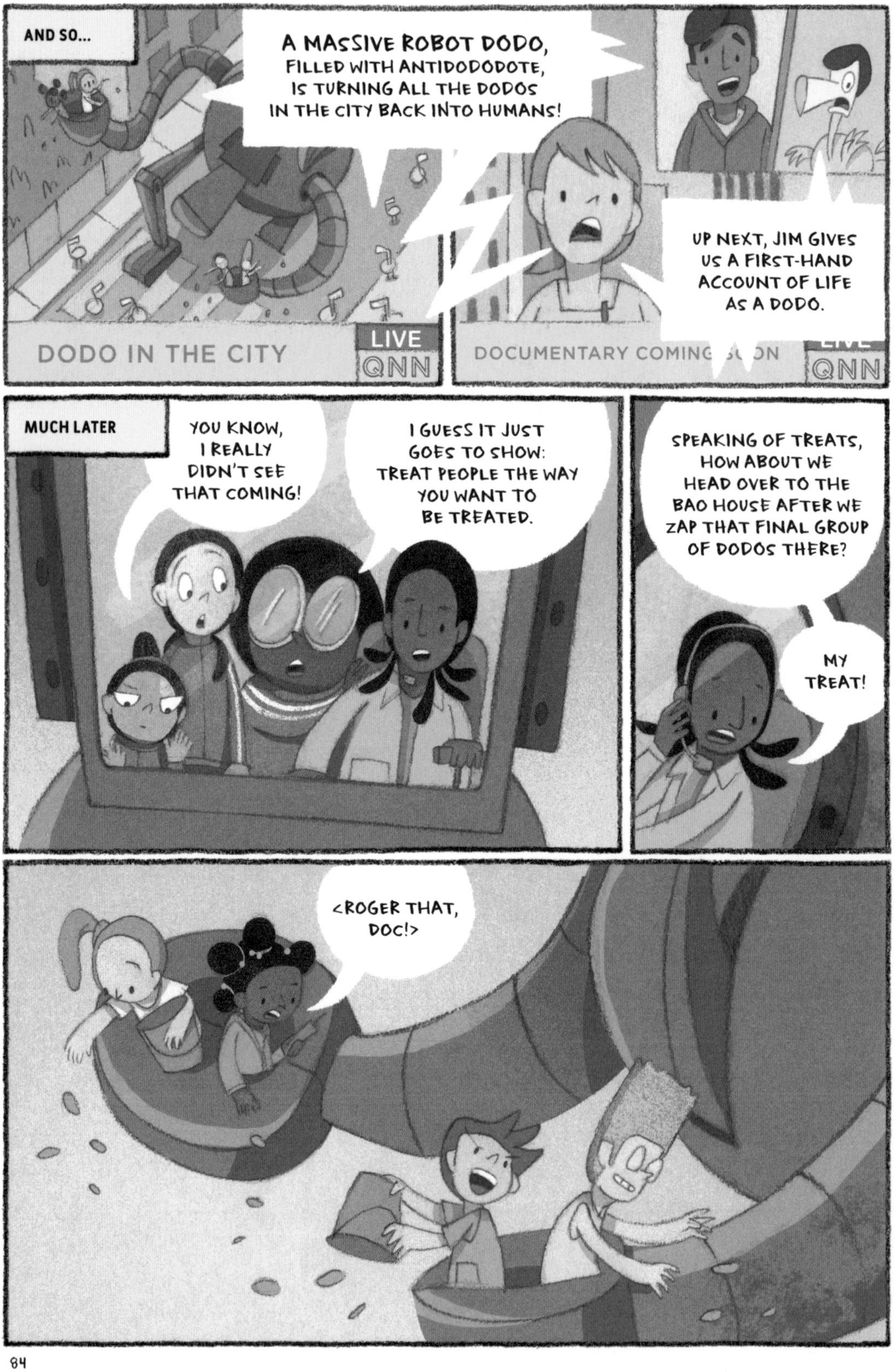
AND SO...
A MASSIVE ROBOT DODO, FILLED WITH ANTIDODODOTE, IS TURNING ALL THE DODOS IN THE CITY BACK INTO HUMANS!
DODO IN THE CITY
LIVE
QNN
UP NEXT, JIM GIVES US A FIRST-HAND ACCOUNT OF LIFE AS A DODO.
DOCUMENTARY COMING
QNN
MUCH LATER
YOU KNOW, I REALLY DIDN'T SEE THAT COMING!
I GUESS IT JUST GOES TO SHOW: TREAT PEOPLE THE WAY YOU WANT TO BE TREATED.
SPEAKING OF TREATS, HOW ABOUT WE HEAD OVER TO THE BAO HOUSE AFTER WE ZAP THAT FINAL GROUP OF DODOS THERE?
MY TREAT!
<ROGER THAT, DOC!>

CHAPTER 9
A FRESH START

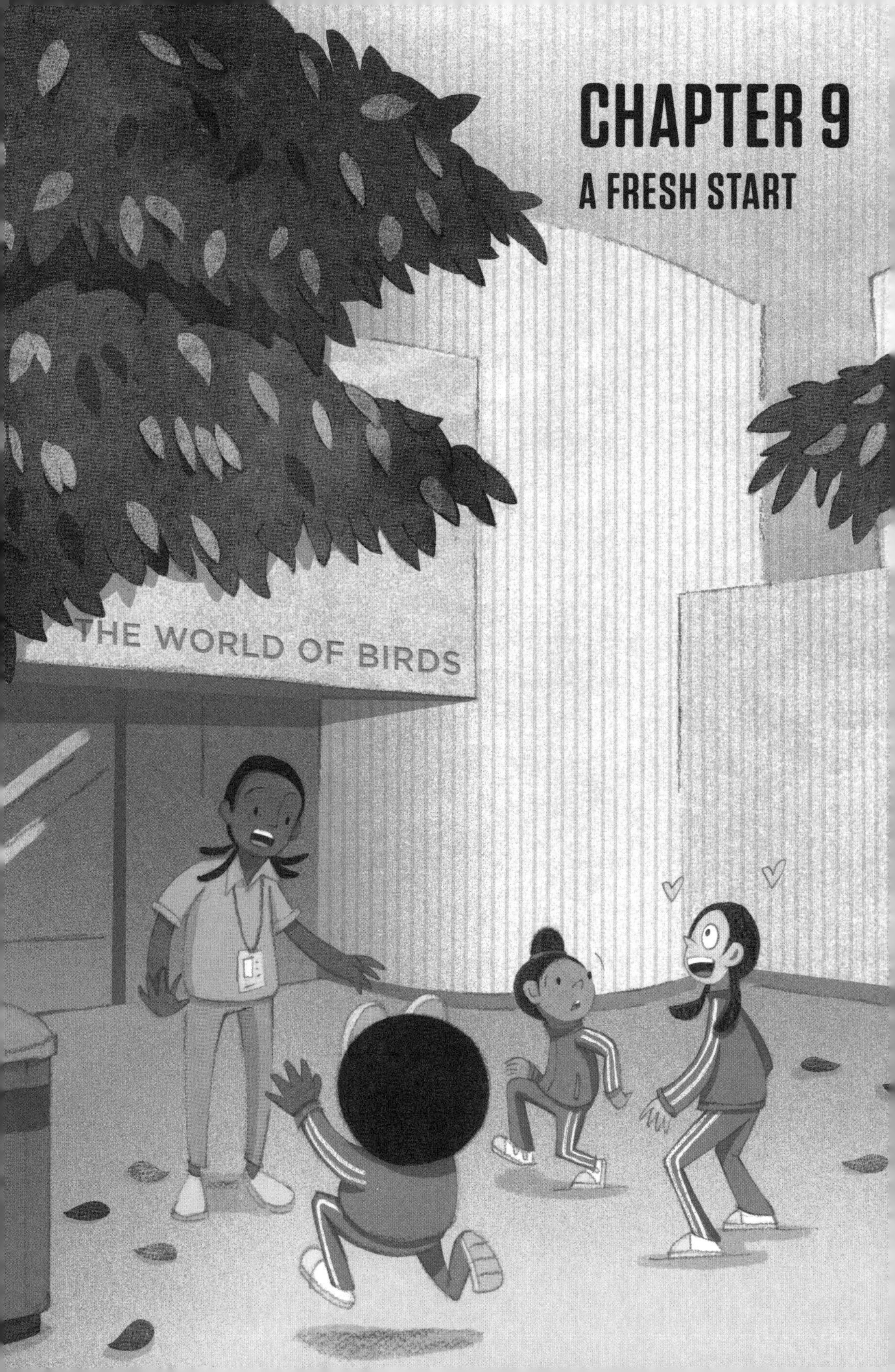
THE WORLD OF BIRDS

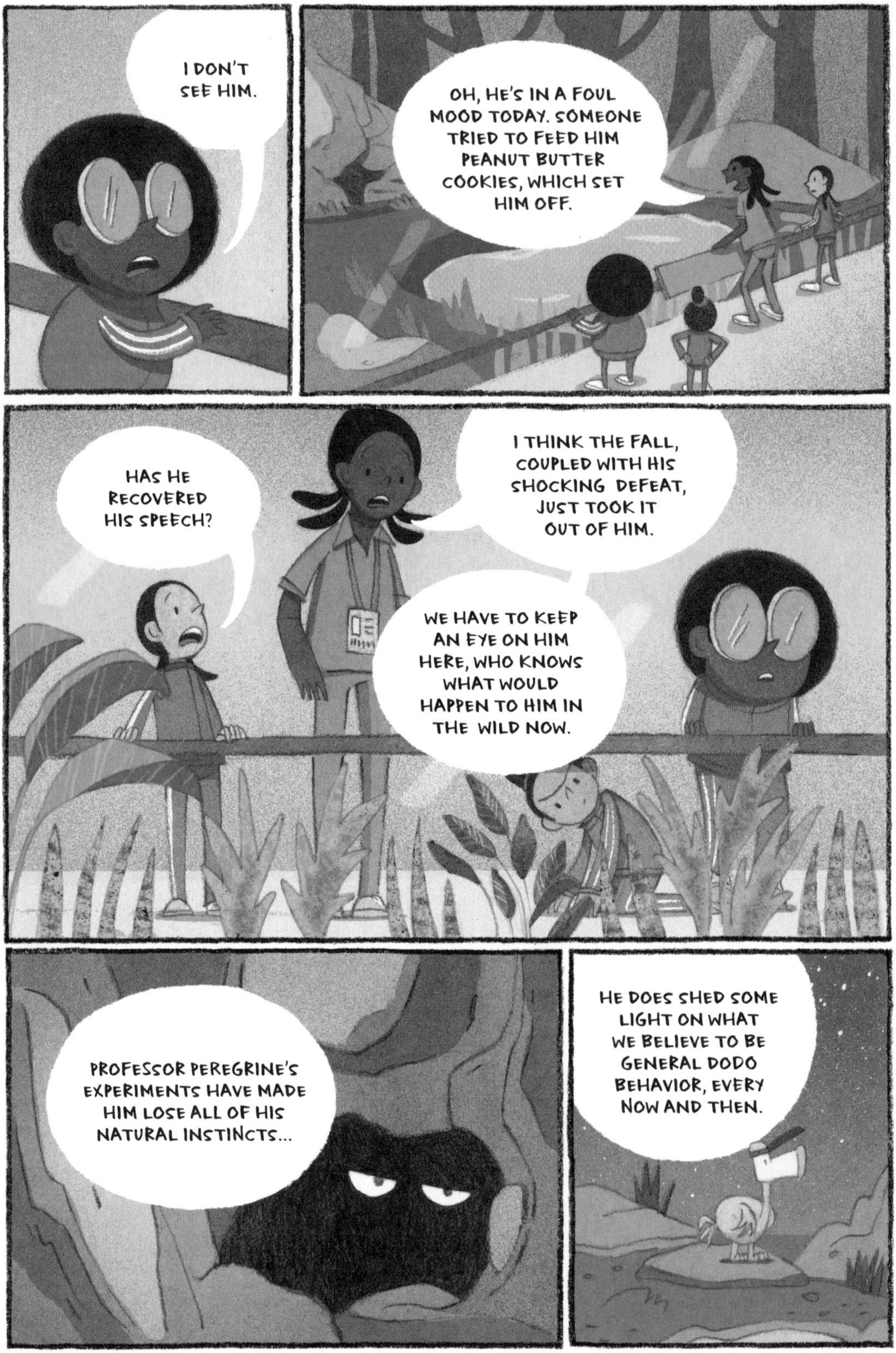
I DON'T SEE HIM.
OH, HE'S IN A FOUL MOOD TODAY. SOMEONE TRIED TO FEED HIM PEANUT BUTTER COOKIES, WHICH SET HIM OFF.
HAS HE RECOVERED HIS SPEECH?
I THINK THE FALL, COUPLED WITH HIS SHOCKING DEFEAT, JUST TOOK IT OUT OF HIM.
WE HAVE TO KEEP AN EYE ON HIM HERE, WHO KNOWS WHAT WOULD HAPPEN TO HIM IN THE WILD NOW.
PROFESSOR PEREGRINE'S EXPERIMENTS HAVE MADE HIM LOSE ALL OF HIS NATURAL INSTINCTS...
HE DOES SHED SOME LIGHT ON WHAT WE BELIEVE TO BE GENERAL DODO BEHAVIOR, EVERY NOW AND THEN.

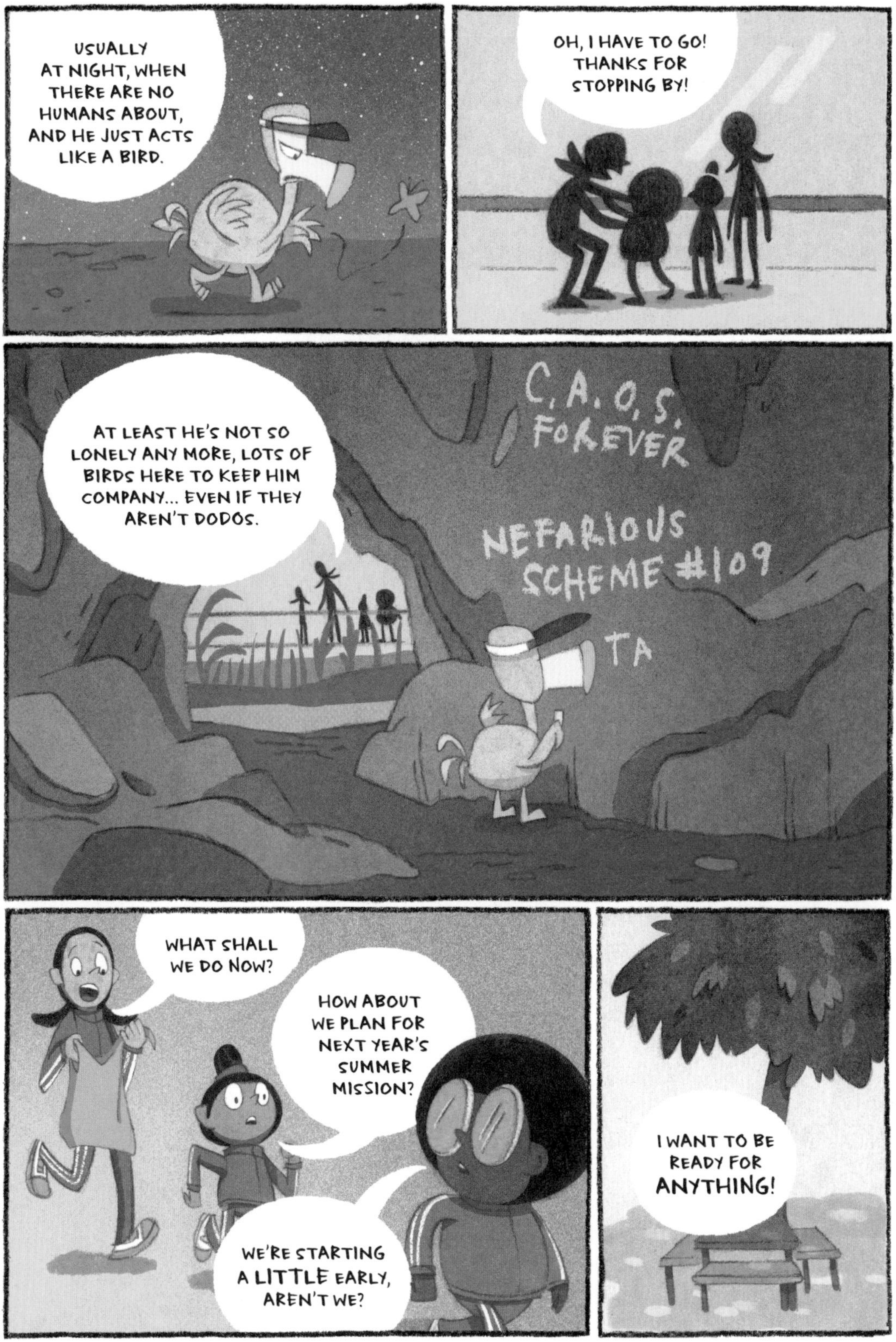
USUALLY AT NIGHT, WHEN THERE ARE NO HUMANS ABOUT, AND HE JUST ACTS LIKE A BIRD.
OH, I HAVE TO GO! THANKS FOR STOPPING BY!
AT LEAST HE'S NOT SO LONELY ANY MORE, LOTS OF BIRDS HERE TO KEEP HIM COMPANY... EVEN IF THEY AREN'T DODOS.
C.A.O.S. FOREVER
NEFARIOUS SCHEME #109
TA
WHAT SHALL WE DO NOW?
HOW ABOUT WE PLAN FOR NEXT YEAR'S SUMMER MISSION?
WE'RE STARTING A LITTLE EARLY, AREN'T WE?
I WANT TO BE READY FOR ANYTHING!

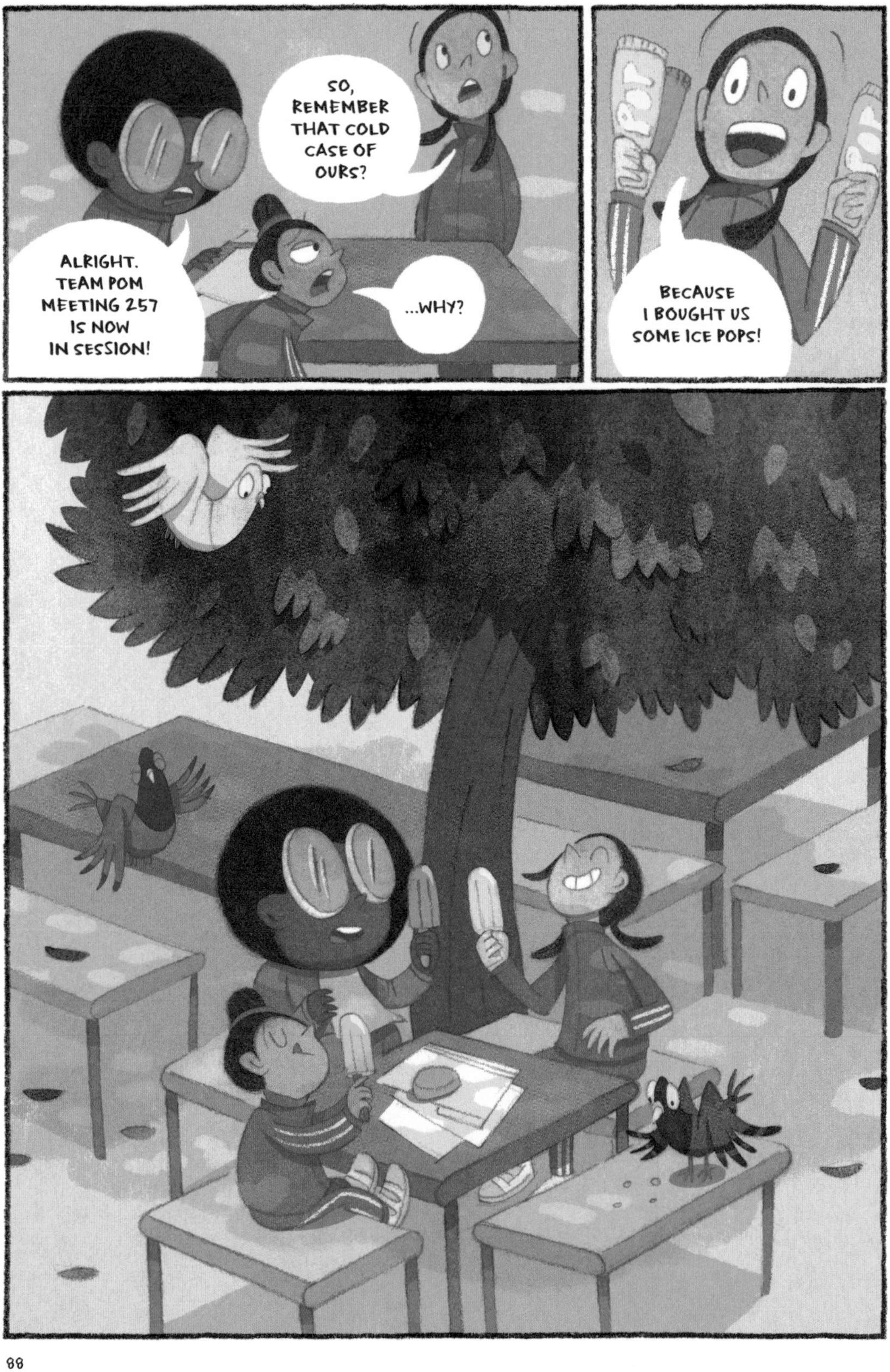
ALRIGHT. TEAM POM MEETING 257 IS NOW IN SESSION!
SO, REMEMBER THAT COLD CASE OF OURS?
...WHY?
BECAUSE I BOUGHT US SOME ICE POPS!

EPILOGUE

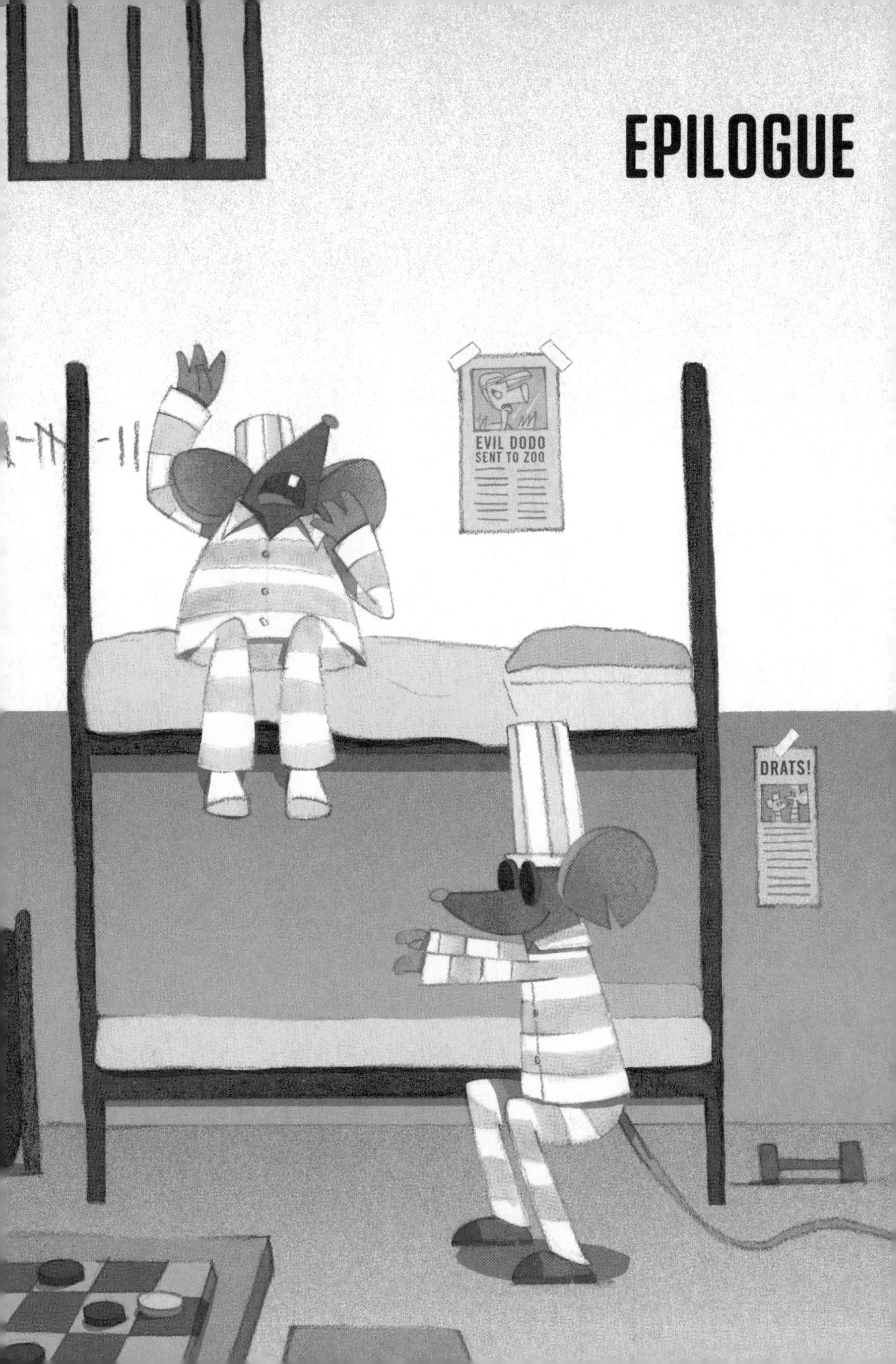
EVIL DODO
SENT TO ZOO
DRATS!

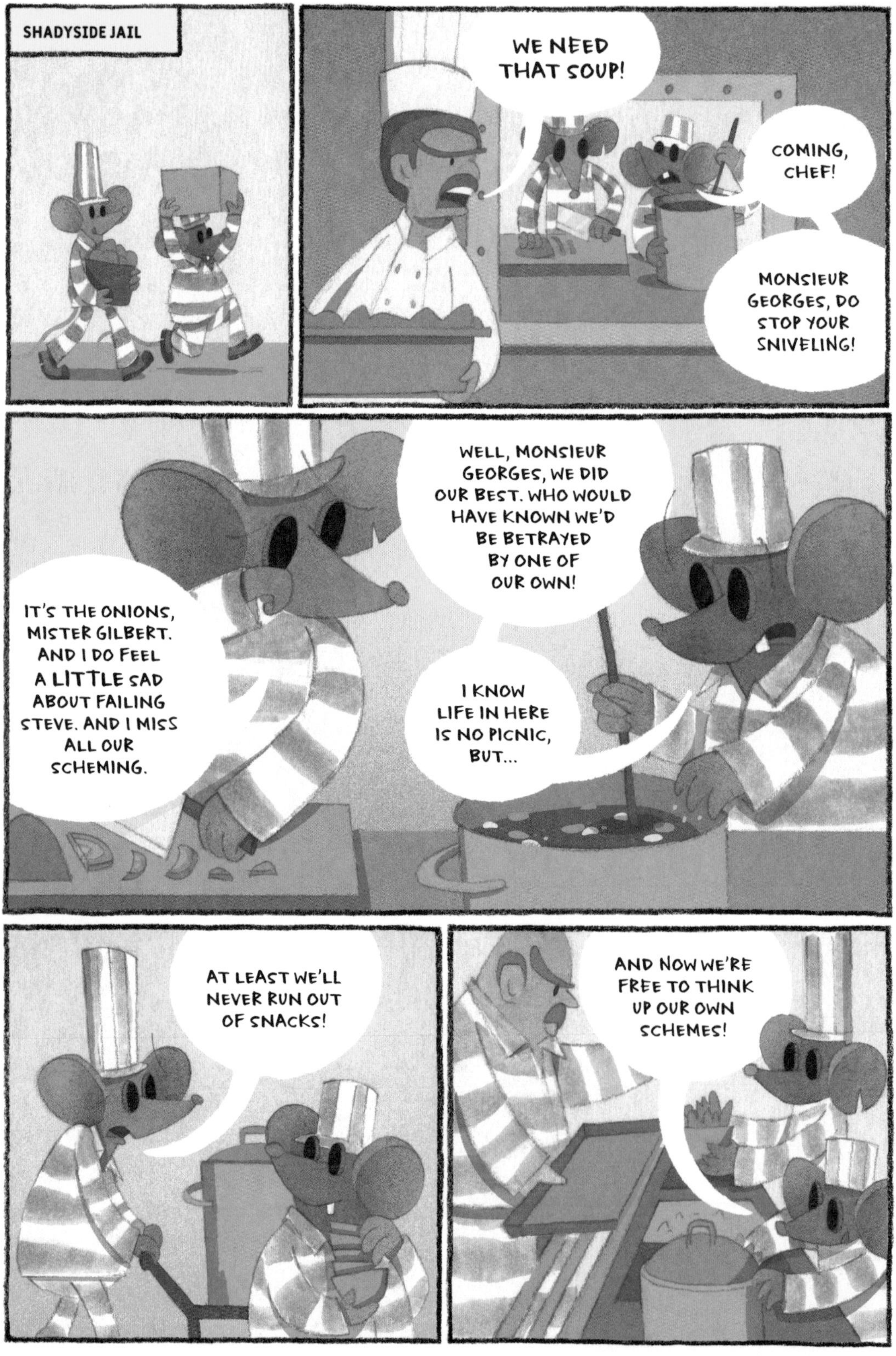
SHADYSIDE JAIL
WE NEED THAT SOUP!
COMING, CHEF!
MONSIEUR GEORGES, DO STOP YOUR SNIVELING!
WELL, MONSIEUR GEORGES, WE DID OUR BEST. WHO WOULD HAVE KNOWN WE'D BE BETRAYED BY ONE OF OUR OWN!
IT'S THE ONIONS, MISTER GILBERT. AND I DO FEEL A LITTLE SAD ABOUT FAILING STEVE. AND I MISS ALL OUR SCHEMING.
I KNOW LIFE IN HERE IS NO PICNIC, BUT...
AT LEAST WE'LL NEVER RUN OUT OF SNACKS!
AND NOW WE'RE FREE TO THINK UP OUR OWN SCHEMES!

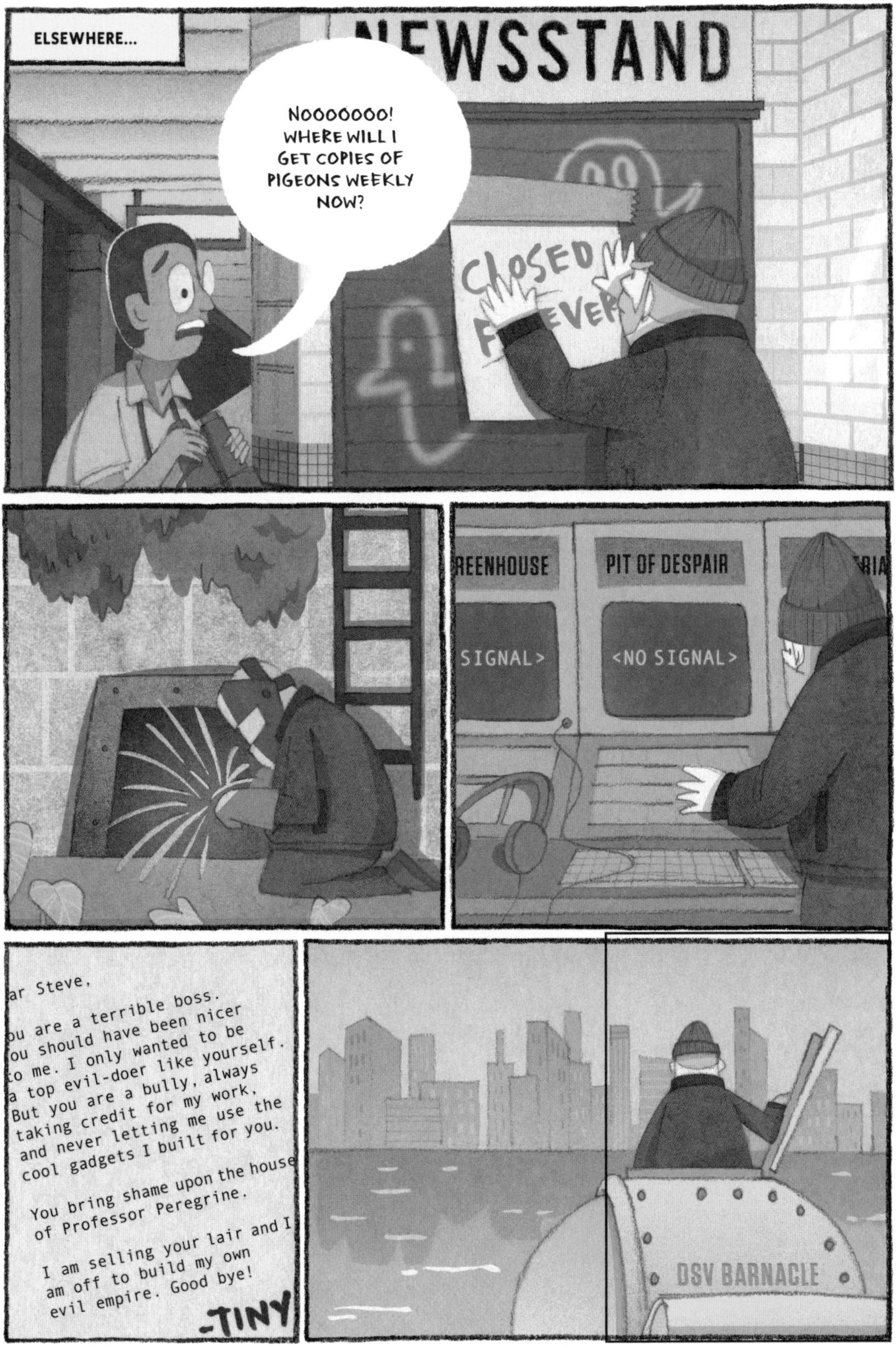
ELSEWHERE...
NEWSSTAND
NOOOOOOO! WHERE WILL I GET COPIES OF PIGEONS WEEKLY NOW?
CLOSED F...EVER
...REENHOUSE
PIT OF DESPAIR
...SIGNAL>
<NO SIGNAL>
...ar Steve,
You are a terrible boss. ...ou should have been nicer ...o me. I only wanted to be a top evil-doer like yourself. But you are a bully, always taking credit for my work, and never letting me use the cool gadgets I built for you.
You bring shame upon the house of Professor Peregrine.
I am selling your lair and I am off to build my own evil empire. Good bye!
-TINY
DSV BARNACLE

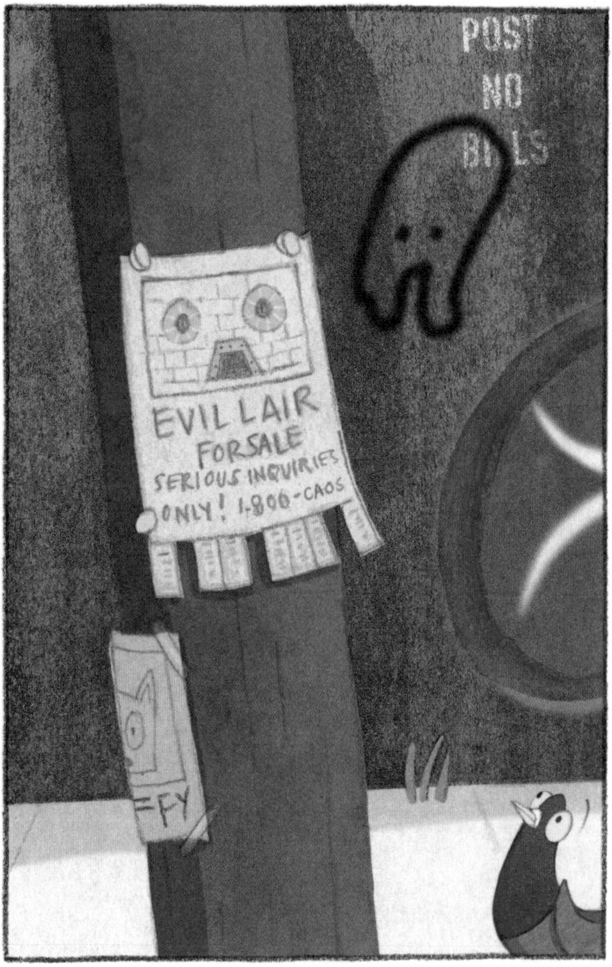
POST NO BILLS
EVIL LAIR FORSALE
SERIOUS INQUIRIES ONLY! 1-800-CAOS
FFY

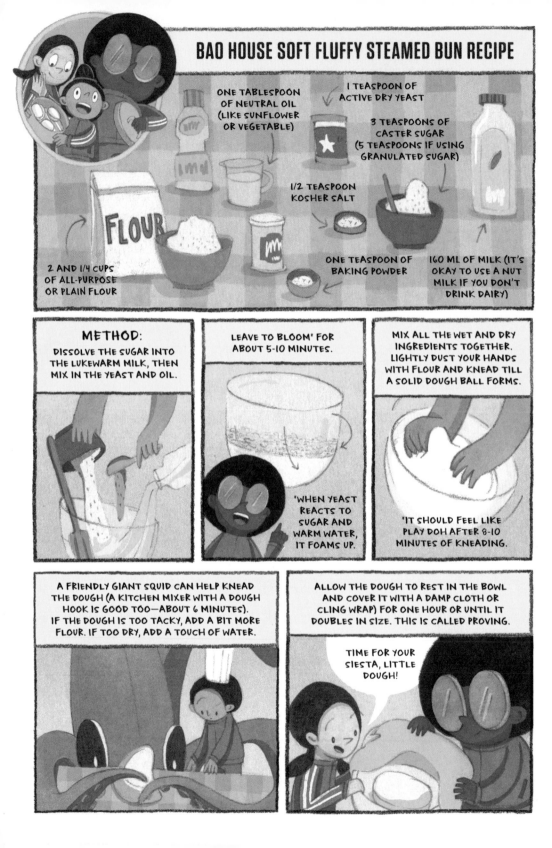

BAO HOUSE SOFT FLUFFY STEAMED BUN RECIPE

ONE TABLESPOON OF NEUTRAL OIL (LIKE SUNFLOWER OR VEGETABLE)

1 TEASPOON OF ACTIVE DRY YEAST

3 TEASPOONS OF CASTER SUGAR (5 TEASPOONS IF USING GRANULATED SUGAR)

1/2 TEASPOON KOSHER SALT

2 AND 1/4 CUPS OF ALL-PURPOSE OR PLAIN FLOUR

ONE TEASPOON OF BAKING POWDER

160 ML OF MILK (IT'S OKAY TO USE A NUT MILK IF YOU DON'T DRINK DAIRY)

FLOUR

METHOD:
DISSOLVE THE SUGAR INTO THE LUKEWARM MILK, THEN MIX IN THE YEAST AND OIL.

LEAVE TO 'BLOOM' FOR ABOUT 5-10 MINUTES.

'WHEN YEAST REACTS TO SUGAR AND WARM WATER, IT FOAMS UP.

MIX ALL THE WET AND DRY INGREDIENTS TOGETHER. LIGHTLY DUST YOUR HANDS WITH FLOUR AND KNEAD TILL A SOLID DOUGH BALL FORMS.

'IT SHOULD FEEL LIKE PLAY DOH AFTER 8-10 MINUTES OF KNEADING.

A FRIENDLY GIANT SQUID CAN HELP KNEAD THE DOUGH (A KITCHEN MIXER WITH A DOUGH HOOK IS GOOD TOO—ABOUT 6 MINUTES). IF THE DOUGH IS TOO TACKY, ADD A BIT MORE FLOUR. IF TOO DRY, ADD A TOUCH OF WATER.

ALLOW THE DOUGH TO REST IN THE BOWL AND COVER IT WITH A DAMP CLOTH OR CLING WRAP) FOR ONE HOUR OR UNTIL IT DOUBLES IN SIZE. THIS IS CALLED PROVING.

TIME FOR YOUR SIESTA, LITTLE DOUGH!

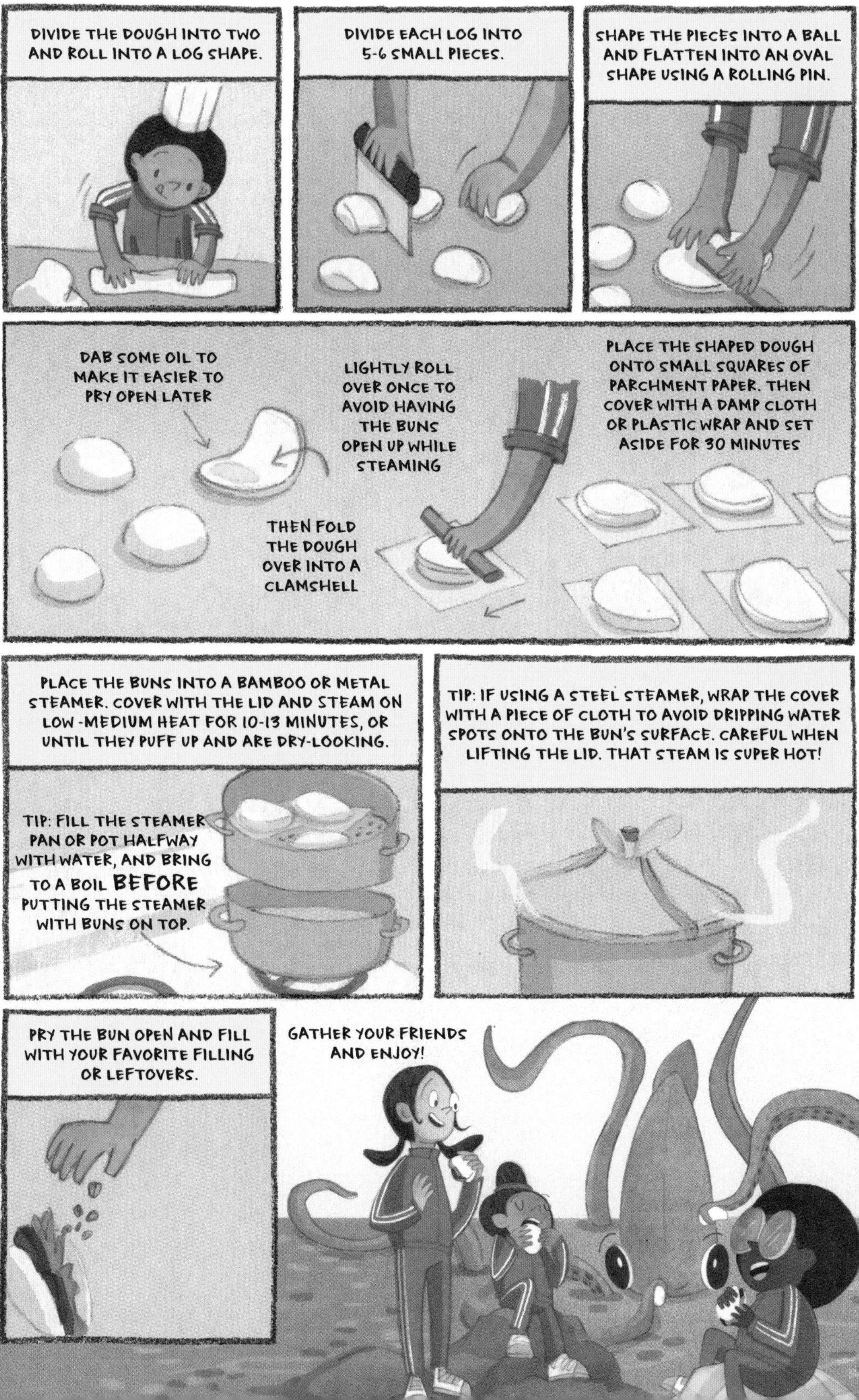
DIVIDE THE DOUGH INTO TWO AND ROLL INTO A LOG SHAPE.
DIVIDE EACH LOG INTO 5-6 SMALL PIECES.
SHAPE THE PIECES INTO A BALL AND FLATTEN INTO AN OVAL SHAPE USING A ROLLING PIN.
DAB SOME OIL TO MAKE IT EASIER TO PRY OPEN LATER
LIGHTLY ROLL OVER ONCE TO AVOID HAVING THE BUNS OPEN UP WHILE STEAMING
PLACE THE SHAPED DOUGH ONTO SMALL SQUARES OF PARCHMENT PAPER. THEN COVER WITH A DAMP CLOTH OR PLASTIC WRAP AND SET ASIDE FOR 30 MINUTES
THEN FOLD THE DOUGH OVER INTO A CLAMSHELL
PLACE THE BUNS INTO A BAMBOO OR METAL STEAMER. COVER WITH THE LID AND STEAM ON LOW-MEDIUM HEAT FOR 10-13 MINUTES, OR UNTIL THEY PUFF UP AND ARE DRY-LOOKING.
TIP: FILL THE STEAMER PAN OR POT HALFWAY WITH WATER, AND BRING TO A BOIL BEFORE PUTTING THE STEAMER WITH BUNS ON TOP.
TIP: IF USING A STEEL STEAMER, WRAP THE COVER WITH A PIECE OF CLOTH TO AVOID DRIPPING WATER SPOTS ONTO THE BUN'S SURFACE. CAREFUL WHEN LIFTING THE LID. THAT STEAM IS SUPER HOT!
PRY THE BUN OPEN AND FILL WITH YOUR FAVORITE FILLING OR LEFTOVERS.
GATHER YOUR FRIENDS AND ENJOY!

About the Author

As well as this book, Isabel Roxas is the creator of the first book in the series, *The Adventures of Team Pom: Squid Happens*.

She has also illustrated several books for young readers, including *Our Skin: A First Conversation about Race* by Megan Madison and Jessica Ralli (ALA Notable Book 2021, School Library Journal BEST BOOK 2021) and *Day at the Market* by May Tobias-Papa (2010 winner of the Philippine National Book Award).

Isabel was born in Manila, Philippines, and was raised on luscious mangoes, old wives' tales, and monsoon moons. She now resides in New York with her husband and their adopted plants.

In between adventures, mini comics of Team Pom can be found online at **www.teampom.team**